JILL KARGMAN is the author of *The Ex-Mrs. Hedgefund*, ~~~~~~
and the coauthor of *Wolves in Chic C*~~~~~~ ~~~~~~
which were both *New York Times* b~~~~~~
numerous publications, including *V*~~~~~~
lives on Manhattan's Upper East Sid~~~~~~

Praise for *Arm Candy*

"Fun and flashy . . . Kargman's quick wit and fast-moving story
bounce along. . . . Kargman gets it."   —*Publishers Weekly*

"Witty."   —*Kirkus Reviews*

"Kargman's third novel is a romance for anyone who has felt that
age is just a number."   —*Booklist*

Praise for *The Ex-Mrs. Hedgefund*

"A cheeky tale for recession-era romantics."   —*More Magazine*

"Puts the fun back in hedge funds."   —*USA Today*

"A lively chronicle of a queen of ka-ching . . . a gleeful little bon-
bon."   —*Publishers Weekly*

"True heart."   —*Booklist*

"Funny."   —*Kirkus Reviews*

"Beach~~~~~~   ~~~~~~o together like
boardw~~~~~~   ~~~~~~*ton Post Express*

Also by Jill Kargman

The Ex-Mrs. Hedgefund

Momzillas

The Right Address (Coauthored)

Wolves in Chic Clothing (Coauthored)

Arm Candy

JILL KARGMAN

A PLUME BOOK

PLUME
Published by the Penguin Group
Penguin Group (USA) Inc., 375 Hudson Street, New York, New York 10014, U.S.A. • Penguin
Group (Canada), 90 Eglinton Avenue East, Suite 700, Toronto, Ontario, Canada M4P 2Y3 (a
division of Pearson Penguin Canada Inc.) • Penguin Books Ltd., 80 Strand, London WC2R
0RL, England • Penguin Ireland, 25 St. Stephen's Green, Dublin 2, Ireland (a division of Penguin
Books Ltd.) • Penguin Group (Australia), 250 Camberwell Road, Camberwell, Victoria 3124,
Australia (a division of Pearson Australia Group Pty. Ltd.) • Penguin Books India Pvt. Ltd., 11
Community Centre, Panchsheel Park, New Delhi – 110 017, India • Penguin Group (NZ), 67
Apollo Drive, Rosedale, North Shore 0632, New Zealand (a division of Pearson New Zealand
Ltd.) • Penguin Books (South Africa) (Pty.) Ltd., 24 Sturdee Avenue, Rosebank, Johannesburg
2196, South Africa

Penguin Books Ltd., Registered Offices: 80 Strand, London WC2R 0RL, England

Published by Plume, a member of Penguin Group (USA) Inc. Previously published in a Dutton
edition.

First Plume Printing, April 2011
10 9 8 7 6 5 4 3 2 1

 REGISTERED TRADEMARK—MARCA REGISTRADA

The Library of Congress has catalogued the Dutton edition as follows:

Kargman, Jill, 1974–
Arm candy / Jill Kargman.
    p. cm.
ISBN 978-0-525-95159-9 (hc.)
ISBN 978-0-452-29698-5 (pbk.)
1. Chick lit. I. Title.
PS3611.A783A89 2010
813'.6—dc22   2009047899

Printed in the United States of America

PUBLISHER'S NOTE
This is a work of fiction. Names, characters, places, and incidents are either the product of the
author's imagination or are used fictitiously, and any resemblance to actual persons, living or
dead, business establishments, events, or locales is entirely coincidental.

To my small band of true friends:

I'd always rather be quirky us than the Beautiful People.

Arm Candy

Why *Forty* Is the Ultimate F Word

1. You feel closer to the people in the Obits section than the Weddings section.
2. You are now in the same age bracket as people who may buy oil paintings of a dog with a monocle or attend a crafts fair.
3. You catch yourself telling young people, "When I was your age, there wasn't any Internet."
4. The reason you keep a diary is to remind yourself what you did yesterday.
5. You have to skip encores at rock concerts because you want to beat the stampede and get home at a reasonable hour.
6. The president of the United States is in your age group.
7. In the newspaper, you look at the real estate section before the party pictures.
8. Two words: sensible shoes.
9. When friends book a reservation for nine thirty p.m., you want to shoot them in the head.
10. Your kid thinks your vinyl records are "antiques from the olden days."
11. You realize there are smart, grown-up people born in 1990.
12. Your joints and scars are starting to forecast rain better than the Doppler 7000 meteorologist Stan Storm.
13. You can admit that when you were your kid's age, you carried a Walkman instead of an iPod, used pay phones instead of cell phones, and typed term papers on a typewriter or "word processor" instead of a computer.
14. You keep telling yourself laugh lines are sexy but then notice that no models have laugh lines.
15. You were once a model yourself, and now the beauty that the world valued you for is starting to fade. And you're seized by the fear that you'll never be able to find love again.

Preface

For Eden Clyde, there was nothing on planet Earth as nauseating as moving boxes. Starting over with new walls and an unfamiliar ceiling to stare at during sleepless nights stressed her out more than anything else. Well accustomed to cardboard paper cuts and packing-tape hell, the stunning but weary model sat, at thirty-nine years old, crying her green eyes out. It was as if she had a bungee cord harnessed around her and was about to take an emotional cliff dive. She didn't know if she could stomach it.

Here we go again.

Despite her breathtaking looks—a more severe, sexier Audrey Hepburn meets a young Demi Moore meets those *Sports Illustrated* bikini girls you want to strangle—Eden Clyde was like so many beauties before her: lottery winner in all twenty-three chromosomes but unlucky in love. But she knew deep down it wasn't so much about chance—it was also about the choices she had made, some of them at an age so tender she couldn't fathom the consequences. But now, after nineteen years livin' in sin (as her small-town, rectangular-shaped Red State neighbors would have scoffed), she sat brokenhearted with a giant hole punched through her chest. It was like someone had shot a cannon through her, but she miraculously lived, forced to walk the misty Manhattan streets feeling empty and miserable. And *forty*. Well, almost. Isn't one's entire thirty-ninth year by nature a reckoning of sorts? A fifty-two-week shadow that is cast from the moment the candles are blown out?

Eden exhaled, her head bending down to her hands. *Deep breaths,* she instructed herself, eyes damp and closed against her thin, ringless fingers. *You have to power through this.* She had never been the religious type, but as they say, there are no atheists in the trenches. Life-changing moments will send even the least pious souls into prayer. A passenger on a turbulent flight or a mother about to give birth. For Eden, the piles of brown boxes were suddenly her unlikely steeple. *Please, God, let me get through this. Please tell me that I will be happy again.*

Eden was a beauty icon. Her career as a model and muse made her recognizable to the fashion and art world cognoscenti all over the globe. She received whistle blows from local construction workers and was the subject of schoolboy fantasies. But what would she do now that the one reason everyone worshipped her was slowly ebbing, day by day, from her without her control? She was hardly the crypt-keeper; it was forty looming, not eighty. But every New York minute, there were girls less than half her age hopping off the Greyhound, staring wide-eyed at the skyline outside Port Authority, just as she had, duffel bag in hand, hope in her heart. It felt like another life. And in many ways, it was.

1

Age is a high price to pay for maturity.

—Tom Stoppard

When Eden, née Szciapanski, hit her teen years, she really started to notice people noticing her. People on Main Street, men, women, children—*everyone* stared at her. As each pair of eyes gazed upon her, they lit a spark inside the girl from the dreary small town, making her feel special, different. Her confidence swelled as she blossomed more and more from gawky and lanky into a sexy, all-American girl, igniting an ambition deep within her soul. Maybe, just maybe, she wasn't like everyone else in Shickshinny, population 3,274. Maybe there were bigger things out there for her.

Her mom, Carol, definitely thought so, a former beauty queen turned courtroom stenographer, whose splurge was weekly French-manicured gel tips. She praised Eden's perfect features and encouraged her to raid her closet and "flaunt whatcha got." Carol hoped Eden's good looks would help her pole-vault out of their tin-rooftop town, bidding adieu to small minds, big asses, and aluminum siding for good.

"I shoulda left this goddamn town when I had the chance,"

Carol lamented to herself one morning as Eden filled her backpack for school. Eden looked down at her sophomore social studies homework pages one last time and zipped up her bag as Carol stared out the rain-splattered window dreamily and took another drag of her cigarette.

"Let's unpack the rest of those boxes tonight, Mom." Eden and her mom had moved eight times in twelve years, all within town limits, whenever the rents would rise. Then they'd fold up their life, find a new place nearby, and unfold it again.

"Yeah, I can't stand looking at 'em anymore," Carol said, looking back at Eden. "Have a good day at school."

"Thanks, Mom. You, too."

"Jason picking you up?"

"Mm-hmm." Eden smiled with an excited hair flip.

"Hold on to him, honey," Carol said between puffs. "He's got it all. The looks, the dough, and he's a good kid."

Eden smiled. She was crazy about Jason. He was romantic (long-stemmed roses in a box at each month's anniversary), fun (surprise adventures like county fair opening night), had a warm smile, and gave the best bear hugs.

A honk sounded in the front yard of Eden's quaint *Edward Scissorhands*-esque street, rows of little houses, except with no dinosaur topiaries and zero color, just white, white, white. The paint and the people.

"That's him, gotta go," Eden said while opening a beat-up umbrella to shield the perfectly groomed shiny, straight brown hair down her back.

Jason was the quarterback of the football team. He had the blond, rugged good looks of an Abercrombie kid, but with a subtle tinge of extra cheesiness. His charismatic dad owned the nearby mannequin factory, and his stay-at-home mom looked like one hot off the assembly line, thin with a platinum do and those fifties-style dresses, cinched at the waist. No stranger to hair products, Jason knew he was the shit. The stud of the town, the local hero. But as Carol had attested, he was also nice. Always the gentleman, he opened the passenger door for Eden and greeted her mom with his wide grin of white choppers that rivaled Nancy Kerrigan's.

"Have a nice day," he said with a wave.

Inside the car, after he'd kissed Eden hello, Jason turned on the radio as they drove in silence for a mile.

"Have you thought about the lake this weekend?"

"Mm-hmm," she said, meeting his gaze. "The weather's supposed to be nice. I'm psyched."

"Me, too," he said with a hungry wink. "I was thinking . . . it might be a good time for, you know . . ."

Eden looked at him and smiled. Jason had had sex before, and he was very gentle with Eden in his coaxing—never with the assholic pressure of a player out to punch her V-card. They'd done everything but the deed, and Eden couldn't bring herself to grips with the pressure. But maybe he was right, maybe it was time.

They pulled into the high school, and Eden looked at Jason as he turned off the ignition.

"Have a great day, J," she said, leaning in to kiss his warm cheek. He put his arm around her and kissed her back.

"You, too."

Inside she met her best friend, Allison, by her locker, their daily meeting place for the morning's goss, picking up right from where they left off gabbing on the phone the night before.

"So, E," Allison said, flipping her blond hair with an arm of Madonna-circa-"Lucky Star" black rubber bracelets. "Whatdja decide? You guys gonna do it finally? At the lake?"

"Oh God, everyone's asking! Why does anybody care?" Eden said, rolling her eyes.

"Because! They just do! I'm not gonna lie to you: Everyone's talking about it. You guys are like the celebrities of the school. I mean you are totally overthinking this. Jesus, just let him perform the Hymen Maneuver already. I can't wait to do it."

"I know. I'm just scared. Megan said it hurts like hell. She said her bedsheet looked like the flag of Japan," Eden said with a nervous laugh.

"It has to happen sometime! And hey, you'll be in those waterproof sleeping bags this weekend. It'll be perfect."

"Do I want to do it in a tent, though?" Eden mused.

"Why not? It's outdoors! The way nature intended."

Eden grimaced and went off to history class as Allison gave her a teasing index-finger-through-hole hand sign that made Eden cringe. She walked down the long hall wondering what the future would bring. Not just the immediate future of the upcoming big weekend, but the real future, like . . . *life*.

She loved Jason. She had dated a bunch of guys when she'd started high school—all seniors, all gorgeous—the basketball forward, the soccer star, the hockey captain. But Jason was different, sweeter, less apt to pat her bum in the cafeteria or make out in the parking lot. She wondered if she'd marry him one day, if they'd be the dream couple forever. It certainly seemed like everyone in town hoped so.

Jason was headed for college at State, which was only twenty minutes away, and she couldn't imagine life without him. If she could save enough money, she would follow him there. He was worth following. But she was also curious what the world outside her town, her state, held for someone like her.

Saturday night rolled around, and Eden and Jason and a bunch of kids loaded up their trucks, drove to a nearby national park, and pitched tents by the water's edge. In the evening, Eden sat on Jason's lap near a campfire, nestled in his arms by the bright orange glow of the flames in the center of the circle of friends. Eden caught Allison's eye, sparkling with knowing mischief. She winked at Eden, as Eden bit her lip and smiled back nervously.

As the silver sliver of moon hung brightly pasted against a blanket of stars, the gang paired off toward the tents. Eden looked around at the hunter green treetops and brightly lit cobalt sky and knew this was the perfect time; it was romantic after all.

Eden and Jason crawled into the tent and started kissing.

"I love you, Jason," she said, searching for his ripped, muscular body. "I'm ready."

"I love you, too. It's gonna be great. Wait—I got music."

He slid across the two red sleeping bags and retrieved a boom box from his older brother's U.S. Army bag. He pressed the play button.

"I made a mix tape of all the songs that remind me of you," he said, holding her face in his big hands. "I wanted you to lose it to something awesome."

Inspired by Lloyd Dobler, he had selected "In Your Eyes" by Peter Gabriel to commence the action. He was slow and gentle and while it was painful like Megan had described, it was hardly the crime scene she'd braced for.

"Eden," he said, sweetly kissing her, "you're the one."

2

The "I just woke up" face of your 30's is the "all day long" face of your 40's.

—Libby Reid

Still together six months later, Eden spent every other weekend up in Jason's college dorm room. When he had an away game one weekend and couldn't see her, Eden decided to do a mini road trip somewhere fun with Allison rather than stick around in Shickshinny. Junior year sucked, and Eden's restlessness was growing. But Allison was a little older and had scored her license, which provided some freedom for the duo.

They headed off an hour and a half away to some semblance of larger civilization, Prairie Falls, home to the Prairie Mall. Some malls euphemistically called themselves shopping centers, or worse, shopping *centres*. But this was not that—no marble, no waterfall centerpieces, no upscale boutiques. This was a straight-up *mall*: tacky, Bedazzled leggings stores, fanny packs galore, a couple movie theaters in desperate need of renovation, and Hot-Dog-on-a-Stick.

As the girls licked soft serve ice cream cones, they walked by The Poster Shop as an image in the window caught Eden's eye.

Normally the window display posters were photos of saccharine nightmares, like a basket of puppies or a kitten dangling from a branch with a script caption of "Hang in There!" But this time, it was a shot worthy of Woody Allen's lens: Manhattan at dusk, a man and a woman running through the street, holding hands.

"Look at that, Allison," Eden said, her tongue circling the chocolate ice cream. "New York City. I love that black-and-white—"

"I'd kill to go there. Like literally. I'd murder someone I don't know."

"Should I buy it?" Eden asked.

"Let's see how much it is," said Allison, walking in, ignoring the NO FOOD sign.

"Excuse me, how much is that framed photo in the window, the New York image with the couple?" Eden asked the guy with Buddy-Holly-slash-serial-killer glasses who worked in the store.

"It's eighty," he responded.

"*Eighty* clams? Forget it, Eden," Allison said, turning on her feet to leave.

"Well, that's framed. I do have it matted for twenty-two," he said.

Eden walked away smiling with her new eighteen-by-twenty poster tucked under her arm as the girls headed back across the food court to Allison's dad's car.

"Excuse me—excuse me, miss?"

The girls turned to find a tall, good-looking man in a black leather jacket. He spoke with a crisp British accent, and with his aviator shades and gleaming smile, he looked nothing like the guys the girls usually saw around.

"Pardon me, I hate to interrupt you," he said with an unbroken stare at Eden, taking off his shades. "I'm Pete MacGregor," he said. "I'm a modeling scout for Ford in New York City."

Carol and Eden packed the boxes while Allison giddily raced around like a jackrabbit on crack.

"Oh my God, this is it. This is so exciting. I can't even deal. I mean, we, like, just bought that poster of New York, and now instead of that dumb photo you're gonna have a *window!*"

"Eden, knock it off with the sulking," Carol said, noticing that her daughter looked like she had just vampired a lemon. "It's gonna be amazing there for you."

"Mom," Eden said, sounding frustrated, "you were the one who said to hold on to Jason. You told me he's got it all."

"Yeah, for Shickshinny. And that was then. This is now."

As Carol loaded her daughter's bags in the car, Allison walked with Eden, giving her a last pep talk.

"Eden: remember when we were little girls and used to watch *The Wizard of Oz* on a loop?"

"Yes," Eden recalled warmly, putting her arm around her best friend.

"You know when Dorothy leaves all that black-and-white boringness? That's this place. You are going to Emerald City."

"Allison, the whole frigging point is that Dorothy missed the black and white," Eden replied.

"Well, Dorothy was a dope. With that dumb apron. Look, you said it yourself in geography: We live in a box. Our state is a fucking rectangle."

"I know," laughed Eden. "I remember thinking the interesting states always have cool shapes. But not us. We just have four straight lines. Whoever made the borders didn't care about fighting for the squiggles."

"That's right. No more lame-ass boxes for you. New York has tons of jagged lines. So pull it together and get in the car."

After a tearful phone call to Jason saying good-bye, Eden

loaded her last bag into Carol's car. At the bus depot, Eden hugged her mom and then turned to give Allison something wrapped in newspaper.

"What's this?"

"It's the poster of New York," Eden said. "You can keep it until you come and get your own window."

Allison hugged her at the bus so tightly, Eden thought she'd snap.

"I'm coming the second I get my fucking diploma, so you better be on your feet," Allison said. "That means a year and a half to make bank. You can do it, Eden! Cindy Crawford can suck it!"

Eden turned with a lump in her throat to climb the three stairs of the bus, then sat in her seat and took a last look at her mom, waving with her cigarette. As the bus pulled away and drove through Main Street, Eden watched as they passed the field where Jason had scored so many touchdowns, including one with her when they had snuck onto school property over the summer. She whizzed by, looking at the quaint rows of houses, the store where she'd worked, the market, and shuddered. Not because she was intimidated by the huge all-caps NEW YORK on the front of the bus. But because deep inside her, she knew she was never coming back.

3

If you're gonna screw up, do it while you're young. The older you get, the harder it is to bounce back.

—Winston Groom

Modeling was not what it had seemed at first. Crammed into a tiny apartment with six anorexic girls, a fat, bulimic chaperone, and three bunk beds, Eden knew right away this was not her dream scenario by any means. She ran around town, headed to go-sees, where they'd look her over, snap a Polaroid, and send her on her way.

To escape the claustro digs, she walked the streets and eventually found her way around. She relished spying through large picture windows in the Village, wondering who the glamorous people were who lived in such lofty locales. She loved sending Allison New York postcards—from the dramatic and dreamily picturesque (Empire State Building at dusk) to the amusingly grotesque (a St. Marks punk with seventy-six facial piercings). She booked two photo shoots for catalogues and continued auditioning. But instead of getting down when she didn't get a job like the other girls would, she still had hope—because the casting people always told her booker that while she wasn't right for this particular gig, she had a striking look like no one else they had ever seen.

She got a part-time job at Tower Records to save money since twice-weekly jobs as a model for fashion designers on Seventh Avenue weren't exactly keeping her in ka-ching, and she was an indentured servant of sorts to the agency, which paid for all her headshots and living expenses.

Her post at the record store allowed her to get almost-free cassettes, and to meet many customers, plenty of whom asked to see her again. She dated several men—a Wall Street banker, an eye doctor, a trust fund baby, each for a few weeks or a couple months. Until one day, in wandered Cameron Slade. Leather jacket, ponytail, pierced ear, gorgeous face. Eden knew who he was; she had seen his local band, Desperate Measures, play in the store at their record release party. He hailed from Southern California, smoked tons of weed, and never met a hairbrush he liked. His fingers burned through the fret, ripping riffs that made guys bang their heads and girls bang *him*.

"Hello again," Cam said to her with a sexy chin jut. "I met you last time I was here. I never forget a face. Well, a face like *that*."

He invited Eden to come see him play at a nearby rock club. As she stood in the front row, watching his fingers grind the guitar, she felt as electrified as the amps he roared over. She saw the girls screaming to her left and right, dancing as if drugged by not only the throbbing chords but also by Cam's hotness. He looked down at her after a string-shredding solo, and she grinned coyly.

She was packing boxes by the month's end, making it almost to the year mark in the tiny models' apartment. And that had been more than enough.

Installed in Cameron's apartment, she felt the hope of things starting to come together.

"I'm wild about you, Eden," he said to her in bed one night, as she stroked his long hair.

"Me, too," she said.

"Can you come with us to Baltimore tomorrow? You know I love having you at the shows."

"I don't know. I'd really like to, but I have a go-see at noon. I'm not sure I can move it . . ."

"Just skip it, then, just this once. Hammerjack's is major."

Eden didn't miss that show, or any others. Or rehearsals. Every day, Cameron would pick her up at Tower and they'd go hang out with the band, and Eden would sit on the side, loving life, swaying to the addictive music of their practice jam sessions in an underground space on Ludlow.

"We're playing Arlene's next week, big gig. It's finally happening, guys!" Cam walked to the side and kissed Eden. "Maybe you can come and sell our tapes."

"Sure, totally." Eden nodded.

"The T-shirts just came in, too," the bassist, Paul, added. "You can sell those, too; they're badass."

"Okay." Eden nodded enthusiastically. She could feel in her bones they were taking off.

"Hey, hon," Cam said with a whispered growl in her ear, his muscular arms wrapping around her waist, guitar slung on his back. "I was thinking of getting a tattoo."

"Oh yeah?" she asked. "Of what?"

"Well, I was thinking, maybe we could get each other's names."

Um . . . yeah, no. "You mean, like . . . I get one, too?" Eden asked.

"Yeah, that's the whole point. I'm yours and you're mine."

Eden considered this for a moment but shook her head. "I don't know . . . I don't like needles," she confessed.

"You don't like needles, or you don't like my name on you."

"It's not that, Cam—"

"All right, whatever," he said, turning to the band. "Let's take it from the top of the set again, guys!"

Things progressed amazingly well for Desperate Measures, whose album was doing better and better as they booked larger gigs in bigger venues. When they were invited to play CBGBs, both Eden and Cam suspected his star was really on the rise. When it sold out in two days, they actually *knew* it.

"This is a new song we're workin' on and it goes out to my Eden," he said through the silver mic over the loudspeaker at CBs. "The foxiest girl in New York."

As Cameron strummed the opening notes, a bolt warmed Eden's chest: It was her first brush with fame. Everyone in the packed club craned to stare at her, off to the side, backstage but visible in the wings. She loved it. It was her first hit of the potent drug of recognition, a high she had experienced only on a microscopic level when students at school would look at her. But this was different. If you could make it here, you could make it anywhere.

Cam's place was way east on Ninth Street, in a neighborhood that was, at the time, sketchy and skeevy. But it was crawling with the young and the vibrant, their seething ambition like a palpable mist in the lamplit air. And as Eden roamed the crowded, hot-blooded sidewalks with Cam gripping her waist, she felt her own ambitions expand exponentially. She suspected, to the core of her soul, that soon she would trade Avenue A for the A List.

4

Live your life and forget your age.

—Norman Vincent Peale

While the months passed, as Cameron's success was growing, unfortunately Eden's seemed to be faltering. She booked fewer and fewer modeling jobs, though ironically, it seemed more and more men were hitting on her. But she was thrilled for Cam and ecstatic to cheer on his string of sold-out shows. Still, there was a growing feeling gnawing inside her; she needed to do something more.

Luckily, just as her rut was growing deeper, Allison graduated. Eden pounded the pavement to find a studio apartment for her nearby, and soon enough the girls were hugging at Port Authority and celebrating Allison's arrival in 212 land over drinks before Cameron's concert.

"Cheers," said Allison, raising her glass. "To the window instead of the poster." The girls clinked goblets. "Even though it's facing a brick wall."

"Thank God you're here," Eden said. "I am so ecstatic I can't even take it."

In the packed Irving Plaza, Allison and Eden stood with their credentials in a VIP section of the mezzanine along with record executives and allegedly someone from MTV. The label was considering investing in a video and wanted feedback on their sound. Eden and Allison screamed and clapped when the band came onstage and afterward Cameron gave them a quick hug before darting off to the side with his managers.

"So what now?" Allison asked.

"Now I usually just kinda wait for him."

A couple more months passed, and while Allison's fabulous arrival had sprung Eden from her worries temporarily, she started to feel a pit growing inside her stomach.

One night after a party off Houston Street, Cam and Eden headed up the Bowery.

"Let's get some food," he said in a moody tone.

"Okay."

They strolled in silence.

"Are you . . . all right?" Eden asked.

"No, not really," he said, pulling open the door to a diner on the corner.

Inside, Eden looked at Cam's annoyed face. A guy with a sketch pad and a yellow pencil took notice of them and moved down a stool at the crowded counter so the couple could sit together.

"Thanks," Eden said to him with a smile.

"Sure," he replied.

She turned back to Cameron. "What's bothering you?" she asked.

"You were ALL OVER that guy Rick at the party!" Cam fumed at her.

"I was not," she retorted.

"You were."

"That's ridiculous."

Eden unfurled her muffler and took off her hat. Her fiery green eyes blazed against her chilled cheeks.

"Come on, you were practically throwing yourself on top of him," Cam accused. "It was pathetic. You were so flirtatious."

"Excuse me. I wasn't flirting with him! This—is in your head," Eden stammered.

"I can't take this shit anymore," he said, enraged. "There are a ton of girls who would kill to be with me."

At this, Eden's face turned red with anger.

"So let them." She shrugged, her voice not rising to meet his fervor.

"What do you mean?"

"Honestly, Cameron, I don't need to be accused, and frankly, I don't need to follow you around, selling T-shirts, waiting in the wings. I've had enough," she said, shaking her head. "I guess we both have."

"Are you fucking joking me?" he fumed, standing up. "Are you breaking up with me?"

"I guess."

"You *guess*?" he screamed, his face reddening. "Why are you so fucking detached? What are you, like, some robot?"

"Nope," she replied matter-of-factly and turned to the counter as the short-order cook approached to take their order and see what the drama was about. "I just think it's time." Eden turned away to face the waiting chef. "Hi! I'll have a large coffee, black, please. And also a hot chocolate. And an oatmeal with extra raisins, please."

"Ma'am, no more raisins, sorry."

"No raisins? Oh bummer." She grimaced, dejected. "I'll have pancakes, then."

"Am I going crazy or are you literally more upset about fucking raisins right now than me?" Cameron raged, steam coming from his multiply pierced ears.

Her flippant, silent stare confirmed that, yes indeed, plain oatmeal would be a greater tragedy than this one-way express ticket to Splitsville.

"I'll be out tomorrow so you can come get your stuff," he said like a child and stomped to the door. "Have a nice life."

Eden exhaled and unzipped her windbreaker nonchalantly as the guy with the sketch pad watched her casually hang it on a nearby hook on the wall next to her.

"You guys always have that large red box of Sun-Maid raisins up on top of that coffee machine," Eden said to the guy behind the counter.

"Oh yes, yes, we all out. Tomorrow, tomorrow."

The guy next to Eden couldn't take his eyes off her as she waited for her pancakes, unfazed by the breakup. She looked up to meet his glance as he looked down. He was wearing a worn-in, well-loved navy hooded zip-up sweatshirt.

"Hot chocolate? Coffee?" the short-order chef called out.

"Yes!"

"Thank you."

Both Eden and he replied at the same time, reaching for the steaming cup of coffee.

"Oh, sorry, go ahead, I got the same thing—you take it," the guy on the stool next to her said.

"No, no, no, don't be silly! I'll get the next one. Look, here it is!" She smiled, reaching for the second cup placed on the counter.

They sipped their scalding mugs side by side.

"I like raisins, too," he offered sweetly. "In half my childhood pictures I swear I'm holding one of those little red boxes."

Eden was charmed by the innocent interjection of the guy with the sketch pad.

"Me, too," she replied, swerving her stool to face him. "I think my mother thought it counted as part of the fruit group."

"I moved from California to Tennessee when I was four, and my mom said that on the drive I asked if there would be raisins in Memphis. It was like the little red box would make it all okay," he said with a smile.

His book-packed messenger bag was slung across him, his blue eyes beaming through his little circular gold glasses. He was one of the kindest-looking men she had ever seen.

"I'm Eden," she said, extending her hand.

That figures, he thought. She was perfect. Of course he could never say that, as he knew instantly she had heard it a million times over.

"Hi, Eden, I'm Wes."

"Nice to meet you," she smiled. "Cheers."

Their ceramic coffee mugs bumped and they chatted the hour away about everything from music (he favored The The) to the best secret little streets in the city (Grove Court, MacDougal Alley, Washington Mews). Before long it had become clear to Eden that this guy had somehow tripped an invisible wire inside of her. He wasn't quite like anyone she'd met before.

As a young architecture student, working late in the libraries and at the drafting table with his little gold glasses over his bright blue eyes, Wes Bennett found that he learned more by following his feet than by following textbooks. Wes loved buildings. He explored every last alleyway, each cozy row of mews, every looming skyscraper. He was a passionate intellectual, drinking in every last gargoyle, arched doorway, and Doric column.

While most of Wes's classmates were funneling beer and keg-standing till they got their graduation sheepskins—ripping and rolling *lambskins* each Saturday night, getting lucky, Wes spent most of his time alone. He had elected to live off campus, away from the pricier meal plan and in an apartment by himself in a less-than-desirable neighborhood on Tompkins Square Park. He could barely afford the tiny studio apartment on the junkie-packed Avenue B, where heroin needles were more common than diagonal-slung book bags. But he had befriended his blind super, Max, not knowing he was also the owner of the building. Max was a fifty-three-year-old African American from the neighborhood who, as a child, also loved to build towers and structures with his blocks before he lost his sight. And when the older man took a liking to the earnest student and kind, responsible tenant, Wes found his lease renewed with a yearly increase of 0.00 percent.

It was an unlikely friendship, marked by weekly walks around the city during which Wes would describe the architecture to his sightless friend, who relished the eloquent, detailed descriptions of cantilevered design and shiny new materials. Wes was breathless and excited to share his passion with a like-minded person.

"Okay, Max, we're rounding the corner onto Park Avenue," Wes would say. "I'm looking at a row of buildings, each set back so that people can walk the expanded pavement. There are fountains to the right."

"I can hear 'em," Max said.

"Across the street is the Lever House," Wes explained, drinking in the gleaming façade. "It's a tall, steel and glass prism and has really clean and simple geometries. It's sleek."

"What are the fountains under?" asked Max.

"They're part of Mies van der Rohe's plaza for the Seagram Building, which is also glass, but more of a warm-toned wall of translucent, coffee brown. There's a man sitting on a bench with his family eating lunch," Wes said. "They're unfolding tinfoil-wrapped sandwiches. Maybe the dad had to work on a Sunday and I guess the wife and little kid came to meet him for lunch."

Max beamed. He shook his head, knowing no one else but Wes could or would have done that for him.

During his downtime, Wes loved to discover inspiring places, big and small, from the main reading room at the New York Public Library to the Temple of Dendur at the Met to his favorite hole-in-the-wall diner, where he'd sit and study and draw.

In the buzzing fluorescent light of the shitty Bowery diner, Wes couldn't fathom a more beautiful paradise. It was as if the nasty dead-mosquito-covered lightbulbs were pale moonlight, the gnarly heater blowing bacteria-laced air on them were an ocean-front breeze, and the glazed hams in the cold-cut window a lavish buffet fit for kings.

Likewise, Eden felt so at ease with Wes. It was the days before venti-soy-half-caf-skim-mocha-triple-shot-'cinos, and their light conversation budded into a nice evening of add-water-and-stir instant connection. She found comfort in the warmth of a stranger so sweet that Eden didn't even care that the next day would bring moving boxes bound for Allison's apartment.

After chatting and nursing their bottomless cups of coffee for over an hour, Wes got the courage to reach for a piece of paper from his bag.

"It's been really nice to talking to you," he said, fishing for his pencil. "Could I, um, get your phone number? Maybe we could get another coffee sometime."

"You're not going to believe this," she said, shaking her head. "But I don't have a phone."

"Guess what?" said Wes, smiling. "Me neither."

"Hmm, I'm kind of . . . in transit, as you could see." Eden smiled, staring right into his eyes. He was so cute. "But . . . I would love to see you again. How do I find you?"

"How about here?" he offered with a smile.

The two agreed to meet again for coffee again, same diner, same time, the next evening. It was probably a waste of time, but Eden felt so drawn to Wes that she needed to see him again.

When Eden arrived the following night, she groaned when she saw the hordes packing the joint. The line looked ridiculously long, even for takeout, but she was pleasantly surprised to see Wes already awaiting her outside. With two large cups of coffee.

"It's so much milder tonight," he said, relishing the fifty-five-degree air. "I thought we could maybe walk a little."

"Perfect! I'm so in the mood for a nice walk."

They strolled down the street, passing halfway houses and homeless shelters, a soup kitchen, a rat. But it may as well have been the Champs-Elysées. Their chemistry was instant and heightening with every pace. Wes wanted the night to never end. When Eden randomly suggested they go across the Brooklyn Bridge, Wes was delighted, not because it was one of his favorite paths, but because he knew it meant a return walk back: His time with her would be doubled.

"I've never done this, have you?" Eden asked, relishing the newness of speeding cars underfoot as they stepped over the wooden beams.

"Sure, all the time," replied Wes. "It was one of the first places I came when I arrived in New York. I love this bridge."

"Really? I wouldn't ever think to cross it, unless I had to get to the other side, I mean."

"Oh no, I just walk across and come back. Just for the view."

"The whole journey-and-not-the-destination thing?" Eden smiled.

"Exactly." Wes grinned. "You know, when John Roebling died of tetanus, his son Washington took over with the construction of the bridge, which began in 1870. When he got the bends, his wife, Emily, took over and completed the project and she was actually the first person to walk across it. It was really a family affair, a true passion project. I hope if I'm lucky enough to build anything, I can be as into it as they were. Hopefully without the dying part."

"How do you know so much?" she asked, feeling a spark ignite inside of her.

Wes shrugged, embarrassed. "I don't know," he said sheepishly. "I'm alone a lot. I read a ton. And take lots and lots of long walks."

"You know what I think?" Eden asked, stopping him and putting her hand on his shoulder. "I think I want to come along."

5

Ah, but I was so much older then, I'm younger than that now.

—Bob Dylan

Eden barely unpacked into Allison's studio when she began spending every night at Wes's apartment down the street. Her heart pounded every time she was headed to see him. Wes was almost too good to be true. He was softer, more nurturing to her than other guys had been. He never tried to control her; they never quarreled. He was wise, sweet, and most of all, he respected her.

Each night he'd study, his blue downward-gazing irises behind his glasses as he sketched and traced blueprints through the night while Eden danced with a glass of wine in the background to her The The vinyls. He gave her that feeling in her stomach, like she felt on the swinging pirate ship ride when she and Allison snuck into a traveling county fair as children: nauseating and thrilling at the same time.

Could this be the L word they talk, sing, write, and scream about? Eden moved in within four weeks. And as the months blissfully passed, she saw no end in sight. They spent every free moment together. He taught her all about architecture; she took him to outdoor free concerts where they would lie in each other's arms. They seemed to have their own language, and even had a special nickname for each other, which they hatched after only a few months together.

One night at their late-night haunt, the diner on the Bowery where they first met, Wes was signaling Eden inside from her cigarette break. Like everyone in New York at the time, she had started smoking, despite years of having called her mom the Chimney.

"Honey, the burgers are ready," he said, sweetly tapping on the glass.

"Thanks, honey," she said through the window as she threw the butt on the ground and came in.

An older Greek guy who sat on the stool beside them laughed as he ate his fries.

"This is very funny, you calling your lover 'honey,'" he said in his thick Mediterranean accent, swiveling toward the cute couple. "In my country, this word is not used for affection, it is ingredient. This is like in your country calling your lover 'maple syrup.'"

Wes and Eden cackled out loud, totally getting how random calling a beloved "honey" might sound to a foreigner. Wes moved Eden's hair from her cheek and kissed it.

"You're absolutely right," Wes said to the man. "Everyone says honey. I actually like maple syrup much better," he proclaimed with a smile. He looked at Eden and smiled. "I now christen you Maple."

"Okay, Maple."

"Eden is in looove," Allison teased.

"Shut up, I am not!" Eden said sternly.

But in truth, when Wes would tickle her back as she fell asleep or make her pasta with the best marinara sauce outside Naples, Eden couldn't help imagining what it would be like to grow old with him.

On deadline for his next project one freezing snowy Sunday, Wes finally put down his pen and paper to take a break. Dazzled by Eden's sensuous dance moves around the apartment as music played, Wes took off his glasses and flopped down on the bed. He lay on his stomach, his pencil grazing the paper gently as he watched Eden in her camisole and panties as she spun around. He smiled as the graphite perfectly rendered what he had intended.

"What is that you're drawing?" she asked as his pencil dotted the pad. "A constellation of stars or something?"

"Nope." Wes smiled. "It's all the beauty marks on your back."

He showed her the pad. The little brown spots were sweetly mapped with expert precision.

"Shit, I have that *many*?" She lay down next to him.

"Yes, you do. Serious mole cartography," he teased.

"Great," she said sarcastically.

He leaned over her and kissed each one down her whole back as she giggled. Her cheek lay happily on the feather-leaking pillow as she smiled.

"You're such a weirdo," she teased. *"I'm not a boobs or a leg man! Me? I'm a birthmark guy!"*

"I'm not some freak fetishist, I just like the whole package, that's all," he replied, laughing. "I love everything about you, don't you know that?" His fingers walked up her camisole. "Every. Little. Last. Weirdly shaped mole."

Eden smiled, rolling over to face him.

"How the hell did I get so lucky to find you?" she asked him, looking up at his face. "Do you know that I've never been able to sleep through the night, for as long as I can remember? I sleep like a baby here."

"I stuff my mattress with opium, didn't I tell you?"

"Shut up."

"Well, you've been a little nomad for a while. Maybe you sleep well here because it finally feels like home."

She reached up to his neck and pulled him down to kiss him as he ran his hand down her neck and shoulder, her arm, taking her fingers in his. She loved to fall asleep with him like pretzels, glued together and intertwined.

"I'm so happy with you," Wes said as they watched the shadows of their hands on the opposite white wall. "Is this the happiest you've ever been? 'Cause it is for me."

"Yeah, I guess." She shrugged playfully. She looked into his blue eyes and knew how much he loved her; he wanted to protect her, take care of her, and his every gaze, from the first in the morning to the last at night, was full of devotion.

"You guess? You *guess*?" He jumped on top of her and tickled her. She giggled and guffawed until her high-pitched laughter turned to shrieks, begging for mercy.

"Okay! Okay! I know it is!" she said, breathless.

"You better!" he said, whacking her butt with the pillow.

"I do, Maple. I love you. So much," she said. "This has been the best nine months of my life." She *was* home.

Wes poured two last glasses of wine from dinner, which they sipped in the sheets.

"Cheers," he said, knowing in that moment, watching Eden sip her wine with rosy cheeks and bed head, that no human could ever be as happy as he was. "You know, Eden, this lousy, el cheapo Chateau Screwcap I bought at the corner bodega tastes like a sixty-seven Margaux," he smiled, patting her.

"You've had that?" Eden asked, playing with the zipper on his navy hooded sweatshirt.

"Nope," said Wes. "But I know it couldn't be better than this."

He reached for her and kissed her clavicle and chest, returning to her face, which he drank in like more wine, kissing her deeply as she curled her arms around his neck, her fingers through his brown wavy hair. Their tongues, wet with grapes, melded in a heated embrace. Life couldn't be sweeter.

As Eden and Wes's magical cocoon together approached the year mark, their happy rainbowed love life couldn't have been more sublime.

And then, little by little, reality started, ever so softly, to tiptoe into their rhapsodic nest.

Zzzt! Zzzt. Zzzt. The light above flickered on and off and then went out.

"Oh shit," she said. "The electric bill."

"Whoops. I'll take care of it tomorrow," Wes said. "I worked some extra hours at the library and get my paycheck then."

"Okay," she said quietly.

"Don't worry, I'll take care of it," he said, kissing her forehead. But she knew he was strained as it was.

"I'll help out," she offered. "I mean, I can work some more hours at the record store." She was starting to hate her job at Tower. Especially when the Desperate Measures album went gold, thanks to their hit single, "Heart-Smasher," based on her.

"No, no, no—I've got it," Wes comforted.

They lay in the darkness in each other's arms. Wes wanted to provide for her, take care of her, love her. And Eden loved Wes right back, so much that it hurt. But when ConEd switched off that current, she couldn't help but be reminded of her life in Shickshinny, and her early days in New York in that overcrowded apartment. Her fears of being destitute started to kick in, and the girl who never cried got a lump in her throat. So she locked down, like when Batman whispers "shields" and a thick armored coating suddenly clamps down on the Batmobile. She had to secure herself, reinforce the casing she had her whole life and suit up, protecting the inner strength that got her on that bus out of Shickshinny in the first place. After all, it was all she had.

6

It takes a long time to grow young.

—Pablo Picasso

"Happy anniversary," Wes said, smiling as he came in from the cold and sat across from Eden at a quirky new candlelit café near their apartment, an early harbinger of hipification to come. Wes hadn't even realized it was the hot new joint when he had made the reservation. But its trend factor was not lost on his girlfriend, who loved the people-watching. Eden scanned the industrial-chic high-ceiled space, with rows of hanging cords, each with a vintage lightbulb with clear glass through which you could see the firefly filaments within. Friends air-kissed each other, attractive waiters brought fancy cocktails, and Eden drank it all in.

Wes leaned over the table and kissed her cheek. "Can you believe it's been a year?"

"I know, it's crazy! Wes, I love this place, great choice, it's so cool in here, I'm obsessed," she observed, reaching for the menu. "Yum, this looks so good, I'm starving!" Eden's eyes widened as she beheld the prices on the right of the parchment paper, which was presented on rustic vintage clipboards. Shit, it was pricey. She looked at Wes, who was also noticing.

"This place is kind of expensive," Eden said.

"Hey, it's a special occasion, Maple, it's worth the splurge." Wes smiled warmly. Eden reached for his hand and held it.

"Jesus, your hands are freezing, let me warm them up." Wes took each of her pink hands and rubbed them quickly with his.

"Thanks," Eden said, feeling his warm hands comfort hers.

"So how was your day?" Wes asked.

"It was fine, Wes, but we really have to deal with the roach problem in the apartment."

"Oh no. You saw *another* one?"

"It was literally bigger than a taxi."

"I'll have Max send the exterminator again," he promised, shaking his head. "Did you kill it?"

"Hell, no! I sprinted out of there!"

"I'll get him when we get home, don't worry," he said, kissing her now-warmed hand. "I have so much work tonight anyway on my term project that I'll be awake to defend you from crazy vehicle-sized insects."

"Thanks, Lancelot." Eden smiled and sipped her water from a taupe-hued glass goblet. "Gosh, can you believe this place? Everyone is so . . . beautiful."

"That's why they call them the Beautiful People." Wes shrugged. He honestly hadn't really noticed. But Eden spied the scene—the edgy and chic fashionistas, the cool young musicians carrying guitars, the offbeat vibe. It was everything she'd fantasized about New York all in one room. Of course she'd seen people like this all the time in the record store, just not all at once, with this lighting, at night, dressed up, being fabulous. Frequenting their hives was hardly within her financial reach.

"I'm going to just run to the bathroom, quickly," said Wes, popping up. Before he walked away he kissed her cheek once more.

After a moment, the door of the restaurant burst open and in walked a noisy, colorful crew. A girl with spiky purple hair and a ton of piercings, two gorgeous male model types, a tall black woman with cheekbones in drastic angles that rivaled Mount Everest, and behind them all, Mr. Otto Clyde: the most famous living artist in New York, perhaps the world.

Eden sat up straight, instantly noticing the famed artist who already, at thirty-seven, was an international sensation and one of the most collected painters in the world. She had heard he resided and worked nearby in a double-width townhouse he had renovated from scratch, and she knew he ran with a crowd akin to Warhol's Factory—kids coming in and out, posing for him, clubbing with him, snorting with him.

As the crew was ushered immediately by the chain-smoking host to a huge table nearby, Otto's dark eyes washed casually over the scene. And then . . . his eyes darted back, in a lightning-fast double take, to the most striking creature he had ever seen. He suddenly stopped still, inhaling his cigarette and staring down at Eden in her booth. While many women would quickly look away, Eden simply gazed back, unfazed. She was used to it. Her green eyes shone in the low light, and her long shiny hair cascaded down her shoulders and back. Though she was still chilled from the air outside, she delicately took both hands to her shoulders and pulled off the crimson cardigan, which revealed her sensuous body under a tight-fitting, lace-trimmed ivory tank top.

"Hello," he said, approaching her, fixated.

"Hello."

"I'm—"

"I know who you are," she said in a monotone way, not letting on whether she was impressed or not. (She was.) "I'm Eden."

"Of course your name is Eden, how fitting. You're too stunning for the earth as we know it."

"Please. Is there also an angel missing in heaven?" she teased, batting her lashes. "Or wait—is my father a thief because he stole the stars right out of the sky and put them in my eyes?"

Otto was stunned. Here he was, a legend who could bed any skirt in New York, and this young girl mocked his advances? He felt himself getting hard just hearing her verbal slap. "Touché, my dear. I suppose you have heard such words before."

"A few times."

"Hello," said Wes, returning to the table. "I'm Wes. You a friend of Eden's?"

"I hope to be," he said slyly.

"Wes, this is Otto Clyde," she said, introducing the two men.

"Oh, wow, I'm a huge fan of your work, sir." Wes beamed, in awe that he was face-to-face with the world's most celebrated painter.

"'Sir'? Hey, guys, I'm a *sir*," Otto yelled to his table with an amused grin. "Why, how old are you two fresh-faced young ones?"

"Nineteen," answered Eden.

"Well, almost twenty," added Wes.

Eden shot him a look. For a young model like Eden, twenty was a dreaded threshold. She had been born January 1, 1970, the first day of a new decade. Wes's stork flew three months later. And there, in that restaurant, in the final weeks before her twentieth birthday and the dawn of the 1990s, Eden caught her first glimpse of her first *real* celebrity in New York. Sure, Cameron had his legions of fans, but the German-born artist was known uptown and down, by art lovers old and young, across the country and across the world.

"Well, then, happy birthday, Eden," Otto said, leaning down to kiss her hand. "It was truly a pleasure." And with that, Otto Clyde turned and walked toward the rest of his party's table, where he sat facing Eden, and Wes's back.

Throughout their anniversary dinner, Eden's eyes locked with

Otto's as he exhaled smoke and narrowed his eyes, as if to Xerox her visage into the labyrinthine cortex of his brain. For spank bank or for inspiration, he didn't know. But he knew one thing for sure: He was obsessed. He couldn't get her face, her body, out of his mind. And as an artist whose unique portraiture had a style all its own, there was no way he could easily get over a visual lightning bolt like that; he would have no peace until she flashed in front of him once more. Otto was determined to run into her again.

After the lovebirds left, Otto asked the restaurant's owner what the name on the reservation had been, and the next day, he had one in his cadre of assistants find all the nearby Bennetts. When they determined the right address, Otto went to the espresso bar downstairs and nursed a cup of coffee until he spied Wes at the foot of the steps, rubbing his little gold glasses on the bottom of his sweatshirt as he adjusted his messenger bag laden with texts and drafting papers. Bingo.

Not long after, his girlfriend emerged, even more breathtaking than before; her black jeans were tight and sleek, her long hair flowing over a sexy blouse she wore with the sleeves pushed up and a ton of bangle bracelets. Like a proto–Kate Moss, she had a style all her own, which cost little and was the trademark confident type that money can't buy. She tucked a lock of long hair behind her ear and walked smack into Otto.

"Miss Eden," Clyde said in his British-inflected, light German accent on her street corner as she was on her way to Tower Records. "How would you like to do some modeling for me?"

"Sure." She shrugged nonchalantly. She played it cool with her relaxed body language, but inside she was doing Romanian-caliber triple back-handsprings. They walked to a pay phone on the corner and she called in sick to work. She hung up with a big smile and turned to Otto. Otto took her hand.

"Follow me."

When Eden first arrived in the enormous, bustling Clyde studio, she was blown away. There were gorgeous, gamine hangers-on, rock music blaring, eyeliner-heavy assistants preparing a canvas with gesso. Otto showed her how to do the various poses, which came quite naturally that morning and over the next few technicolorful days. It was like a big, loud, raucous party that never ended, and Eden, lying on a white couch as Otto sketched her, was at its center. There were whispers from his circle of onlookers about her exquisite beauty, her perfect body, the fierce soul in her eyes.

She started going to the studio every day, and each night she would come home and gush all about the day's "work" to Wes, whose expression lit up as he watched his girlfriend excitedly describe her incredible day modeling.

"This is huge," Wes said beaming. "He is such a brilliant artist."

"Yeah, he's kind of as big as it gets right now," Eden marveled.

Wes was thrilled for her—he was so proud of Eden, not just because she had been noticed for her amazing beauty but because of her uniqueness, the fire in her eyes, her penetrating, burning soul, and the charm she emitted. She was enchanting, and together Wes knew they would make great art. But little did Wes know that Otto was a pair of shiny, searing hot scissors that would soon leave his heart in tattered ashen shards on the Bowery.

"What the fuck is your problem?" Allison asked, astonished when Eden said she wasn't sure if she'd stay with Wes long-term. "You guys are made for each other. By the way, news flash: He's the greatest thing to ever happen to you!"

Eden scoffed, taking a drag of her cigarette.

"Wes *is* amazing," Allison continued. "He cares about you.

And stop smoking! Didn't you promise him you were through with those Satan Sticks?"

"I can't quit now. Things are starting to happen for me! I just want to see where all this goes. If it works out and I join Clyde's studio, then I'll quit."

"If, if, if!" Allison teased. "Don't always look to the next thing, Eden; you've been doing it your whole life. It's a very bad habit."

"Oh yeah? Guess who I learned that from? You were the one goading me on," Eden said, flicking her ash, annoyed. "You told me I could make it here as a model. Is it so wrong to hope the wish we hatched back home comes true? What's so awful about looking to the next thing?" Eden asked.

"I'll tell you," said Allison, staring down her best friend across the table. "You miss what's right in front of you."

Everything appeared to be perfect with Wes: They made love at all hours, kissed in their rusty tub with Johnson's baby shampoo as bubble bath, lounged outside in the spring and picnicked on the Brooklyn Bridge on warmer nights. But would this be it *forever*? And while their little dumpy apartment was certainly romantic, was this all there would be for her?

Eden loved Wes deeply. She loved his passion for his architecture, the way he'd hold her hand as he taught her about design. She loved his warmth and shy humor. She even loved his adoring family, especially his mom, Penelope, who occasionally came to visit, taking the couple to Broadway shows and on fun excursions. She loved watching Wes study and sketch his projects for school, the large vein that ran down his wrist as he earnestly drew blueprints for class. Eden loved everything about him. But after years of dreaming of a career of her own, she knew one fierce unwavering truth: She loved herself even more.

After a month of Eden's modeling for Otto, poor Wes Bennett's exodus was written all over Otto's brushed canvases.

"I don't know," Eden confided in Allison. "When Otto's

painting me, I feel this . . . strange attraction to him. He says I'm his muse. I think he really likes me. He said he wants to do more canvases of me and that his gallery was obsessed with the paintings." Eden exhaled guiltily. "I care about Wes, I do, but . . ."

"*Buts* aren't good. Love is supposed to be unconditional, no buts—"

"I'm young. I have a future. We didn't come to New York so I could struggle my whole life. Look, I said before I *think* Otto likes me. But, Allison, I *know* Otto wants me. He ravages me with his eyes. And frankly, I kind of miss being worshipped like that. Wes is so gentle and sweet and loving but he's a student; Otto is aggressive, a manly man. He's bold and strong and—"

"Are you out of your mind? Poor Wes practically has a shrine to you! He adores you. And not because you're hot."

"I know," Eden said, sadly. "You know, I almost feel like Wes is the perfect person for me but that I met him too early. Like I was supposed to meet him later in life or something. We're too young now. I have, you know, *dreams*. Okay, that sounds so cheesy but it's true."

"Why can't you accomplish them together?" Allison asked, crushed.

"That's a long, long road. And I'm impatient. Otto is like that magic card in Candy Land that shoots you to the top. Wes is the long winding path."

"But it's a colorful path! It's fun with him," said Allison, devastated for poor Wes, who she truly thought was the best thing to happen to her best friend. "E, you *love* him."

"Maybe he's the right person, but it's the wrong time."

"Bullshit," said Allison, shaking her head. "If it's the right person, then I believe there is no such thing as the wrong time! If you really and truly believe it's the wrong time, than it means it's the wrong person."

"Then I guess he's the wrong person," Eden said.

"I really don't think you're right," Allison protested. Eden sat in silence. "So . . . what are you gonna do?"

"I know what I can't do. I can't sit and feel guilty and terrible about pursuing my own goals because of Wes."

"So is the hatchet falling on this relationship for real?" Allison asked, brokenhearted for sweet Wes.

"I don't know," Eden lied. She knew damn well it was.

7

The really frightening thing about middle age is that you know you'll grow out of it.

—Doris Day

While the little diner on the Bowery was really all that Eden and Wes could hack wallet-wise, they also continued to go there because of the sentimental history. It was *their* place. There were so many nights when Wes, laden with books in his messenger bag, snow falling all around him, would see Eden through the window across the street and feel as if he were coming home.

As he warmly kissed her hello after a freezing day apart, Eden felt a bolt of heat soothe her chest.

"Let's go get some sandwiches to go and sit in the park and see if those blues guys are out there singing," he suggested excitedly.

As the street band strummed their bass and crooned in harmony and light, fluffy snow started to dust their flushed faces, Wes knew, as Eden swayed in his arms to the music, that he could never be more elated than he was in that moment.

"I love you, Eden."

"I love you so much," she spat out guiltily, abruptly, surprising herself. "Come here." She threw her arms around him and kissed him as the mingling voices of the singers swelled. As much as that moment made her pulse rise, she still had her own seething drive to contend with, and the lure of fame made her heart beat even faster.

After growing chilly standing still as the snow fluttered, they decided to get walking again. They strolled the wooden walkway of the Brooklyn Bridge, their favorite place to go together, as they had on their second date. They walked under the majestic Gothic arches, drinking their coffees, looking upward in silence.

"I have something for you," Wes said.

He reached into his pocket and pulled out a little red box of Sun-Maid raisins.

"Aww." She leaned in and kissed him, taking the box.

"I wish—" Wes stopped in his tracks as his voice broke. He suddenly looked serious and then choked up.

"What?" Eden asked, stopping also, surprised by the emotion in his face.

"I wish it were a box of diamonds," Wes said.

Eden looked into his eyes, saying nothing. She thought she would cry.

"You deserve the world. I love you so much, Eden. I'll love you always, for the rest of my days. You make me want to give you everything I have, and even everything I don't have yet. I want to marry you," Wes said, holding her cold hands in his.

Eden didn't know what to do. She panicked. She leaned in and kissed him. They kissed and kissed until the tears Eden was fighting won their battle and welled in her eyes.

Eden never answered him that night. She just put her arms around him and squeezed him harder than she ever had before. When they returned home, they made love with a fervor so intense it was as if they would melt into each other; she gripped his back as he moved over her, as if she could hold on to him forever, but deep down, she knew she wouldn't.

Wes collapsed on top of her in a euphoric state, kissing her dewy neck while Eden lay on her back. Staring at the ceiling, the tears streamed out of the corners of her eyes down toward the tops of her ears. Wes didn't notice, but if he had, he would have mistaken them for tears of joy.

"I love you so much," he panted, wiped out.

"I love you, Wes," she replied as she patted his fluffy head of hair and choked back the sadness welling inside her.

8

Thanks to modern medical advances such as antibiotics, nasal spray, and Diet Coke, it has become routine for people in the civilized world to pass the age of 40, sometimes more than once.

—Anonymous

One warm day, after a month of sessions during which Otto Clyde very cautiously asked Eden to shed, say, her sweater, or even her skirt, Otto took a deep breath and walked up to his dream model. He had done his whole rigmarole before—pick out a new gorgeous girl, make her feel pretty, get her relaxed, maybe get her some booze, play some music, work her down until she feels calm and comfortable, not to mention a little tipsy. Then get her to show some skin.

He knew exactly what to do. He came in close for a gentle whisper.

"So, my dear," he started carefully. "I was thinking that today—"

Without a word, and unflinchingly maintaining eye contact with him, Eden pulled her black T-shirt over her head, revealing her perfect, pert breasts with no bra. Otto gulped. She stood up and calmly pulled down her panties with zero self-consciousness, as if she were a mannequin, but with a twinkle of confidence that proved she couldn't have been more alive. She was so at ease with her body, unlike the shy virgins or awkward ingénues off Amtrak whom Otto had to coax into the buff. Eden stood stark and relaxed as sweat began to gather on Otto's brow.

"I'm speechless. Your beauty is so rare, so flawless," Otto said to her as he ran his hand through his hair, nervously walking back to his easel and turning to face her again. "You truly make one understand how Helen of Troy's visage could have launched all those damn ships."

"Well, I'm glad we're making art and not war," she joked, rolling her green eyes.

"I believe the hippie dippies say make *love* not war," he countered flirtatiously.

"We can do both," she retorted.

His eyes flashed from behind his canvas. There it was, desire. Lock and load: Eden knew she'd hit the target. He was all hers.

Poor Wes didn't know what hit him.

"I'm so sorry, Wes. It's been . . . such an amazing time, really, I just . . . this is an amazing opportunity for me and I—"

"You're seriously leaving me? After last night?"

She flushed the thought of their final night together, a last walk on the Brooklyn Bridge, the red box of raisins, their final sex, all out of her head for fear she would lose her resolve. She choked back tears and proceeded, in a Tasmanian-devil-style whirlwind, to sweep up her things as she spewed sincere apologies with no eye contact. As Wes stood there withering with shocked grief, Eden swallowed hard and tried to speak as she finally looked at his face.

"I just think it's time to move on. Part of me will never stop loving you," she said as her voice cracked. "But I need to go."

Wes stood silently staring at her, decimated, like in a bad dream where you want to scream but nothing emerges. He had not seen this coming at all. As she turned to the door to leave their apartment for the last time, she saw Wes draw breath to speak his parting words. Dewy-eyed, he simply said quietly, "I hope this guy loves you as much as I do, Eden. And that you love him as much as I have loved you."

Eden's eyes swelled, but only for a second before she gathered her composure.

"I'm sorry," she said simply, before closing the rusty door behind her. And with that, she was gone.

9

They say that age is all in your mind. The trick is keeping it
from creeping down into your body.

—Anonymous

Any latent guilt Eden had about Wes was drowned in her
immediate joy when Otto told her *The New York Times*
Magazine wanted to photograph her for a story on his
new works. Her renewed ambition trumped any lingering grief.
And then Otto showed her to her own room, massive and clean,
gleaming white, and a huge marble bathroom just for her.

Things were finally happening. No more record store. No
more roaches. She could smell the next step, taste it. She'd come
a long way from her roots as a brilliant but bored rural high school
dropout from the wrong side of the wrong town, itching to get
out. And now here she was, posing for Otto Clyde and *The New*
York Times.

Eden couldn't help but pinch herself. While everyone would
be dead and disintegrated in a century's time, her image would
still stare down from museum walls spanning the globe, tantalizing viewers forever. After her glum childhood and dreams of bigger and better things, here she was: She had pulled it off.

Later that night, after the other studio hangers-on and one of the dealers left at nightfall, Eden and Otto remained, as he was on deadline for his new show at the Lyle Spence Gallery, which would feature the first finished canvases of his new muse. Eden, newly single, was supercharged and ready to pounce. As the sun was setting and the pair shared a snack in the industrial, skylit kitchen, Eden suggested they get back to work.

She opened her robe and let it fall to the floor. She walked back to her chaise and lay down as Otto went back to his easel. The artist was fully clothed in khaki pants and a white button-down shirt, sleeves rolled up a bit, with dabs of paint on it. After an hour of painting, and with Eden's heated gaze alone raising the temperature, they were both even more flirtatious than before. Eden's back was arched, her brow cunning. Otto unbuttoned his shirt a bit.

"Is it hot in here?" he asked.

Without a word, Eden sexily swung her legs over the edge of the chaise. She got up and casually walked over to his easel and faced him. She took the paintbrush out of his hand and chucked it on the floor, red paint from its wet bristles staining the wood. He was clearly stunned: He was used to sexual hunts with beautiful women, but usually *he* was the predator, not the prey. Eden stepped toward him and pressed her naked body onto his clothed one and kissed him forcefully. Otto shuddered, then molded into her grasp, feverishly returning her kiss. As the great artist breathed and sighed, Eden recognized the texture under her fingertips. She'd known it from the first guy she made out with at a spin-the-bottle party in seventh grade: putty.

Eden and Otto stumbled against the large white wall behind him as she put a smooth, young leg around him. He turned her around and he kissed her against the wall as she slowly moved her hand downward. The normally in-charge Rembrandt was positively enslaved. His hands shook, and he felt his heartbeat in every pore of his skin. He needed to be inside her. It was the sexual equivalent of a gulp of oxygen after being forced underwater. If he didn't fuck her that instant, he would die.

He lived.

And sadly, that first time Eden and Otto had mad sex on the floor of his studio, the red paint from his hands smearing her breasts and waist, poor Wes, her love of nearly a year and a half, didn't even enter her mind, not so much as a cameo in her unfolding, color-splattered, libidinous drama. As Otto flipped her over on all fours, Eden had flipped a mental switch. She ravaged Otto, knowing she had her talons in and she would not let go—she would be riding this celebrity train to the finish line, never looking back.

Just as Otto gasped in climax and screamed Eden's name, the word echoing in the cavernous loft, her fate was sealed. She had made it: Not only was she in Oz as she had once dreamed, but she was in the arms of the Wizard.

Va-Va-Voom!
Artist Clyde and New Muse
Take City by Storm

Get a Room! Famed painter **Otto Clyde** kicked up some paint at an exclusive party at the Plaza Hotel on Wednesday night as he engaged in Tonsil Hockey with a mysterious model. Awed onlookers gazed in amazement as the frisky pair pawed each other in a PDA-palooza. "They couldn't keep their hands off each other!" marveled one reveler. "I thought he was going to eat her face off."

Said another in the crowd of chronic-heartbreaker Clyde, who has been linked to **Debbie Harry** in the early '80s, plus models **Cheryl Tiegs** and **Tatjana Patitz**, "You can't teach an old dog new tricks." Not so, says a source close to the artist, whose last show sold out opening night, fetching seven-figure price tags: "He's smitten. He wants her to have his baby. He's obsessed with her." Clearly, so was everyone in attendance; the crowd couldn't take their eyes off the doe-eyed vixen, whose first name was rumored to be **Eden**. "She's the hottest girl I've ever seen," said art collector **Thor Quackenbush**. "She's pretty much as perfect as it gets."

10

The first twenty years are the longest half of your life.

—Robert Southey

Fifteen years later.

In a sea of black-clad, tattooed, faux-'hawk-sporting Sprockets, Eden and Otto clinked wineglasses in a cavernous white gallery on West Twenty-ninth Street. Steps from where tranny hookers with wigs and protuberant Adam's apples had tottered on six-inch red patent stilettos only a decade back, the NoChelSoHell (North of Chelsea, South of Hell's Kitchen) rectangle was now not only un-scary (b-bye to countless taxi garages, heroin dealers, and canine-sized rodentia) but actually borderline *posh*. The packs of rats had been replaced by Rat Packs of fancy high rollers on the prowl not for a White Castle crust or errant Sabrett hot dog remnant but to scavenge high-priced art, their eyes wide, mouths foaming, and wallets open.

Schmucks abounded. There were pompous art historians spewing postmodern theory about race, class, and gender; insecure but wealthy collectors racing to put holds on various pieces; art students wearing serial-killer thick-framed glasses; and of course dealers, rubbing their hands together with glee as the show sold out before opening night.

Tonight was a magnetic draw like none other: the opening of Otto Clyde's provocative latest works, lauded by critics, chased by buyers as marquee must-haves for their collections. His fame had only ballooned in recent years, as he dabbled in film like Julian Schnabel, his debut lauded and his second feature nominated for a Best Director Oscar. Like Jasper Johns or Andy Warhol before him, his work had a signature, graphic style—part pop silkscreen, part Edward Gorey grisaille. Mostly portraits, his images had a look all their own, one unmistakably Clyde, like a big fat fashion logo for collectors to show off. They loved showing that they could afford a seven-figure Clyde canvas above their couch. It was Otto's seventh solo show in The Eden Series, which featured the striking, mysterious, and brazenly sexy Eden Clyde, his sassy younger partner, muse, and best friend. Her job was lying nude on his mesmerizing canvases and playing a version of herself in his two movies. Otto had become not only the most famous artist in New York but also the world over, and Eden propelled him to new heights.

And vice versa. Eden's ascent by Otto's side was so rapid, their fame was cometlike. Magazines, television, fashion shows, celebrity friends . . . the world was hers. She'd fallen fast for Otto (and his fast-lane lifestyle), and by her twenty-first birthday she had become pregnant with the child of this thirty-eight-year-old budding international star. She was thrilled to have his baby, a son they named Cole. Despite their frenetic lives, the globe-trotting travel, from the Venice Biennale to fairs in Basel, Maastricht, Toyko, and Miami, to museum openings of his work, Cole was Eden's passion, and she made sure to create a stable base for him. She wanted him to be centered, despite the dartboard-on-a-map existence they led. While Otto gave gallery talks or had speaking engagements at various arts clubs, Eden would try to sneak off with Cole and weave in and out of winding city streets, discovering tucked-away churches and hidden architectural gems in all the nooks and crannies.

All the while, Eden didn't mind the lack of bended knee and ritual rings—Otto always made it clear that matrimony was for the masses, a biblical opiate to tame the rowdy hordes into little submissive units. It wasn't for him. And that was fine. It wasn't for her, either.

The years passed and she remained cool with it, even as friends like Allison, at twenty-nine, happily walked down the aisle with her doctor boyfriend, Andrew Rubens, reciting vows with dewy eyes and jubilantly tossed bouquets. At each white wedding, a longing for a tulle veil flickered like lightning in Eden's brain, stealth and momentary between two of her heartbeats. Occasionally she would flip through the *New York Times* Weddings section and smile warmly at the "Vows" column, a story of how that week's featured bride and groom met. And then, instead of becoming an emotional thunder crack, the dull temptation vanished. Allison was a radiant bride, showered with petals and presents, embarrassed by the spotlight but relishing her day in the sun. Eden, however, knew that was not her path. She and Otto were the hip couple with the cute growing son, the offbeat stars of their galaxy, like Brangelina but with a much better brand of fame: the kind where only cool people in the know recognize you. She didn't need to be in the spotlight for a day; she was already basking in it all the time: red carpets, gallery openings, a sexy, grainy campaign for the Marc Jacobs Collection, fashion shoots as a guest model when an editor called for "real" people— she didn't need to be swathed in organza and snapped in glamorized perfection. That was her job on a daily basis.

"Look at us," said Otto, his arm around her as the paparazzi of Europe gathered at the Musée d'Orsay in Paris for a much-hailed retrospective. "We are the toast of the Continent! You are their muse, too."

"I can't believe this," Eden said, stunned by the hordes of French press and fans, toting cameras, pads, and pens. Her hand cramped from the autographs, her eyes saw orange circles from the blitzes of light from cameras capturing her celebrated visage.

As the Clydes' fame and fortune increased through the years, so did Eden's euphoric high. She had it all: her precious son, Cole, who traveled the world with his parents and aced school when he was home, a partner who worshipped her in Otto, and a career of her own: part mother, part muse. And as more and more canvases of her naked body and fierce stare sold at higher and higher and higher prices to museums on every continent, Eden knew she had not only climbed to the heights she'd once dreamed of, she'd transcended them.

11

*When I passed forty I dropped pretense, 'cause men like
women who got some sense.*

—Maya Angelou

Meanwhile, on the same island of Manhattan but in a
milieu so drastically different it may as well have been
Abu Dhabi, two other lovers were at the top of their
game. Chase and Liesel, both twenty-five, had been introduced at
the Ball for New York Hospital, where both of their mothers
served as trustees, and were instantly the toast of the diamond-
paved philanthropic circles of Manhattan. The It Couple. The
heads of every junior committee, the most invited guests, the
boldfacers on social columns and best-dressed lists. Their eve-
nings were filled with grand parties, opening-night theater tick-
ets, and tête-à-tête cocktails. Their weekends featured jaunts to
their families' country homes, friends' lavish destination weddings, and little getaways to the Wheatley in Lenox, Massachusetts, or the Mayflower in Washington, Connecticut. Not to
mention dinner every night in a capital-lettered ZAGAT estab-
lishment: As any discerning eater knows, a restaurant in all-caps
means TOTALLY YUMMY BUT FUCKING EXPENSIVE.

"You look beautiful tonight, Buttercup," Chase said, taking Liesel's hand as she stepped from their chauffeur-driven car. He had nicknamed her that not for the gold-hued flower but for her resemblance to Robin Wright Penn.

"Aw, thank you, sweetie," she said, lifting her delicate wrist so he would notice the thin emerald-laced links. "Look, I'm wearing my new bracelet!"

"You wear it well."

"I love it!"

"I was thinking we should go up to Blantyre this weekend, what do you think?" Chase asked. "It was really great last time when the weather was freezing."

"Hmmm . . . what about the Wheatley?" Liesel asked, tilting her perfectly coiffed head in serious consideration. Ahh, decisions, decisions. "That food was so delicious. Plus remember that massage therapist who came to our room? Oh, I just love that place. It's so cozy. But the Blantyre's great, too. Up to you!"

"Then the Wheatley it is," Chase said, as if they had just settled on a strategy in a business meeting. "I'll have Pam book it in the morning."

When the backdrop for time together is so romantic, lubricated with Dom, sparkling with gems, and scented with peonies delivered weekly from L'Olivier, relationship cracks take longer to emerge. In five-star hotels, anyone could feel misty eyed and hit in the ass by Cupid's arrow. Hot meal, hot tub, hot sex.

Also, Chase was as gorge as he was loaded. Chase DuPree Lydon's facial architecture was so refined that you could slash your wrist on his chiseled cheekbone, and his eyes were so blue you'd bet the Vineyard compound that they were colored contacts. If a *New Yorker* cartoonist were commissioned to create a caricature of his perfect visage, it would be the artistic equivalent of shooting a fish in a barrel: too easy. He was almost too handsome, too perfect. Not that he was ridiculous like Gaston in Disney's *Beauty and*

the Beast, overmuscled with Leno's chin and beefy 'roidy chest.
No, his handsome beauty, innocent and cold, was like a child's,
gripping and hypnotic. When Chase walked into Waverly Inn or
Da Silvano, everyone—from Graydon to Anna to countless
celebs—turned to look at him. Even tourists who didn't know
who he was wondered, "Who's that?" sensing instantly he was at
least B List.

Like JFK Junior before him, this scion of a world-renowned,
prominent political family had been in the public eye since a very
young age. His attractive, popular maternal grandfather, Price
Hutton DuPree, had been a United States senator, ambassador to
the Court of St. James, and then head of the United Nations. His
mother, Brooke DuPree Lydon, had married his father, Grant
Lydon, in a grand society wedding at the University Club in
Haute Couture, chronicled in *Vogue*. Brooke was a Hitchcock
blonde, picture perfect, pulled together and full of pronounce-
ments, be they political ("I'm to the right of Mussolini and
proud!") or fashion-related ("People over ten who wear Crocs
should be executed."). Brooke had three sisters (Paige, Blair, and
Lynne) and followed in her family's tradition of curt, monosyl-
labic names for her three sons: Price, Pierce, and Chase. The four
DuPree girls had been blond photogenic catnip for the press, waving beside their parents at the Republican convention or riding
their thoroughbreds in Millbrook, and now so were Brooke's
three sons. They were constantly snapped by shutterbugs—on the
beach in Massachusetts or at a polo match in the Hamptons or at
a black-tie ball on New York's benefit circuit.

Truth be told, Chase didn't really care for the air-kissing scene
of Manhattan's elite. He had been educated at Buckley, Groton,
Princeton, and Harvard Business School, with classmates at each
institution whose family names were synonymous with those on
the Fortune 500. But while he had never cared about any of that
crap, and even sometimes wanted to bag some of these sometimes

twice-weekly rituals, Chase was dutiful. He was the model son who never got into trouble at school (whereas Price has been expelled from Andover and spent his senior year at a public school in Southampton, near the family estate). And forget about the entitled generation: Chase exhibited what his mother, Brooke, called "the work ethic of a Filipino," laboring for his family firm till all hours, while Pierce had been "between jobs" for six years (read: does jack shit). Both of his brothers rolled in the proverbial hay with blond tits-on-sticks with head shots and their own Web sites who may have shimmied by a greased pole or two, and had names that ended in the letter *i*, the classy nomenclature kiss of death. But good Chase dated a shining star of Mayflower descent on par with the DuPree Lydon pedigree: Liesel van Delft. No Brandis or Candis for him.

Yet as the years passed, the union that would have had his forefather's fossils cheering from their cobwebbed graves, all was not well. Though it was a sunlit, romantic courtship, by twenty-eight, Chase and Liesel were coasting on a cross between love and inertia.

"Sweetie," Liesel said one night as they undressed for bed. "I feel like you don't even notice my new matching lingerie. I splurged at La Perla and you barely looked up."

"Oh, it's beautiful, honey. I'm so sorry, I'm just, I have a splitting headache."

"I have seventeen sets of perfect matchy-matchy sexy stuff. I even went for this magenta set, and it's like . . . I may as well be wearing my eighth-grade Calvins."

"Not true, Buttercup. I'm just in agony, that's all. I need to take some Excedrin."

The truth was, he had hardly noticed her pinup getup. Under her cream-colored cashmere twinsets, strings of pearls, and proper pencil skirts, she always paired together a lacey confection. Part patrician kindergarten teacher and part burlesque, Liesel made an effort to rock some titillating lingerie beneath her ho-hum one-notch-above-Talbots WASPy attire. But no such luck tonight for her hope to have her longtime boyfriend crave her. Within a few minutes, after bringing him the two capsules and a drink of bottled water to wash them down, she had slipped a silk floor-length nightgown over her head and was over it.

The next night, Liesel tried her luck again. Perhaps soon she could get a sense of what her boyfriend's intentions were.

"Mother says we make quite the handsome couple," Liesel mused as the duo caught sight of themselves on the mirrored door of an elevator up to the Rainbow Room on yet another glamorous date night.

Feeling guilty for being less affectionate with her, Chase kissed her up sixty floors until the ding of the roof destination sounded. As the double doors were about to open, Liesel abruptly pulled back and smoothed her hair, lest, heavens forbid, someone spy their unseemly PDA.

"Liesel, come here," Chase said, trying to kiss her again.

"Chase, people are looking!" Liesel unfastened the toggles of her Dennis Basso fur coat. "Sweetie, will you check this for me? I'm going to run to the Ladies' quickly."

Chase knew her lipstick had to be refreshed; Liesel simply couldn't make an entrance without being preened to perfection.

As he waited, Chase surveyed the scene, watching one couple cuddle sweetly, while another was reunited across the bar with a huge hug and passionate kiss.

"I'm back! Did you miss me?" she cooed in an almost childlike tone.

"Like the Sahara misses the rain," he said sarcastically, hand on heart.

"Stop teasing me!" she squealed jokingly, mock-whacking him with her Fendi clutch.

As the years wore on, Chase started to get a creeping feeling

about that allegedly perfect word: satisfaction. Isn't life supposed
to be more than "satisfying"? Isn't there supposed to be an elated
surge of heated passion, a crazy, scream-from-the-rooftops, jump-
on-Oprah's-couch epiphany of utter besotted *amore*? Little by little, the white peonies on Liesel's birthday, the bracelets from
Tiffany at Valentine's Day, the necklaces at anniversaries, and the
trips for Christmas felt rote. He had tried, a few months back, to
do something crazy and surprise Liesel with a helicopter ride, but
she had declined, saying she didn't much like surprises. Or choppers, apparently.

Throughout Chase's entire life, any latent impulses toward adventure had been summarily quashed by his family, and now Liesel was doing the same thing. When he wanted to travel abroad,
The Family warned him of cousin Barrett, who had gone to the
Amazon on an ecotour and disappeared; no one knew if he had
fallen into a ravine, OD'd on drugs, or encountered some tribal,
bone-through-nostrils headshrinkers who rendered his aristo-
cratic melon the size of a clementine. Barrett's disappearance,
along with his great-aunt's falling asleep cuddling her boyfriend,
Jack Daniels, and a cigarette, plus his uncle's bungee jump gone
awry, caused speculation in the press of a DuPree curse. So para-
noid was this family tree that its powerful branches swayed with
fear when even the slightest threat appeared on the horizon. When
Chase subtly floated the idea of parasailing by the family home at
Round Hill in Jamaica, Brooke looked at him with squinted
eyes.

"Surely, you jest."

"Mom, please: It's no big deal! Countless people have busi-
nesses doing parasailing all over the island. It's their living. If people got killed, they wouldn't do it," he pleaded.

"Do what you must," Brooke said with a crisp, passive-
aggressive shrug. "But if you smash into the dock and shatter both
legs, don't come running to me."

Needless to say, Chase decided to skip it.

Sometimes Liesel was, in a far less manipulative way, similar to Brooke in her slight puppeteering.

"Really, you want to play golf today?" Liesel would say with a sad face. It was clear that little pout had worked with Daddy since babyhood. "Okay, fine. I was so hoping to play tennis together with Wills and Becky, but it's fine, we'll do that another time, sweetie. You go play golf."

"No, no, no, you're right," related Chase. "I'd be psyched to play tennis, too. I'll call Wills."

But while Liesel gently floated one café over another or perhaps a different activity instead of the one Chase had envisioned, she found ever-so-annoyingly that forcing her boyfriend's hand to take her hand was proving slightly more difficult.

"I'm so excited for Phoebe Nordstrom," she said at La Goulue one night. "She and Roddy got engaged! She seems sooo happy."

"She's a nice girl," Chase replied, not sensing the nudge-nudge. "Roddy's fine, though all he wants to talk about is business. I'm not sure if he has any other interests."

Liesel felt her face growing red. "Well, he's interested in Phoebe, *clearly*."

All of the pressures came to a head one cold January evening. Chase had just walked into his parents' apartment for the weekly family dinner, when Brooke soberly took his arm and sat him down, relaying to him the sad news that Ruthie DuPree, his maternal grandmother, had just suffered a stroke. He was devastated. Chase was extremely close to Ruthie, a whip-smart firecracker of a woman with an old body but a young soul. She always inspired him, conspired with him, and made him laugh out loud.

"You know what keeps grandkids and grandparents so close?"

Ruthie once asked him, rolling her eyes as Brooke prattled on to the staff about florists. "We have a common enemy." Life with Ruthie was filled with winks and code speak. She and Chase had their own unique rhythm and bond, a close-knit connection that he cherished, especially now: After decades of political programming and social censorship, Ruthie's edit button had started to jam, and she just said whatever the hell she wanted. Sometimes it enraged Brooke to hear her mother and son laughing hysterically at the dinner table, wielding swear words and whispered jibes. She felt left out of some wildly hilarious, and often dirty, joke.

"Your mother has to, what do you kids say? *Chill* the hell out! Why's she so angry all the time? Always complaining, your mother. Never had a dish she didn't send back to the chef. Twice."

Once, at dinner at the now-shuttered La Caravelle, Chase reeled in embarrassment as his mother cruelly berated a waiter publicly over undercooked meat. Equally horrified, Ruthie leaned in to her favorite grandson and said under her breath: "Brookie's karma's so bad, when she was little and I gave her a bowl of alphabet soup, the noodles all swam together and spelled out FUCK YOU."

Chase almost spat out his soup en croute.

"What's so funny?" Brooke probed, aghast not only at her silly food issue but also more gravely over the generational conspiracy that repeatedly had her feeling like the left-out monkey in the middle. "You two are always thick as thieves."

Chase loved it. While he remained ever respectful of his mother, that didn't mean he didn't love listening to his beloved grandma Ruthie slinging a little shit on occasion. No one had a grammy as cool as Ruthie. Sometimes Chase would laugh so hard he had stomach pains, which then morphed northward into his throat, forming a sad lump in recognition that his days with her would be numbered and he couldn't imagine life without her clever barbs.

As Chase digested the shocking news of her stroke, he was grief-stricken. Brooke put her arm around her son.

"Who knows how much time she'll have left now," Brooke said ominously. Offering comfort was never Brooke's strong suit.

"Maybe you should consider proposing to Liesel sooner rather than later," she continued. "You know Grandma's ring is ready when you want it."

Chase knew a vault on Madison and Sixty-second held the birthright for the hand of his intended, three D Flawless boulders for each of the boys, all collecting dust. And while it was an enormous privilege to not have to hit cheesy Zales like so many other knee-bending grooms-to-be, the silent presence of Ruthie's Cartier-designed ice rink in Box 2736 felt like a huge burden. A rock, so to speak, that weighed heavily on his shoulders and conscience. He loved Liesel, sure, but he always secretly dreamed of a woman who had a bit more chutzpah, a bit more sass, more edge. Someone who understood him the way his grandmother Ruthie did versus the way his mother saw him. Someone who challenged him. Someone who made him feel a longing so strong it was akin to an ache. He had no idea what that would be like. But something boiling within his blue blood was dying to find out.

12

*You've heard of the three ages of man—youth, age, and "you
are looking wonderful."*

—Francis Cardinal Spellman

The zenith of Otto and Eden's fame came when he painted
her (not her likeness but her actual body—boobs, pubes,
and all) for a historic cover of *Vanity Fair*'s Art Issue when
Eden was thirty-five. It was her apex—of beauty, of confidence.
Her shiny chocolate brown hair was waist long and flowing, and
she was buck naked but for his impassioned brushstrokes on her
breasts, torso, and long legs. Otto stood beside her in his jeans and
paint-splattered T, running a hand through his trademark shock
of prematurely gray hair. The photograph, shot by Annie Lei-
bowitz during the peak of exorbitant canvas price tags harvested
by hedge funders, became nothing short of iconic.

Inside the thick issue was a twenty-page portfolio of the world's
top artists and their muses, inspirers who ranged from children to
friends to lovers to a cadre of sexy sycophants hoping to be in the
presence of the next Francesco Clemente. They lolled around
shirtless, doe-eyed, and languid as the old CK One ads of the
early nineties, overbred and underfed, gamine and gorgeous. But

of all the muses, it was Otto Clyde's who was the most striking. Even on the page, she was charged and alive. The glimmer in Eden's piercing mint green eyes, the arch in her thin brow, and a sexy pout on her full lips rivaling Angelina's obsessed many a reader. Her Latin cursive tattoo down the inside of her upper arm—*more certa, non vita*: "death is certain, life is not"—lent her a live-in-the-moment passion that made her seem to jump off the cover and inside pages.

The magazine sold more issues from the newsstand than ever before, launching a nationwide wave of interest in Eden; she had always been famous among the intelligentsia and fashionista clan, but now it seemed the whole country wanted to know more about her, as the name *Eden Clyde* yielded millions of Google hits, and prices for Clyde's portraits skyrocketed.

Eden couldn't believe how far she'd come.

It was the height of heights. But the problem of reaching that coveted summit is of course that there is nowhere left to go . . . but down.

Not that the thought even entered their minds at first; they were still flying high. Unlike It Boy artists who came and went, Clyde had reached quasi-Picasso, godlike stature with his alluring persona and boundless talent. Photographers snapped pictures of him and Eden, holding hands or eating dinner at Da Silvano with handsome Cole. There were legendary parties in warehouses where the backdrop was cocaine, deafening mixed music, and blinding hues of fashionistas' too-bright wardrobes. When Eden wasn't spending time with Cole, taking him to and from school or to museums or to the park, she was part of the Otto Clyde machine. She was entertaining their friends or collectors with Moroccan feasts, Chinese New Year celebrations—any excuse to have a bash. Otto needed the buzz of people around him, fluttering their wings to stroke his ego, their voices building to a chorus of how talented he was.

But what onlookers might not have known was that Otto and Eden's relationship was very, ahem, *alternative*—although what Otto did (fucking countless women) couldn't be called *cheating* because they weren't married, and Eden knew all about it. He was a sexual omnivore who worshipped Eden but craved variety. She couldn't know for sure since Otto was as discreet as he was lustful. But the first time he actually admitted it was probably right around when Cole was twelve or thirteen, and Eden was cruising into her mid-thirties.

"Sweetness," he said, kissing her hand. "You look ravishing. This has nothing to do with you, but . . . ," his voice trailed off.

"I know. Daddy's gotta get some," she finished. She pretended to be chill and shrugged as if she hadn't a care in the world.

"See? There is no one like you. You get it," he said, kissing her. "You're a modern woman. How did I get so lucky?"

"I don't know, you are pretty damn lucky," she said, flopping on the bed. He climbed on her and kissed her neck. For the first time, she felt sick about her complicit participation in this lousy deal. He was sucking the best years out of her and still getting some on the side.

"I love only you, though," he said each night, sliding into their bed in the darkness. Sometimes she pretended to be asleep. "There is no one like you, my Eden."

Eden knew by that point he had plenty of lovers, but one by one she'd bested those beeyotches and had him to herself at the end of every night. That was their unspoken rule. Roll in the hay but come home to roost. Eden knew that this was the deal she had made in exchange for her life, one people would kill for. One that exceeded her wildest Shickshinny dreams. But the truth was, she hadn't been dreaming much at all lately, because she hadn't slept in ages. She had been a total insomniac her entire life but it was getting worse than ever. Not even the latest drugs could help her. She consistently woke up at 3:13 every morning, heart pounding.

She'd toss and turn for an hour, flip her pillow over, do Jane Fonda–style leg lifts to combat cramping and even a yoga-esque bridge to crack her stressed back. Then, after her mind raced till 5:00, she'd fall back asleep as the sun started to pierce the gray night.

"How is my darling, sweet little honey this morning?" Otto kissed her awake.

She slept in the nude and sat up in the sheets to give him a kiss hello.

"Fine," she said, rubbing her eyes. "Tired."

"I've made us some espresso and Alonzo just brought in some fresh pains au chocolat. Let's get to work!" He clapped.

Yeah, sure, she thought. With his hot lay last night of course he's charged and ready to go. As she hauled herself to the bathroom mirror, noticing the grooves in her forehead looked slightly deeper than they had even yesterday, she rubbed her neck, which was incredibly sore. How ironic, she thought, kneading the painful spot on the right. The body echoes the mind. She had been looking the other way for far too long.

13

The spiritual eyesight improves as the physical eyesight declines.

—Plato

In a sunlit East River–facing room of New York Hospital, Ruthie DuPree lay in her Craftmatic, watching soaps. Not one, not two, but seventeen flower arrangements from L'Olivier, Renny & Reed, and Plaza adorned her suite, the cards from various charity boards Ruthie sat on all sending well wishes and hope for a speedy recovery. Chase sat beside her, holding his grandmother's hand as the nurse drew blood from her left arm. He watched a huge tugboat move up the river in silence, its wake muted by the thick wall of glass. But the quiet moment was punctuated by beeps from the IV and various calls on the speaker system as the vials filled with a dark red liquid that J. Crew would call oxblood. But it wasn't an ox, it was his beloved and frail Grammy, and it pained Chase to see this strong, vibrant woman with tubes and needles stuck in her papery skin.

After the nurse exited, she turned to Chase, gesturing weakly.

"Promise me you'll yank the plug if I get all loony," she said seriously. "I don't want to be some drooling vegetable like Helen Sinclair from Maidstone. If I ever get to the point where I don't recognize you or your brothers, just rip it out. Promise."

"Grandma, please. Don't talk like that, I can't stand it." Chase winced. "You're going to be fine."

"C'mon, Chasie. I'm ninety-two, I've lived my life! Why stick around and have the personality of a hothouse tomatah?"

Some say tomayto, some say tomahto, but Ruthie said tomatah. She was sophisticated New York but was so down-to-earth and no bullshit; she almost sometimes sounded off the farm. Chase took his grandmother's thin, veined hand and held it tightly, saying nothing.

"You know," she said, looking at her beautiful grandson's perfect but somewhat sad face. "You're too darn serious. Why so serious? You're young. You've got the world in your hand."

"I'm . . . not so serious."

"Baloney. Always the good son. Since you were a little boy with your poncy little suit and your violin case. You were always so serious. Maybe it's because those darn brothers of yours were so damn reckless. Your mother put too much of a burden on you. So much pressure! I told her, 'Brookie, let the boy breathe,' but you were her star, always."

"I don't know about that," Chase said bashfully.

"Take it from me," she said with a wink. "It all goes by so fast, Chasie. You've been old since you were a kid! Even with your young face, up here, in your head, you've always been an old fogey. Don't wait till your body is, too. Don't wait till you're in this bed hooked up to all this junk to realize you could have had some fun, could have lived a little."

Chase sat quietly, digesting his grandmother's words.

"Look, I loved my life, I've had a great run," she said, smiling. "But if I could do it over, I'd live it up a little more, go nuts. Rock the boat," she confessed. "I had so many obligations to your

grandfather, so many duties, the campaigns, the political fund-
raisers, the attention. It was all wonderful, but sometimes I was
itching to break free—just a bit—and I hope you will, Chase.
Everyone—all the people you know—will be old, lying here like
me one day. What's it all for, unless you eat it all up? Devour each
day. Loosen up, my boy! You don't know how to have any fun."

"That's not true. I can have fun, Gram." He smiled, trying to
assure her with his boyish grin that he wasn't some robotic drone
drowning in duties.

"You can't really have fun if you've never broken a rule or two.
Now I don't mean laws, don't go getting arrested, not like your
dumb brothers. I mean *rules*, the way things are. The status quo.
Your schools, your job, your gal are all things that Mom and Dad
wanted for you. But do you want that for yourself?"

"Sure, I mean, what's not to like about my life?" he asked
somewhat defensively. She had touched a nerve.

"*Like?* You just said it yourself. You think you should like life
or love it? Ya know how I spell *like*? B-O-R-I-N-G. Like is bland.
Like is yellow cake without the chocolate frosting. Dress it up.
Rev it up a notch, kiddo!"

Chase looked at her hand in his. He was so hardwired to be
The Good Son that he couldn't even divorce his wishes from
those of his parents. They were deeply intertwined, like two
necklaces that get tangled into a ball of indistinguishable links.

"I'm . . . happy, I am."

"You don't sound so convinced to me."

"No, no, I am . . . everything's great."

"Careful there, Chasie. You keep telling yourself that and you
might believe it."

Dr. Smith knocked as he opened the door.

"Mrs. DuPree, good afternoon!" he bellowed as Chase rose
from the bed to shake his hand.

"Hello, Doctor," Chase said, shaking his hand. "I should be

getting back to work, Grandma. I'll be back later, before dinner."

"All right, darling. See you later, sweetheart."

"Love you."

He closed the door gently behind him and got back to work just in time, as always.

14

We know we're getting old when the only thing we want for our birthday is not to be reminded of it.

—Anonymous

As Eden stared down the barrel of thirty-nine, she began to look back on her life and her choices and consider her future needs. Fall was approaching, and soon Eden and Cole would order twelve moving boxes to pack him up for college. She cried as she left him at JFK to head off to Stanford, where he had been accepted early decision. The house seemed empty, like when she had first moved in. Except that back then, the massive home was filled with the bubbling energy of the pair's joint excitement, both for their artistic endeavors and for each other.

That was long gone. As Eden walked around the living room, picking up a sweatshirt Cole had left behind, she feared that she was falling slowly into an abyss of frustration and depression. Those Prozac ads with the little cartoon blobs with sad frowny faces started to speak to her.

"Are you not enjoying the things you used to?" Check.

"Are you feeling like an outsider?" Yup.

"Are you dreading social engagements?" Hell, yes.

"Is your partner making you feel underappreciated, invisible, and, oh by the way, is he fucking twenty-somethings behind your back?" Ding, ding, ding! Okay, that one wasn't in the commercial, but it was starting to be difficult to ignore as fact. Little by little as the weeks passed and she took stock of Cole's departure and her empty nest and empty chest, Eden weighed her fate. And then she weighed her options.

But where would Eden go? What was she going to do? Leave this life? Start all over again like old times? *Hell-to-the-No.* She would do what everyone else did: Deal with the fact that you can't always have everything. And how spoiled was she? She had it all!

Here she was, at the height of fame and fortune, in a place where everyone would want to be. But like Sheila E. once crooned about the glamorous life, "Without love, it ain't much." Eden always thought love was for naïve Hallmark card buyers, a kick-in-the-pants cocktail of pheromones. But in the complete and total absence of romantic love, which she now realized her relationship was, she starting to have a feeling she never had known: longing. She didn't know what that intangible lack was, what it was she yearned for, but she knew the growing emptiness inside her was getting worse as time quickly passed.

Eden popped more happy pills, drank more wine, but they were only temporary fixes for what she would inevitably face in the morning: an even bigger pit in her gut, not to mention the bed she shared with Otto. She slept only on her left side, her back to him. And even if her every muscle wanted her to roll onto her right, she fought it. She couldn't bear to face him, knowing full well he slept beside so many others. For years she truly didn't care. But more and more lately she found herself getting suckered into romantic stories, movies about true love, and she would even find herself staring at older couples holding hands or dining together.

Sometimes she went to films by herself to pass the time, watching the tilted heads of couples watching the screen, their hands touching the popcorn, or resting on each other's thighs. She started to realize that all those romantic stories she'd dreamed of as a child were tantalizing her again, filling the voids they once had. And this time, it wasn't with the hopeful glimmer that she had watched Molly Ringwald kiss Jake Ryan as she had as a kid; it was with a nostalgic sadness that she may never know such a pure love like that again. She realized she was experiencing a brand-new feeling: envy. Sadly, it seemed Eden, the woman everyone wanted to be was starting to want to be someone else.

Eden tried to exhale any thoughts of moving on out of her head. It was too far-fetched and too silly; her childhood resilience, she feared, had evaded her more and more as her age ticked upward. But little by little, Eden began to think the allegedly perfect world she had built for herself might splinter into a thousand meteors if the pressure welling inside her were to grow stronger.

"Otto, we need to talk," Eden said one night as he slid under the cover in the pitch-black of night. "I don't think I can do this anymore."

"My love. Don't be silly! You know I love only you. You are my whole *world*!"

"I'm starting to feel more like Pluto," she said. "I've been de-accessioned, downgraded from planet status."

"Oh, Eden, don't be so dramatic." He cackled casually.

"I'm serious," she replied. "I can't take it. I'm tired of being the 'cool, modern' woman. Maybe I want to be old-fashioned!"

"You? Impossible," Otto scoffed.

"We'll see," she trailed off, hating being goaded by him. She used to love a challenge, but at her age she feared one.

"Good night, Eden," he said, rolling over. His snoring soon sounded like a foghorn that could easily register on the Richter scale. Nice. Now she had to fucking lie there being tortured by his soundtrack that was akin to a nasal chain saw. She put a pillow on her head. She rolled back and forth. She tried to dream of a different life, something romantic, something new. But she never achieved freeing slumber that would send her traveling away from the life she was entrenched in. Instead, by the lavender light of dawn, she was still staring at the ceiling with red eyes.

"I'm just a little down, that's all," Eden told Allison over coffee when she inquired about bloodshot retinas and her seemingly blue demeanor.

"Why, because Cole left for school?"

"Maybe. That, and I just . . . get this feeling that maybe I'm in a rut right now. A really deep one. And it's growing deeper as more time goes by. I'm not happy. It's been a while now, to be honest. I just never said anything until now."

"Why do you think?"

"I'm getting old. I can't sleep at night. I'm getting more and more restless."

"That's why you're down? 'Cause we're getting older?"

"No. Well, yes, that and I'm also growing upset with Otto's . . . dalliances. Maybe there's more out there for me. Otto's, you know . . . being Otto."

"That never bothered you before, you two are upfront, open."

"The problem is," Eden said, looking out the café window, "it's starting to bother me now."

"Interesting," Allison said, sipping her coffee. The other sexy strappy sandal was about to drop. Allison always knew Otto's ways might be a heavier burden on Eden as the years wore on, and she feared this day would come.

"There's this new girl in the studio. Mary. I could be her mother. She's blond, beautiful, and so . . . young," Eden said to her black coffee, sadly. Mary had been around a few months and was like any new model or part of the entourage, except that Eden recognized in her eye the very same twinkle of ambition she once had. Or blazing fire was more like it. She had her talons into Otto, and Eden suspected he was beginning to wilt in her grasp. She was Eden, only younger.

"So? He's always been into mixing it up, you know that. He is still obsessed with you and fully devoted, right?"

"I'm not so sure anymore. You know, I look back and I feel like an ungrateful idiot because I got everything I thought I wanted but it doesn't feel quite right," she said, trailing off.

"Well, E, you have to be realistic. I mean, I am madly in love with Andrew and it's not like we are rabbits pawing each other every single night. Day-to-day life is about companionship and respect and love, not necessarily boning."

"It's not that. It's not just about the sex; it's a connection that has flickered and faded out completely. I'm getting really lonely. I'm just starting to realize that I'm hitting middle age and I have my own needs. It's been a long time coming. And it's starting to scare me."

"So what, are you seriously telling me you might split with Otto? After all these years?" asked Allison, incredulous.

"I'm thinking if I ever want to be truly happy, now is the time I need to take a step away from him, from this relationship."

"Let me tell you something, Eden. When I was single and screwing all these guys and you asked me about it like you missed it, what did I say? I said, *It's hell out there! You are missing nothing!* Once the sex sparks burn out it's all about companionship anyway."

"Well, I don't even have that. Not anymore, anyway. And plus, come on, there has to be more than that, Allison! I mean I'm turning thirty-nine, not eighty-nine. Yes, I want companionship, but can't I have both? I can't be invisible to him for the rest of my life."

"At first when you met Otto and had Cole, I was still lonely and single and I thought all you couples drank the Kool-Aid and were skipping in rainbow slow motion, walking your unicorns. And then when I got married I realized: It wasn't a fantasy! It *is* so much better to be part of a couple! You just have to work through the dry patches. That's normal—peaks and valleys."

"This is a big fucking valley," Eden said. "I'm talking Grand Canyon."

"You'll get through it!" Allison said, patting her friend's arm. "Trust me."

"I guess."

"No, you don't *guess*. You have to *make* it work, try. What are you fantasizing about, anyway? Now you're having this vision of what it's like to be single! Again: It sucks out there."

"Maybe you're right," Eden said, confused and exhausted. "But it's starting to be pretty miserable for me as well. Now the freedom of being single and hopeful is the side with the pegasuses or whatever."

"Unicorns."

"Same thing," said Eden, rolling her eyes.

"No. One has a horn, one has wings."

"I'm just so tired," complained Eden. "I can't sleep. I lie awake obsessing about life, aging, death . . ."

"Cheerful," Allison teased.

"I know, it's pathetic," Eden admitted. "That's what I'm saying! I'm in a rut." Great. Now even Allison thought she was being dramatic, just like Otto had said.

After they left the café, Eden sulked homeward and climbed into bed listlessly for a nap. When she woke up, Mary and a bunch of young people were there at the studio. This was starting to become the routine lately, and Eden had always sucked it up and joined them. But as Otto more frequently mentioned a new film Mary adored, or a new café they must try on her recommendation ("All the young people are going there!"), Eden started to suspect that Otto and Mary were enmeshed more than his other rolls in the hay.

Her suspicions were confirmed one rainy day, when she arrived at her local yoga studio to find it was closed due to a water main break. She did a disappointed 180 and wandered back home. When she opened the door, she found Otto in their marital bed with Mary. Clearly, post-coitus. This was a first.

"Honey! I . . . didn't know you'd be home."

Mary pulled the sheets up over her mega breasts and resembled a young Marilyn Monroe.

"IN OUR BED, REALLY?" she fumed.

Eden turned and stormed out. Otto left Mary and followed her into the cavernous stairwell.

"Eden. Come on, love, you know I love you. We were just painting and things got . . . come on, love, Mary is just—"

"Just the one who tells you where all the *young people* are hanging out? What the young people are listening to? Huh? FUCK YOU, OTTO. I can't take this anymore."

"Let's not be immature, Eden. You knew I had my needs—"

"AND I HAVE MINE."

Otto stopped, looking surprised as his brow furrowed.

"Honey, this never bothered you before."

"IT BOTHERS ME NOW. No wife in America would put up with what I have. I should have known! *Marriage is just a piece of paper, right?* Now what?"

"Eden, calm down."

"Don't tell me to calm down!"

"This is madness!" Otto laughed with an evil cackle. "You know we are meant to be together! Mary is nothing," he said, looking away. His downward gaze betraying his lie.

"Otto, she's fine. She's cool, even. But you're into her. I can tell."

"I'm not 'into her.' How juvenile this all sounds. Into her. What are we, ninth graders?"

"Fine, so tell yourself that if you'd like. Anyway, it doesn't even matter—if you're not into her, you'll be into others. There will be more young girls who make you feel recharged and immortal. And we need to be honest about this: You and I are running on fumes here. I have struggled with this for a while and I know now, seeing her IN OUR BED, that I need to go."

"Eden, don't be dramatic."

"I'm not. See, you didn't smash my heart like a sledgehammer with Mary overnight," she explained sadly. "You broke it slowly, like putting it through a cheese grater. No, it was even slower, wearing it away like sandpaper each night, with each woman you fucked. And now I've taken a new shape. And I don't like what I see."

"Honey—"

"I have to go."

Otto didn't fight the fight. In fact, he let her walk without any resistance.

Eden, who hadn't cried in years, walked like a teary-eyed windup doll onto the uptown subway, exited and walked to Allison's apartment, and collapsed into convulsive sobs Allison had never seen from her best friend. After decades of holding the water back from her eyes, Eden let loose, crying not just for Otto but for everything in her whole life.

"Let it out, sweetie," she said as she handed Eden tissues and rubbed her bony back, which racked with sobs.

She could see the flashes of Eden's whole life in those tears, all the disappointments. It pained Allison immensely to see her friend's resolve disintegrate before her eyes. Allison prayed that her friend would have the strength to deal with the flood the way she had in her youth. She had to pull herself up and soldier on.

"We are going to get you sorted out," Allison promised.

"Here's what's going to happen. You will stay here this week in Kate's room and she'll stay with the twins. I am calling Schlepper's Movers. They are hot Israelis. They will come in like a tornado and pack you all up. You'll move up here near us. You'll start over."

Eden nodded blankly, happy to hand over the reigns for the first time in her life.

She was catatonic over the next week as Allison (and Gadi and Asa, the movers) helped pack her things and move her into a small rental apartment uptown. She nodded at the broker as a signal of "I'll take it," as Allison scurried about settling her in with a bed, furniture, and fresh-cut flowers by the window.

After Alison left with a long hug to go deal with the kiddies' bath and dinnertime, Eden was left alone to face the four walls of her first solo apartment ever. Drowsy with a mixture of grief, dread, and that mental bungee jump, she sat down and sobbed. She bent her head to her hands to wipe the streams from her eyes with her palms as there were so many tears a mere finger wouldn't cut it. After a few minutes of making sounds not unlike a cat being strangled, she knew her cries had to stop. *Okay . . . deep breaths.*

Eden wearily surveyed the brown landscape of corrugated cardboard. She knew from her many moves that if you don't power through and unpack every last box, then you'll carry that pit of dread with you until you do. Enough blubbering, it was time to rip open that tape. *Power through*, she told herself. Every last box. Eden opened her first one in a blur. But then she opened the second and started to figure out where each thing would go and she began to get focused. By the fifth box, she was getting organized. By the next, she had located her speakers and iPod. She limped to find a wall socket. She plugged in her gear and put on some eighties music, starting to sway as she slashed the next box with her cutter. As Duran Duran swelled, so did her hope; despite her fragile state, she recognized in the distance the feeling that everything was not going to shit. Nick Rhodes's synthesizer triggered an ever-so-slight memory of looking at herself in the mirror at seventeen and knowing that she was going places as she packed those first boxes in Shickshinny. If she had that strength and confidence in her then, surely she could tap into it now, even if it had laid dormant for a while. After she finished unpacking the seventh box, Eden's despair was beginning to be eclipsed by a tiny glimmer of hope. Maybe, just maybe, she would be okay.

Splitsville for Painter Clyde & Muse Eden!

Record-breaking artist **Otto Clyde**, fifty-five, and his longtime companion and muse, **Eden Clyde**, have called it quits, sources say. The duo, who have a teenager named **Cole** and have been together for nearly twenty years, have long dodged questions of their apparently open relationship as rumors of the Picasso's infidelity have long dogged the dynamic duo. But now friends say the pair have split for good after Clyde's paintbrush was stroking more than the canvas: He allegedly has been spotted with new studio model **Mary McGregor** out and about at hotspots downtown. Sources in the artist's circle say the pair will remain friends and continue to work together for his upcoming show at the Lyle Spence Gallery, one of his biggest to date. No word on where the aging model, Eden, nearly 39, will wind up but she has vacated their large loft and will remain in the city.

15

Perhaps middle-age is, or should be, a period of shedding shells; the shell of ambition, the shell of material accumulations and possessions, the shell of the ego.

—Anne Morrow Lindbergh

As Eden exhaled, New York City gasped.

The onslaught of awe and gossip was atomic in scope, even mushrooming abroad among Clyde's international collectors. His most recent work had just fetched $7 million. And of all his masterpieces, it was always the Eden series that kept him in ka-ching.

Afire with shocked revelations of his new flame, Mary, and the power duo's split after almost twenty years together, the world's film cognoscenti and art elite waited in breathless wonder to see where the paint chips would fall and whether Clyde would still paint Eden. But Eden was never one to give a rat's ass what people thought; there were no cheeks rouged from scandalous embarrassment, simply tears shed for an empty bed. Wagging tongues from the press never hurt her, since she and Clyde were bound together forever not just by their deep friendship but also by Cole, who was now eighteen.

Otto called Eden in her uptown haunt, which was now settled into.

"I wanted to check on you, see how you're doing," he said with concern. His worried tone pissed her off even more, as if she were a child who couldn't hack it out of the studio she virtually grew up in.

"I'm fine. I mean, people here spend five dollars on a tomato but it's been okay."

"When can I see you? I want to paint you. Lyle needs me to finish this show."

She said she would oblige, only if it felt comfortable. She wanted to be mature and the fact was, she liked posing for him and wasn't quite ready to abandon the world she had grown so accustomed to. Uptown she was a Martian transplanted, as if she'd parked her saucer by Central Park and tried to assimilate.

Allison introduced her to two of her single friends, Sara and Callie, both divorcées who were addicted to Core Fusion at Exhale, Botox and Dr. Reed, and with boobies that could act as flotation devices to get them across the Atlantic. They lunched at Via Quadronno, Eden in a flowing gray dress and black wool Mayle coat, the other three in fur coats over gym clothes. Eden guessed Sara and Callie were a bit older than she, around forty-four, though she couldn't be sure since their foreheads were motionless and as smooth as their post-lipo'd ass cheeks.

"I can't stay long; I have an appointment at the gyno," lamented Allison, looking at her watch.

"Ugh, the worst," said Callie, adjusting her leopard-print D&G cardi over her old-school implants, the kind that slope up before they go back down.

"I know," said Allison, rolling her eyes over the dreaded exam.

"It's like being raped by the Tin Man," said Callie.

"So glad I only go yearly now," said Sara. "During the pregnancies I was always in that fucking office! Ugh, so glad my eggs have passed their sell-by date."

"Totally! See, Eden, that's the beauty of dating at our age," explained Callie. "The girls who are thirtyish, they're in this big rush to hijack some sperm and get their asses knocked up. But us? We're already mothers, we've been down that road. We're not out on a DNA safari. So the guys know it's just for fun."

"There is something happening with women our age and these younger guys," Sara seconded. "It's like the whole Upper East Side's doing it! It's the ultimate symbiosis, really. Both groups want FWOF, fucks without fetus. It's so liberating! And guys know that we deliver way better than those young girls who don't know what they're doing. They love us!"

"All those young girls want is a ring on their finger!" Callie added.

"They want bling, we want booty," said Sara.

"They want diamonds, we want dick," Callie roared mischievously, her long red nails newly tacky from polish.

"Ew, you guys please stop," Allison said, prudishly cringing over her brassy pals' sexploits. Of course her pink cheeks only goaded them on further.

"They want carats, we want cock!" Sara teased.

"They want weddings, we want ween," Callie continued.

Allison looked at Eden, who looked like she had just sucked on a lime.

"Maybe I want someone who's my own age," Eden offered nervously.

"Sorry," Sara snorted. "Doesn't happen."

"Wait—didn't Shandra McCraw wind up with some guy her own age?" Allison asked, not wanting Eden to get freaked out.

"Urban myth," Callie corrected, shaking her head. "You either marry a rich geezer or bang a young hottie."

"Or both!" Sara shouted, raising her glass.

"I'll drink to that!" laughed Callie.

"You guys kill me," chortled Allison. Her friends totally amused her, but she thanked goodness she had Andrew at home.

"We'll totally hit Bar & Books on Lex and troll for young bankers," said Sara. "These guys work like dogs and just want to get laid. They don't want drama. Callie's right, they don't want some young bitch looking for a rock. They want an older woman who'll rock their world! They know we're not out to get knocked up—we're too old!"

Eden looked at Allison. These women were funny and all, but they creeped her out. And while they claimed to have all the power, something about them still seemed desperado. "I'm not so sure I'm ready."

But her best friend knew better. "E, you're always ready."

"Come on, girl, come out with us!" pleaded Sara sweetly. "We may be cougars but we don't bite."

"At least not outside the boudoir!" Callie howled.

"I'm not so sure this time. It's different now. I mean I'm . . . I'm turning thirty-nine next week. January first."

As sexy as ever to outsiders, Eden still felt worn, physically and emotionally. It was a new year, the first time in many she wouldn't be at a huge blowout bash—drunk or dancing on tables or both. With a birthday on New Year's Day, the world toasted her each year. But this time, as the ball in Times Square plummeted as she did into the murky well of thirty-nine, Eden was a mess. Her little tea party with Allison's friends had only made her feel worse.

It was arctic on the day of December 31. Eden woke up too lazy to even go out and get her coffee, so she just lounged in bed, trying not to cry or to acknowledge how incredibly lonely she was. She stared at the ceiling, trying to figure out what the different cracks resembled, like a child on the beach lying in the sand, examining the passing clouds. But without the innocence or the hope. She slumped on her couch and flipped on TBS, always there for her when she needed a laugh or a good John Hughes movie. Bingo: *Some Kind of Wonderful.* She watched it attentively, as if she were seeing it for the first time, though in fact she'd had countless screenings. But somehow, this time, rather than feeling like she was Amanda Jones—the gorgeous girl from the wrong side of the tracks—as she was entering the last year of her thirties and feeling more invisible than ever, she was like Mary Stuart Masterson: there to be a friend, undesired, taken for granted.

Halfway through, Allison stopped by to check on Eden.

"LOVE this movie! Move over."

Allison flopped next to Eden. At the end, when cute Keith makes his dramatic run down the lamplit suburban road, into his BFF Watt's arms, Eden's eyes welled up. They were one of Eden's favorite movie couples of all times. She exhaled as she watched their young, apple-cheeked embrace in the romantic finale.

"You know what freaks me out about being old?" Eden asked Allison over the credits.

"What?"

"We can only *hope* we have that feeling again," she said, gesturing to the screen. "When you're young you see this, you just *know* you will find love one day and you just have to be patient. Now I'm not sure I'll ever have a love like this again."

"Oh my God, speaking of first loves, I heard Jason Price's wife is prego with her *sixth.* They're like all platinum creepy Children of the Corn."

"Great," Eden said almost wistfully.

"Come on, you would never want her life! Anyway: new year,

new start. I have a good feeling," Allison said, kissing Eden good-bye as she left to meet Andrew. "You sure you don't want to come out with us?" she asked.

"Yeah, I'm sure. Thanks, Allison."

At 9:00, Cole rang to wish her a happy birthday and happy new year. He had decided to stay in California and go to L.A., where his roommate was from, to celebrate.

"Thank you, honey," she said, feeling tears burn their way to her retinas. She missed him so much it was agonizing, especially now. She had often felt lonely with Otto, but she had always had Cole. "Are you going out tonight? Any fun plans?"

"Yeah, a bunch of us are all going to this huge party in West Hollywood. It's crazy here, Mom. We went to this house last night overlooking the whole city"—Eden heard his friends in the background calling his name—"Wait, you guys! Hold on!" Cole said.

"Sweetheart, you go and have fun with your friends. Drive safe, please."

"Have a great night, Mom."

"Okay, I will."

"Mom, I love you. Next birthday will be better. I promise."

"Thanks. I love you, too," she said, trying to sound upbeat. Next year. *F-F-F-Forty*. Ugh.

As her son ran off with his friends, Eden put the phone back in its cradle. She wished she could put Cole back in his. She missed his fat feeties. His sweaty bangs she'd brush off his face as he slept soundly. He hadn't had a traditional childhood with Little League and hockey sticks; he'd blown out birthday candles in the Court of St. James's ambassador's residence rather than Chuck E. Cheese. But because of their myriad journeys, they had always been together, meeting Otto or flying back home, seats A and B.

"ONE HOUR UNTIL THE NEW YEAR!" Ryan Seacrest yelled as crowds cheered.

How did all this time pass? It was like Allison's husband had once said of those weary years of parenting: *The days are long but the years are short.* Cole was out on his own, the human glue that kept her fused to Otto for so long. Eden flopped back in her pillows and cried herself to sleep.

She woke up the next morning feeling as if she had been out all night, even though she didn't even stay up long enough to watch the ball drop on New Year's Rockin' Eve. She stared again at the cracks on the ceiling. No. She refused to allow herself to lie there any longer. She couldn't spend another night like the one she just had. No way. She would simply have to move the hell on.

She forced herself to get out of bed and meandered zombielike to the bathroom. She splashed water on her face, then reached for her new miracle moisturizer she'd splurged on at Bloomie's. The salesgirl had given her some spiel about it being made in a rural Japanese monastery, where the monks all had shriveled and wrinkly and disgusting raisin faces but their hands looked shockingly smooth and infantile. It had sounded better than the whale sperm and sheep's placenta crap Allison slathered on for $600 a pot. In this new chapter, a new year, Eden would have to start taking care of herself. She closed the mirrored door of the medicine cabinet and beheld her clean, lined face in front of her. There she was: one year from forty.

As she slowly rubbed the moisturizer onto her cheeks, she tilted her head, looked at herself, and found her lips beginning to smile. Workmen still hollered, and more than one of Clyde's friends had made a pass, confessing an enamored heart after a drunken dinner party. She would be fine. She still had it. Right?

She would not waste time. She would take Allison's friends up on their offer to go on the prowl, even if she was ambivalent.

If you want to get hit, you gotta go out in traffic! The many fish in the sea were not going to fly through her window; she had to go and hook 'em herself. And deep down in the vast ocean of her mind, Eden scuba'd to the bottom to summon the hope she still could.

16

You know you are getting old when the candles cost more than the cake.

—Bob Hope

It was nearly five thirty when Chase got the call.

"Chase, it's your mother."

His mother, who never wept, simply had to say his name through a wall of tears, and Chase knew. He had been finishing the piles of work on his Midtown desk, watching the clock out of the corner of his eye, hoping to get back to his grandmother's bedside. But it was too late.

He staggered to his parents' apartment on Fifth Avenue, awash with grief. As always when there was a crisis in The Family, cousins, advisers, and old friends gathered in lockdown mode in the penthouse. *Here we all are again*, Chase thought, surveying his uncle Johnson, aunts, the family lawyers, and Dewey Riley, the head of DuPree Family Office, who managed and controlled Brooke's and her sisters' lives.

After Chase greeted everyone with a somber, shocked tone of despair, he saw Liesel enter the room, her face downcast.

"I'm so sorry, sweetie," she said, hugging him. "I know how much Ruthie meant to you."

He hugged her in silence and looked down at her face. Her pristine preppy beauty remained intact despite her sadness; her shoulder-length blond hair was crisply pulled back in a short ponytail, a Hermès scarf tied around her neck. At twenty-eight, she had the aura of a fortysomething grown-up, in charge and ever pulled together. She embraced Chase and offered her polite and sincere condolences to his mother. Brooke hugged Liesel and grasped her son's hand as they shared a silent moment acknowledging the loss of Ruthie.

"Well, I hope you all took the bus," said Grant to some chuckling guests. Chase smiled, recalling how his grandmother, who always had a driver, loved taking the bus and would often still take it to remind her of her childhood on the Upper East Side, even though she could be in a quiet and far less crowded chauffeur-driven Denali, or, as she called it, "a living room on wheels." Chase recalled her saying once that if she wanted to be in her living room she'd stay at home, but that she preferred to be in the outside world, among the people. Brooke always scoffed at this, saying that it was ridiculous for a high-profile political wife to choose public transportation, but only on occasion over the years would someone stop her on the bus. In her old age, though, she rarely ventured out without her nurse. Her few short blocks' stroll each day made her feel part of society, like a citizen of the world instead of a holed-up hermit.

And now she was gone. Chase was beside himself, and while he also grieved for his mother and aunts, deep down he felt like no one had had the connection with Ruthie that he had. No one else had her irreverent sass, her sailor's tongue, her desire to be real, unedited, unencumbered by rules. And no one knew him the way his beloved grandmother had. Theirs was a special bond that no one could possibly understand.

Liesel hugged him and offered bland words of comfort. "She led such a good life, sweetie, you were truly the most devoted grandson."

"Thanks," he said quietly.

"Ninety-two is a ripe old age," she continued. "It's really a blessing she didn't suffer for longer."

She was right; pain is always relative, and sure, losing someone who is young is much worse and more tragic. Chase knew Ruthie was old, and he had been expecting this, but that didn't change the fact that he lost someone who was such a huge and guiding force in his life.

"Honey," Liesel said, patting his head as he lay in bed later that night, fighting in vain to sleep. "She lived a long, fulfilling life! It's a blessing she didn't suffer. You know she didn't want to suffer." Chase blinked back any emotion, swallowing the growing lump in his throat, and he rolled over and pretended to fall into slumber.

17

A diamond cannot be polished without friction, nor a man perfected without trials.

—Chinese proverb

Of all people, it was Otto who tried to fix up Eden at his birthday dinner in March at Moto in Brooklyn. She thought it would be the right thing to attend and help him celebrate, as they were still friends, so she went, but she cringed as Mary giggled at Otto's every word. John Cavett Morley, a famous writer who had come of age with Otto and was in the Clydes' circle of friends, had asked if he could bring his old pal Rory Sussman, her fix-up, who was not-so-subtly seated next to her.

"So what do you do, Rory?" Eden asked in a bit of a revenge-fueled flirt.

"I'm actually a hotelier. I just opened a boutique hotel in West Hollywood. Starck designed it and Kelly Wearstler decorated it. You should come for a visit."

"I always thought it was funny how people could be a *hotelier* instead of what they called 'em back home in the sticks," Eden said.

"Oh yeah," said Rory, turned on by her not-giving-a-shit-about-him tone. "What do you call them at home?"

"Innkeepers."

Rory grinned. Most girls threw themselves at him, but this gal was trickier, more confident. He was worldly and grand, a sexy scenester presiding over countless special events at his Hollywood haunt, with multiple slashies (model slash actress slash massage therapist slash whore) roaming his lobby. He'd suffered a freak heart attack after two helpings of foie gras, and it changed his life. Now he lived for the moment, indulging in everything (minus the pâté) and doing two things he never would have dreamed of: He bought a yacht, which he christened the *Triple Bypass*, and now, he hoped, he would screw Eden Clyde.

Naturally, Rory took to Eden instantly, and their flirtation carried on through the meal as Otto looked on, teasingly winking at his ex on occasion. He wasn't at all jealous (well, maybe a little); he just wanted her to be happy.

But alas, Rory was too slick, too pretty. Eden wasn't feeling it. She knew when she was being used as a pawn, a collectible asset to check off his list. She wasn't wrong. Her image was so famous around the world, it would be the holy grail of lays. The old Eden wouldn't have minded being used as a prop, as long as it got her places. But now she didn't care.

She didn't need to be someone else's arm candy. Not anymore.

After Otto's party, Eden and Otto continued speaking one or two times a day on top of their painting sessions. Even though part of her was wounded about the roll in the hay with corn-fed farm girl Mary, she no longer held it against him because somewhere deep inside she was grateful. She knew she wanted more and would have probably coasted indefinitely. It had been so long in the making.

Sometimes she had to act casual when she was steaming inside (like when Mary would yap in the background) and other times she felt a warm comfort in Otto's voice like catching up with an uncle or old teacher. They spoke not just about Cole but about anything and everything. Some nights they'd chat till all hours, even once or twice suggesting that maybe they should just stay together for the companionship and convenience.

"Nothing would be different." Eden shrugged. "I really think you're more into Miss Mary than you let on."

Otto was silent. A mute confirmation of Eden's suspicions that deafened her on the line.

"I just miss you sometimes," he said sadly.

"Well, maybe I want to be missed *all* the time," she said. "There was an era when I couldn't walk to Gourmet Garage without twenty questions about when I was coming back."

"So why did you blow off Rory? He seemed nice. Lots of ducats in the bank."

"I'm not looking, Otto. Actually tonight Allison's friends Callie and Sara are taking me to Cipriani."

"Just don't have too many Bellini," he teased.

"CHEERS!!" The third round of peach nectar–infused Prosecco clinked together.

"Oh my god, we're like The First Wives club but without the rings floating at the bottom!" said Sara.

"Yeah, and I was never married," said Eden.

"Oooooh, eye candy three o'clock," Sara whispered. A bunch of Wall Streeters in blue button-downs walked in after a long round of squash at the Racquet Club followed by Chinese "Special Massages" at a Third Avenue second-floor jerk joint, where, before the Happy Ending, they tell you to "frip" (as in "flip over").

All the guys were calm as cucumbers (thanks to Li and Ling having taken care of their cucumbers) and ready for some Italian food. These nights were a preppy tradition—Squeal and Veal— "frip" rubdowns and eats.

"Check it out, bro, look at the cans on those broads," one said between gobbles of veal parm.

"Hells yeah! Holy flesh melons!"

"Talk about happy fun bags," added another.

"Try happy *meal*."

Overhearing enough to Sherlock the guys' convo, Callie beamed. "They're checking out our racks," she said proudly, sitting erect.

Eden looked at the guys, then back at her friends. It was like two sets of Big Bad Wolves licking their chops, and she was innocent Red Riding Hood in the middle.

One of the preppies raised a glass to the ladies' table.

"What is going on?" Eden asked.

"It's called flirting. Geez, you really do need to get out more. You've lost the moves, girlfriend!" Sara teased.

"Mesdames," the waiter said, approaching their table. "The gentlemen there would like to send you a bottle of wine."

"Oh, terrific!" cooed Callie, red manicured hand on her heart as she tilted her head in thanks to their table. The waiter poured the wine, and the two bolder of the three women sipped it seductively, lifting their glasses.

"Bottoms up!" Callie said.

"Hopefully mine!" Sara laughed.

"You guys are like predators," Eden said.

"Why shouldn't we be?" asked Callie a tad defensively. "Why should guys have all the fun?"

"No, no, I didn't mean it badly. I just . . . guess you're right. I've lost the tools, I suppose."

"They're not tools," Sara explained, delicately touching her décolletage as the guys looked on. "They're weapons."

"Would you ever want to get a little lift-a-roo?" Sara asked, surveying Eden's perky but semi-low-riders.

"I have better tits now than I did in my saggy thirties nursing two babies," Callie confessed. "Now *these* babies defy gravity!" she said proudly. "Thank you, Dr. Baker."

"Mine are Hidalgos." Sara shimmied.

Eden had noticed the 9.81 meters per second pull taking its toll on her hooters, but she couldn't imagine slicing them open and inserting some foreign body into them. She was such a baby that a paper cut yielded moans and Band-Aids.

After a while, the crowd started to thin and the table adjacent to them became available. The three guys sauntered over.

"Can we join you ladies?" one asked.

"Of course," Callie said, adjusting the seats to face them.

"So," said Sara. "What're your names? Chip? Biff? Chad?"

"I'm Court," said the cutest one, smile wide.

Eden laughed. Same thing.

"Court, eh? Like this Court is in session?" Callie asked as he nodded. "Is your jury hung?"

Eden spat up the wine she was sipping and knew this was her cue.

"Uh, pardon me, so sorry, I should be going," she said, abruptly getting up as she fumbled for her clutch.

"No, don't leave so soon," one of Court's cronies begged. Crap, three dudes, two poons left. It was like muff musical chairs. And the hottest was leaving.

"Yeah, sorry, I'm not feeling so hot," Eden apologized.

"You look hot to me," the other dude said.

"Oh, uh, thanks. Sorry—Bye, girls—bye, have fun."

Eden's legs couldn't run home faster. Yuck. Sara and Callie

were amusing with all their cock talk, but it was so not her. She
had been with a grown man of fifty-five; she couldn't very well
prey on preppy boys with the maturity level of a Dora viewer. *She*
wanted to be the cute young one; she wanted to feel new and coveted, not be the crusty, grateful one. Shit, this growing old thing
sucked.

18

By the time you're eighty years old you've learned everything.
You only have to remember it.

—George Burns

For the next two months, Eden flew solo. It was the longest sexual drought in her life. The groundhog got freaked out by his shadow and wigged, adding more frozen windows and slushy streets. Once or twice a week she would take the train down to Otto's and pose, but she didn't get the same joy from it anymore. When she wasn't downtown, Eden was getting into her new neighborhood groove and enjoyed her hours with *The New York Times* and Allison's close-knit family.

"I can't thank you enough, Alli," she told her best friend over a glass of wine at Daniel. "I realize now what a mess I've been, and you saved me."

"Bullshit," Allison said with a wink. "You're the strong one who got us to New York in the first place. You saved yourself."

"I'm not there yet." Eden sighed. "But it's getting better every day. Instead of waking up and starting to cry, I just wake up *wanting* to cry!"

"E, it will get better. Trust me."

"I'm sorry. I caught myself complaining. No one likes a sad sack. Thank you for listening to me bitch."

"Hun, I love you happy or sad. There are some friends who are only there in the happy times and others who creepily get off being the shoulder to cry on so they can feel needed. I love both. That's what real friends do. You don't have to thank me."

"Still. I'm grateful."

"Hey, Sara and Callie want to plan a group dinner with some of our other mom friends from school. They LOVE you," Allison said proudly. "I knew they'd have girl crushes on you, and they fully do."

"They're great," Eden said, appreciative of Allison's hooking them up. "I just think I'm not quite at their level of—"

"Hormones?"

"Yeah. They're hard-core."

"We don't have to go on the town. We can just get lunch or manicures or something."

"Done."

Eden relished her time with Allison and even, increasingly, her time alone. Her long walks through the snow-filled park reminded her of a time when she often strolled the city, and little by little she began to feel more and more like her old self. On the first warm day after a particularly sleet-filled winter week, Eden woke up refreshed and, for once, didn't think about her age, or a new wrinkle here, a deepening crevice there. She had slept soundly and realized that with a solid night's sleep, her skin actually looked way better. *Shit, I guess that's why it's called beauty sleep*, she mused.

The Canadian on NY1 said it was an unseasonably warm March 1, and she put on black tights and a silk print dress from Jane Mayle from before the designer had shuttered her doors on

Elizabeth Street. She walked outside and took a deep breath: It was the first day she felt happy in a long, long time. She walked the streets for hours, nursing a large coffee, savoring every flavorful sip. Flowering dogwood trees and blush pink cherry blossoms, their branches bedecked with buds heralding the end of the chill, sprang up all over the city. Soon enough, there would be four weeks of April showers, and afterward, she could taste it already, would bloom the darling buds of May, and everyone joyfully eschewing sweaters.

19

Inside every older person is a younger person—wondering what the hell happened.

—Cora Harvey Armstrong

The soundtrack for the sunshine was the Good Humor truck's childlike tune. Brooke DuPree Lydon rarely partook of desserts, and if she wanted a caloric splurge, it would only be gelato from Sant Ambroeus, where a small cup ran five clams. Even then she'd probably sample only half, then pass on the cup to her husband. But quirky Ruthie loved that crappy ice cream truck with the jingle that could either sound cute and innocent or like the creepy backdrop to a serial killer à la Buffalo Bill's bloody spree. Once she'd gone with her Tobago-born nurse, Inus, to wait in line by Seventy-second Street and Fifth Avenue, behind schoolchildren in their various uniforms, headed to the playground to blow off steam. Brooke was carrying shopping bags from Ralph Lauren and was aghast when she spied her mother requesting a chemical swirl.

"Mother! You may as well ingest frozen Drano! Do you know what's in that? How in God's name can you ingest toxic garbage served from some vile vehicle?"

"Hey, ya gotta live a little." Ruthie calmly explained that she simply couldn't pass one of these trucks without ordering a chocolate cone with rainbow sprinkles, cream swirled high to a joyful point, which she'd bite off while awaiting her change from the window on the truck's side.

"Plus," Ruthie said with the ever-present twinkle in her eye, "it just makes me happy."

"Great. I'm so glad you derive such pleasure from Styrofoam shaped into cone form," Brooke sneered. "Inus, you should know better. Mother should not be eating this refuse."

In a flurry of navy shopping bags embossed with Polo's logo, she walked off in a huff.

"Sometimes I'd like to get a polo mallet for her," Ruthie joked to a grinning Inus, who clearly concurred.

Chase missed his grandmother terribly. It was a pang in his side like when he ran too fast around the reservoir, splitting and rendering him off-kilter. In crowded Midtown, Chase took an abbreviated lunch break after working until two thirty and saw the season's first ice cream truck and thought of his grandma. He smiled sadly and found his feet wandering toward it, despite his complete lack of sweet tooth. The woman in front of him ordered none other than a chocolate cone with rainbow sprinkles, and dug into her huge Hobo bag to retrieve her two smacks.

"Uh-oh," she said, cone in one hand while the other furiously dug through her massive brown suede satchel. "My money! Hold on, I thought I had money. Wait, I have, like, a zillion quarters, one sec." The woman dug madly through her bag and retrieved piles of change, which was rather difficult to sift through with her cone in her hand.

"It's on me," Chase said, handing the ice cream man a five. "I'll have the exact same thing."

"No, no, no, it's okay, I have money. It's just kind of scattered in here—"

"Honestly, it's my pleasure," Chase responded. He squinted, finding her face familiar but not able to place her.

"Seriously, I have money," she said, frazzled. "I'm just so clumsy. If you hold my cone, I can—"

"Nope," he interrupted. "It's the first real day of spring, and it would make me very happy to get you that cone."

"Hey, what about me?" an old lady behind Chase joked.

"Yeah, me, too, Romeo!" joked a burly construction worker and his friend.

Chase smiled as he watched the beautiful woman happily lick her ice cream. "Cones for everyone!" Chase erupted spontaneously and handed the Mister Softee guy a twenty to pay for ten cones for the line behind him.

Shocked by the rare gesture of goodwill, the crowd in line cheered. It was a great New York moment.

"I'm Eden," she said, sticking out her cone-free left hand to shake his.

"I'm Chase."

He smiled and walked next to Eden as they ate their twin cones.

"That was pretty nice, Chase," she said, looking him over. "You don't see that every day."

"It's not every day," Chase replied, gesturing to the blooming trees and crystal blue sky. "Look at this."

"So what do you do, Milton Petrie?" joked Eden, relishing her cone. "I mean when you're not engaging in frozen treat philanthropy."

"I . . . you know . . . work in finance." He shrugged. Yawn, he knew he couldn't sound more snoozeville.

"Gee, you sound reeeeally excited about that," said Eden sarcastically.

"Well, I'm not, actually. I'd really love to switch gears but . . . who knows. Duty calls. I'm actually thinking of quitting and getting my PhD in history. But it's a secret."

"Ohhhhh. *I* see," she replied.

"See what?" he asked innocently.

"Everyone knows what PhD stands for." She winked.

"What does PhD stand for?" Chase inquired.

"Poppa Has Dough."

Chase had to laugh; he'd never met such a straight-talking woman who was that captivatingly gorgeous.

"Okay, touché."

They walked toward the corner of a block lined with cherry blossom trees. Just then a strong breeze blew. Eden's long hair whipped in the wind and she shivered. As the trees were walloped by gushes of air, thousands of pale pink petals flurried to the ground, enveloping Eden, Chase, and the other pedestrians on that lucky sidewalk.

"Oh my gosh, this is so frigging stunning, it's like a mirage," Eden said, marveling at the gusty swirl of pink. The petals blanketed the street, and her head and Chase's were covered in tiny petals. "Too bad the pollen count is going to make me overdose on Claritin."

Chase laughed. "It's worth it, though, right? This is almost too amazing to look at."

Eden studied his young face. *He* was too amazing to look at. But young, very young. Scary young. We're talking, like, Zac Efron territory. Okay, maybe not quite *that* young, but she was so used to being with Otto, sixteen years her senior, that Chase appeared positively fetal.

"It is quite something," she said. "Especially after this long, gloomy winter."

"I know, right? Where is global warming when you need it?" Chase joked nervously.

Eden could tell he was charmed by her looks, despite the fact that if they each built a tower with a brick for each year, hers would tower over, or probably topple over his.

"Well, thank you for the 'scream," said Eden, stopping to descend the stairs to the subway. "That was very sweet of you. You put rainbow sprinkles on my whole day."

"My pleasure," he said, feeling a warmth in his chest. "Enjoy."

"I will."

"Happy spring," Chase said, studying her.

"Happy spring," Eden replied, practically skipping off, and licking her first cone of the new, sunny season.

20

Forty isn't old . . . if you're a tree.

—Anonymous

P utting her recent uniform of black skinny jeans or casual dresses aside, it was time for Eden to get dolled up. She knew the drill: showtime. Red carpet, Waldorf-Astoria, hair and makeup. The evening's fête was honoring Rock McGhee, whose name sounded like a porn star's, but he was in fact a huge collector of Otto's work. He had four massive canvases in his Fifth Avenue penthouse—all of Eden—and invited the pair and a few of their studio and gallery friends to his black-tie event to sit at his table with his wife, Muffy, and a few high-profile hedge funders.

During the massive cocktail hour, Eden and Otto were led to a small antechamber with paparazzi and a backdrop with the logo of McGhee's charity, EndTesCan, which fought testicular cancer and was jokingly referred to by Otto as the Save Our Balls Ball. The paparazzi snapped shots of luminaries, from indie actresses to Lance Armstrong to a young "virgin" (yeah, right) pop starlet with hot pants and thunder thighs who would be performing one song. Eden and Otto held hands and smiled as the countless flash-bulbs flashed. "Eden! Eden! Otto! Eden!" yelled the shutterbugs, who were insectlike with their incessant clicks and the big eyes of their long lenses.

"Okay, thank you," Otto said sternly when he'd had enough of the glare. He took Eden's hand and guided her away from the firestorm. Despite their separation, he still felt protective of her.

"Thanks for doing this," Otto said as Eden shot him a look. It was obvious she'd rather be hang gliding over a canyon of skyward-pointing machetes. Lyle Spence, Otto's gallerist, said people were getting skittish about their allegedly rock-solid investments in Otto's canvases and that it would behoove them both to put on a brave front and walk the walk. Eden agreed so long as Mary stayed home and played Parcheesi or washed her hair or painted her nails hot pink or whatever the hell she did. Eden was growing weary of these saccharine dog-and-pony shows, but Otto needed to please the longtime collectors who funneled millions his way, including Rock McGhee and his hedge fund partner Jack "Gefilte" Fishman, so nicknamed for his constant bobby-pinned yarmulke.

"It's okay," Eden said, looking for Allison. "I just need a serious drink. Or five."

"I'm right there with you, honey."

Otto put his arm around her and led her into the grand ballroom. It felt slightly strange and poseury for them to enter as their same old arm-in-arm unit, the art world Cover Story duo, but Eden felt almost proud that she could play the role Otto had cast her in so well. *Oh, look, they are such grown-ups, such an amicable breakup.* They walked the walk and greeted high-profile socialites and fauxcialites through the cocktail hour, then made their way to the ballroom. It was there, at the table next to theirs, that Eden noticed Chase and his two brothers. Their eyes locked briefly as they tried to remember how they knew each other, and soon their realizations synced as one mini epiphany of shared cones and a magical moment of light breezes and fluttering petals.

Staring at Chase during a long welcoming speech by the CEO of some investment bank, Eden put up her hand in a blank stationary wave, the gesture everyone learned as kids as the way Indians greeted one another, saying "How." It was a pure child-of-the-eighties reference. By the time Chase was born, the term was Native Americans, and sitting cross-legged was only ever called "crisscross applesauce." But he held up his hand back to her, How-style, and smiled.

As the speech about early gonad scans droned on, Eden shocked the polite Chase by picking up a knife from her table setting and miming it slashing across her neck while sticking her tongue out, as if to say, "Kill me now, please." Chase was surprised and almost snorted laughing, as while he may have echoed the sentiment, sitting through long speeches was commonplace for him. As he stifled his laugh, a coiffed Liesel turned to him, wondering what the distraction was. She had been listening intently, hands crossed on her lap.

"What's so funny, darling?" she asked, patting his shoulder.

"Nothing, sorry." He composed himself.

Eden looked to Chase's side, noticing Liesel, her swan neck delicately covered in a big bold string of Mikimoto pearls, her buttery blond hair coiled into a chic chignon. Eden's long, wild, shiny brown hair, meanwhile, hung loose down her back, and while Liesel wore a prim Oscar floor-length gown, Eden was rocking a sexy, übershort Zac Posen strapless garnet-hued frock. Liesel sat quietly by Chase's side, appropriate, ever composed, pale-pink manicured fingers interlocking and still. With her Hermès scarves, diamond studs, Tory Burch flats, and Burberry trench, she was always the height of sophistication and Upper East Side poise.

Eden had dark bloodred nails, which flashed as she ran her hands through her hair, broke off bites of dinner roll, fidgeted with stemware. Chase looked at Eden's table of arty types; everyone wore black and oddly asymmetrical fashions. Instead of penguin tuxes were black Hollywood-y red carpet attire, plus one guy sleeved in tattoos, wearing a black leather vest. One woman had a platinum blond bob and was talking loudly to Eden across Otto. Liesel looked at Chase with an arched brow as she sipped her wine, wondering what the table of *colorful* people (read: weirdos) to their right was doing there. Suddenly, though, Chase's gaze fell on Otto Clyde. He knew instantly who the celebrated painter was, then immediately that his muse, Eden Clyde, was the icon with whom he shared that ice cream.

Aha. Of course. His grandmother had walked through Clyde's famed blockbuster retrospective at MoMA beside him, a memory he cherished. She had loved his work, and Chase had often stared at those paintings in the catalogue she bought him at the gift store. Amazing. No wonder Eden had been familiar and somehow larger than life. She was, quite literally, on countless canvases he had seen all over.

Intrigued, Chase could not keep his eyes off them the rest of the night. Their table was a bit raucous, clinking glasses en masse several times, chortling loudly over some naughty joke, and asking for more and more wine.

"I love Danny LeMieux's new show at Deitch," yelled Allison. "He is so sexy! I'd shag him rotten if I weren't in love with Andrew."

"Allison, you idiot," laughed Eden. "You OBVIOUSLY did not get the memo: LeMieux is so gay, he sweats glitter."

Allison pouted like a little kid, though it was all for show, as she was a happily hitched mom of three, crossing her arms as the whole table burst out laughing. Otto rolled his eyes, then scanned the crowd for beautiful people.

At the Lydons' table the conversation was more subdued, veering to politics or the editorial in that day's *Times*. While Liesel stuck to her Atkinsy rhythms of a few bites of her filet mignon, leaving a pile of grilled rosemary potatoes untouched, Chase spied how Eden not only cleared her plate but was also spearing extra potatoes off Otto's with her fork.

The two tables, like their two worlds, contrasted on every front. Of course, the art world's Venn diagram intersected with the upper crust in that rich people were collectors. But if those two worlds were marked by blue and yellow circles, that sliver of green in the middle was only the color of the money that bound them to each other. Otherwise, there would be nothing connecting these people, who were practically different species.

And yet across the cacophony of the ballroom, Chase was in a muted tunnel, silent but for the sound that emanated from Eden's tanned throat as she threw her head back in laughter. The room, bursting with shimmering silks and satins, seemed dim but for the glow around Eden.

21

The first forty years of life give us the text, the next thirty supply the commentary on it.

—Arthur Schopenhauer

It was in the interminable line at the coat check that Chase gathered the courage to approach Eden.

"This line is ridiculous!" trumpeted Allison, hand on hip. "They are moving like molasses! I've seen escargot faster than this."

Brooke Lydon was also in a tizzy over the wait. "This is unacceptable!" she huffed. "These moronic people are moving at a pace that is positively glacial." But Chase had never been happier to wait. He watched Eden shiver, rubbing her hands over her bare goose bump–covered arms.

"Not in the mood for ice cream now, are you? It's freezing in here," Chase remarked, approaching her.

"Tell me about it! I'm blue."

Without a thought, Chase took off his jacket and draped it on Eden's chilled shoulders.

"Wow, thanks, that's okay, really—"

"No, it's my pleasure. It looks like it could be a while until you get your coat."

"Thanks." Eden beamed. "So how horrendous was that cheesy wedding band?" she said, rolling her eyes. "Talk about lousy."

"I guess," Chase said, sort of confused. He had seen the same in-demand band a hundred times at every charity ball or party his family had ever thrown. He knew they probably weren't cool per se, but only when Eden commented did he suddenly realize how lame they actually were.

"I mean, ugh! Why is everyone so anti-deejay? Bands are sooo cringe-inducing," Eden said while shivering. "It's always twenty white guys playing that horrible song, *'Ah-eeee-ah say that you re-member! Ah-ee-ah, Dancing in December!'*"

"Now that you mention it, that is true." Chase smiled.

"At least they didn't do that nightmare one that I really hate: *'A little bit of Sheila on my mind, a little bit of Jessica, from behind . . .,'*" Eden sang.

"Really, is that how it goes?" Chase asked scratching his head, not quite sure.

Eden's hawklike peripheral vision kicked in, as she sensed Otto approaching them.

"Honey, who's this?" Otto interrupted, looking Chase over skeptically. The artist's face was so intensely serious, it was as if he were Derek Zoolander doing Blue Steel.

"Hello, sir—Chase Lydon. I'm a big, big fan."

Otto offered a tight smile accompanied by a squint. Eden thought he looked like he was either an X-Men mutant scanning Chase's organs or just a dude taking a dump.

Next the patrician princess joined the fray.

"Chasie, were did you go, I was looking for you!" Liesel fluttered in a worried, birdlike chirp. She darted up behind Chase, putting her arm around his as she smiled at Eden and extended her hand. "Hello, I'm Liesel van Delft."

The unlikely foursome greeted each other perfectly politely but with the warmth that might be found in an igloo. Liesel and Otto were clearly on the outside of the bizarre duo connected by Chase's Ralph Lauren tuxedo jacket resting on Eden's warming shoulders.

"Here, Eden, take *my* jacket," said Otto, removing Chase's from her bony back. "I insist."

Chase looked at him and took it, as Liesel batted her long lashes, confused why this . . . person in the way too short dress was sporting her boyfriend's jacket. She smiled sweetly to bid them adieu and squired her boyfriend off to the line on the other side of the coat check window.

"Did you know that woman?" Liesel asked, curling her fingers with Chase's.

"Oh yeah, I met her once before."

"She poses *naked*. That's Otto Clyde's muse, Eden. Apparently he's with someone else now, though. I saw in the blind items on Page Six that he totally cheated forever. Marriage of convenience, I guess."

"Mm-hmm," said Chase, watching the Clydes claim their jackets. "I don't think they were ever married."

"Typical. These artsy folks, you know . . . not the real world!" she drifted. "So, darling, are you going to play golf at Piping this weekend? Because I have to go to Lily Hearst's bridal shower."

"Okay, I'll play golf, then," he said, still looking across the room at Eden.

"I wonder if she'll take her husband's name. I mean, her mother sure didn't—her biodad's last name is Smith, you know. And all the kids took the mother's name, wonder why!" Liesel mused. "I hear she and Skipper are having five hundred and seventy-five guests at the Library. Glorious Food is catering. Ron Wendt is doing the flowers. Supposedly, Oscar is . . ."

As Charlie Brown's teacher once famously said, *wah, wha wah wha wah wah whaa*. As her glossed lips moved, Liesel's breath whirled in a tornado of frothy descriptions; up in the cyclone were swirling words—"hydrangeas," "emerald-cut diamond," "embroidered, monogrammed linens." Chase, totally tuned out, heard only a peppering of noise, about steak and the band, the honeymoon at some Aman, but it all faded to a muted, unintelligible blather.

He loved Liesel, sure, but she got so caught up in the fineries of their milieu. Her grandmother's ornate emerald bracelet and her bubbly enthusiasm for her friend's Stephen Russell diamond and sapphire ring was in such stark contrast to Eden's pared-down, bling-less beauty—she hadn't wanted or needed jewels and feminine rosettes or ribboned details on her clothes; she had style all her own and didn't need the sugar sweet female trappings of rings or necklaces. Her body was all the accessories she needed. She was now quietly waiting for Allison, standing in a firm stance, thighs shiny with body oil, her hand on her impatient hip, which jutted out provocatively. Her body language could not be more different from proper Liesel's, who stood feet together in patent kitten heels, while Eden shifted her weight to her other foot, to a spike stiletto that looked like it was designed by a dominatrix. Chase could not take his eyes off her. As she moved some hair from her face, he spied a quick glimpse of tattooed ink on her back. "Tattoos are like letting the devil doodle on your body!" Liesel had once exclaimed. "Filthy, filthy, filthy."

Liesel, meanwhile, was prattling on about some masked ball and asked Chase if he had his costume yet.

"Huh, uh, what's this for?" he answered, distracted by his mesmerizing people watching. "The Venetian thing at the Plaza?"

"No, silly! Not the Save Venice masquerade that's next month! It's the MASK ball: Motivate Abandoned Street Kids."

Without acknowledging the difference, Chase stared as Eden,

Otto, and their boisterous friends made their way out to the street. And just under the red exit sign, with Otto's and Allison's arms around her waist, Eden looked back over her shoulder and briefly locked eyes with Chase. He looked down bashfully, then back up, where his brown eyes met her piercing green ones. And just before she turned to face forward again, she gave him a little wink, stealing a beat of his blue-blood-pumping heart.

Are They or Aren't They?

It seems one-time Art World IT Couple **Otto** and **Eden Clyde** like to keep us guessing. The on-again, off-again duo turned heads at the EndTesCan gala by pawing each other with some public PDA. Maybe it was for the paparazzi, but it certainly made several coiffed heads in the Waldorf-Astoria turn and whisper. While one source in their circle attests, "They are *not* back together," others intimate that the team needs to keep up appearances to keep collectors on their toes. "They want to stay relevant," sneers a sharp-tongued onlooker. "And they can only do that if they're together." "Not so," says our source. "Eden is living uptown now and loving it." Let's just hope that despite the seventy-block spread, the pair still paint and pose together—their rabid fans wouldn't have it any other way.

22

The only time you really live fully is from thirty to sixty. The young are slaves to dreams; the old servants of regrets. Only the middle-aged have all their five senses in the keeping of their wits.

—Hervey Allen

Eden and Allison were lunching in the jam-packed Three Guys Restaurant on Seventy-fifth Street, the Mother Ship (tied with Yura on Ninety-second) for the mommy set. Allison loved it thanks to her custom grilled chicken and avocado salad (Stavros the waiter was used to high-maintenance orders) but had just been complaining that everyone on the Bugaboo-wielding mom scene was there at that moment. Most took a break from their salads to stare at Eden and whisper.

"Allison Rubens!!! Hiiii!" exclaimed a 'rexi yummy mummy in sprayed-on skinny jeans, Lanvin flats, and Tory tunic. *"Ça va?"*

"Hi, Jess. This is my friend Eden Clyde. Eden, Jessica Shapiro."

"I know who you are," said Jessica, beaming. "So funny, I always run into people I know here: Saul and I call it Three Jews!"

"How are Madison and Jameson?" asked Allison as Eden carried on eating her grilled cheese and French fries.

"The twins are great!" Jessica smiled. "How are your two little ones?"

"Sam and Sasha are great, thanks . . . they worship their big sister," Allison replied, trying to end the convo.

"Last time I saw you was at that *Wizard of Oz* birthday party at the Sites' new town house, remember?"

"How could I forget?" Allison laughed, nudging Eden. "They painted a mural through all six floors of their town house, where the steps were the yellow brick road," she said to Eden. "And they hired twenty midgets to serve the hors d'oeuvres."

"NO!" exclaimed Eden between mouthfuls of shoestring fries.

"Yes," said Jessica, shaking her head. "It was awful. My kids were crying, *Why do those kids have grown-up heads?!*"

"Yeah, also it was awful 'cause Liza Sites used human beings as props for her three-year-old's party," Allison added.

"So how is Kate?" Jessica asked of Allison's oldest. "Are we gearing up for kindergarten application hell, or what? This process is literally going to be Hades! But the twins both got ninety-nines on their ERBs, so hopefully we're all set."

"Great," said Allison halfheartedly. "Yeah, everyone gets ninety-nines, haven't you heard?"

"Oh, well, okay . . . ," Jessica stammered, unsure of what that meant, exactly. "They miss Kate so much from Baby Beethovens! How is she? Are you applying for all-girls or co-ed?

"Both, you know, keeping options open. Plus, Eden and I are from the boonies. School for us was all metal lockers and linoleum floors, so I don't really care all that much."

"Uh-huh," Jess said, trying to relate (she couldn't). "Well, I'll see you on the open house circuit, then! And give a squeeze to that cute little Sasha! She is such a bruiser!"

Jessica spied her food arriving a few tables away.

"Oh no!" she whined with utter dismay. "I said egg whites only!"

"Barf," said Allison, rolling her eyes, as Jessica sprinted off with a distraught urgency usually reserved for buildings on fire. "What does *bruiser* mean, anyway? That she causes bruises?"

"It means she's fat," said Eden with a shrug.

"Real nice. She's your godchild."

"Alli, she's two. She's supposed to be a chunky muffin. What do you want, a waifish two-year-old? Don't listen to that crazy woman."

"You must be thrilled that Cole is eighteen and you're out of the mommy loop. It's such a pressure cooker now."

"Who is that woman, anyway?" asked Eden. "She stresses me out."

"Her husband's some big private equity guy. I bet they have one of Otto's paintings—all those guys want these days is a marquee artist on their wall as a badge of honor to show they still got juice."

"Intense. How is Kate, anyway? Please do not tell me you are seriously going to stress about schools?" asked Eden, who sent Cole to Friends downtown. "You have nothing to worry about!"

"Please. I love my kid, but instead of Sanders, her middle name should be Trouble. She does stripteases! Seriously, I'm like, where's the pole? She wears those clear Cinderella heels you gave her and looks like a tranny!" she said, shaking her head. "She's four-going-on-whore."

Eden cackled in her trademark guffaw. "It's just a phase, don't worry."

"I hope . . . 'cause I swear, this kid is one strut away from Scores. One grind away from Girls Gone Wild! I found her raiding my makeup while I was on the phone. She had full JonBenét red lipstick and blue eye shadow. The horror."

Eden laughed and ordered another round of fries from the

waiter, who was practically falling over himself to refill her water after each sip.

"Sheesh, Eden, how do you stay so goddamn thin? I can't believe you didn't outgrow our white-trash eating habits. You still chow like a fucking truck driver! Are you sure you're not on the Two Finger Diet?"

"Please. I could never pull the trigger and make myself chunder. I have a thyroid disease, you know that."

"How do I get it?"

"Shut up. It's not good. You can get heart problems."

"But no one can see your heart." Allison shrugged.

After lunch, the pair left Three Jews and walked down Madison, surveying the windows and armies of Stokke-pushing MILFs.

"I can't believe I let you convince me to move uptown," Eden said. "I don't belong here. I think I should be down in Tribeca or Brooklyn. Somewhere else. I feel like a fucking alien."

"Come on," Allison, said, putting a hot-pink manicured hand through her platinum bob. "Look at me! I'm the most punk rock mom at Carnegie! It's actually retro-chic to live here. Uptown is the new downtown. Plus, honey, you need to break away from The Studio, if you know what I mean."

Eden knew her friend was right. She still hung around Clyde's circle of friends, cooking dinner, seeing plays, visiting galleries. By Clyde's side she was Eden, the model, The Muse, but alone, sixty blocks north, she was . . . Eden.

"So, the million dollar question," said Allison. "When are you going to date again? It's been a while now. I don't think you've ever gone this long without a guy. Thoughts?"

"You're right. But I don't know. I still love Otto, you know."

"He loves you, too—he's mad with jealousy at the thought of you with someone else."

"Yeah, well, tough. Not that there is anyone else on the horizon but . . . We're friends, and true friends let each other go."

"So maybe you should cut the cord a little bit," Allison offered.

"I'm trying! That's why I moved up here," she sighed.

"You're not trying hard enough! I think you should sever all ties. At least for a while. Otherwise, how can you figure out what you want? Who you want to be with?"

"Maybe I don't want to be with anyone. You were always spending your twenties partying and hooking up in the Hamptons trying to find your husband, but I was raising Cole and missed out on all that fun you got to enjoy."

"It's not all it's cracked up to be, trust me," attested Allison, hand to gawd. "That Hamptons house was a shithole overflowing with Eurotrash, which is one step beneath even us. Townies are not just an American phenomenon, you know."

Eden smiled, remembering Allison's stories of beach bonfires and beers under the stars while Eden's life was more about being preggers than hitting keggers.

"The truth is, you didn't miss a thing," Allison promised. "It's way more fun to be in a serious relationship than out there. You know that more than anyone. Weren't you the one who said you want a committed, monogamous relationship? Marriage vows?"

"Of course," Eden admitted. "I would love that, you know that. But I'm not in a rush. I probably wouldn't even be able to settle down if I did meet that guy. The wounds are all too fresh; he wouldn't stand a chance. I want to live for the moment, all that Dead Poets' shit."

"So I can't fix you up with Gerard, Andrew's half brother? He's fifty but really young at heart. Just like Otto."

"If and when I meet someone, I want someone totally different from Otto."

"So jump on the strapping young buck bandwagon!" suggested

Allison. "Oh my God, we have this new young hot Latino gardener in Sagaponack."

"No, gracias," said Eden. "No offense to Callie and Sara, but doesn't that stuff kind of gross you out?"

"No, why? Madonna's doing it! It's hot," said Allison, eyes ablaze. "Plus, you're prettier than all those twentysomethings. They all would die to look like you! You could totally cougar out with Sara and Callie."

"Yuck, I hate that term," Eden squealed as they passed by the Whitney, surveying the hip art kids lining up for the biennial. "It's a little creepy how they eat those guys for breakfast."

"Midnight snack is more like it."

"Whatever. It's not for me."

"Why? Cougars are hot! They're all the rage. Anyway, you're technically still in your thirties, so you're not a full cougar yet. You're a puma."

"There are subdivisions of feline female predators now?"

"Yeah. Cougars are in their forties. Pumas are in their thirties, which you still are, I might add."

"Don't remind me," Eden said, shaking her head in sorrow. "We're clinging on for dear life."

"Forty isn't so bad."

"Yeah, when you're married!"

"No, I mean in general," attested Allison. "It's not what it used to be!"

"Liar."

"Women look better than ever, they have longer life expectancies. Forty's the new thirty and fifty's the new forty. Susan Sarandon, Goldie Hawn, all older! It's your brazen cougary sexuality that keeps them wrapped around your finger. Or claw, I should say. Your cougar cub awaits."

"You know why I loathe that word? Because there is no male equivalent. It is sexist and crass. It's like saying 'slut.' What's the male equal of that? There is none. Men have been dating younger women since they lived in caves, and there's no term for it. It's offensive and I don't want to think of myself as some trashy wild animal who preys on someone else's young."

"Whatever, I just thought since Otto's so much older and you don't want older, maybe the pendulum could swing the other direction this time. I think it's a great idea."

"Honestly, I just want to meet someone who I can love, who loves me. Not this second, maybe, but in general. I don't need to have 'fun.' I did that with Otto for so long. I'm over partying!"

"Of course! I know you would rather fall in love and be swept off your feet, and I agree, you deserve to find true love! I'm just saying while you're waiting, enjoy some rumpus rather than trying to fast-forward to a relationship. Fill the void now! What better way to live in the moment than to roll with a young stud?"

The pals walked in silence for a minute. Then Eden smiled to herself.

"What?" Allison asked, intrigued by the beguiling grin on Eden's lips.

"There is this one guy I met," Eden said, raising an eyebrow carefully.

"I knew it, you slut!"

"Shut up! I'm not. Anyway, it's too embarrassing to even entertain. I have never felt so old. I met him on the street and then saw him again last week at that Waldorf testicles benefit. He's with some girl, I think. I was probably going to first base already when she was born!"

"Oh, who are you kidding? You went right to sex, you lying trollop."

"He was incredibly charming and Old World. I actually have never met any guys who are chivalrous and old school like that. Except Wes. You know, who I used to date before Otto."

"Of course I remember Wes!"

Eden suddenly envisioned a hazy, distant image of her young self with Wes, like a grainy black-and-white photo in a slide show, a staticky Super 8 film, or a tattered postcard. Worn-out media that hardly boasted the high-def sharpness of today but that somehow captured soul so much more.

"So who is this young guy?" Allison asked, snapping Eden back to Madison Avenue from Avenue B.

"Oh, I don't even know him. I just saw him staring at me through most of that benefit at the Waldorf."

"Honey, everyone stares at you. When I first met you in grade school, I thought I might be a lesbian."

"Shut up."

"Kidding. I love you, but not that much. Okay, I gotta pull an Usain Bolt and pick up Kate. I'm telling you, E, don't be afraid to cougar out! If Madge can do it, so can you!"

"Meow," Eden deadpanned, doing an air scratch with a mimed paw.

23

Just remember, once you're over the hill you begin to pick up speed.

—Charles M. Schultz

"What's on your mind, darling?" Liesel asked, lying across Chase's chest, touching his cheek with her Mademoiselle-manicured index finger.

"I don't know, I'm just sad about my grandmother."

"She was a wonderful woman," Liesel said, her long lashes looking down at the Frette linens for a beat of silence. "I just don't want you to be so depressed. You've always been the strong, silent type, but your grandmother wouldn't want you to mope over her."

Liesel's words made Chase ache; she had no idea what Ruthie would have wanted. And, yes, maybe it was true, she wouldn't want him mourning, but she *just* died! He couldn't just sweep away his grief and frolic down the street as if nothing had radically changed. Chase feared, correctly, that Liesel was secretly selfishly bummed at the timing of Ruthie's passing, because Chase's deep sadness would stave off a possible engagement. When one is down, it's hardly the moment to pop Champs corks and celebrate the future; Chase was too bereaved.

"You know," said Liesel, kissing his chest, "my lease is up next month."

"Already? I feel like you just moved in there."

"No, it's been a year, can you believe it?"

"Mm-mm."

Liesel drew breath to fill her lungs with courage. She had to tread delicately. "I was thinking I shouldn't re-sign the lease, right? I mean, I'm here so often that it's basically just a five thousand dollar locker for my stuff, but Mummy obviously would never allow me to let my own place go until . . . things were . . . settled."

"Well, it is a great apartment. And you've made it lovely. I wouldn't let it go."

"Oh," she replied, disappointed. "Okay, then."

The next day, further heightening the mounting pressures, Chase met with his family's lawyer and chief of staff, Laughlin Wilton Taft, at the Family Office, which housed their money managers, DuPree Capital and Lydon Partners as well as the DuP/L Family Foundation. The philanthropic arm was chaired by Brooke, who had just come from an endowment grants meeting when she met Chase and his brothers in the large conference room on Central Park South, overlooking the sweeping vista of a sparkling rectangle of green trees.

"Good afternoon, gentlemen. Mrs. Lydon," started Mr. Taft. "I have here the last Will of Mrs. Ruth Weatherly DuPree."

After he read the particulars—where the Monet, the Picassos, and the Gauguin were going, who would inherit the various pieces of furniture and how the assets would be dispersed to the foundation and various museums—the group got up to leave. But before the somber Chase could make his way to the door, Mr. Taft asked him to remain.

"Whatever for, Laughlin?" asked Brooke, surprised.

"Mrs. Lydon, I do apologize, but I'm . . . afraid that is between me and your son, Chase," replied Taft.

"I beg your pardon? That is preposterous! There is nothing my mother would leave Chase without telling me. She wouldn't mind if I were here. . . ."

"It's not an object, just a letter. A private message to Chase. And as executor of her estate, it is my duty to see that he gets it alone. Again, I am quite sorry, Mrs. Lydon."

In a huff, Brooke exited, her eyes boring a hole through the manila envelope that Laughlin held.

"Chase, your grandmother insisted that no one else give this to you but me. Have a seat."

"All right." Chase nervously opened the envelope.

"Take your time," Laughlin said, exiting the room, closing the door delicately behind him.

As the trees swayed forty-four floors below and three miles in front of him, Chase unfolded the note, written in his grandmother's trademark tiny handwriting. A growing pressure ballooned in his chest. As always, she began writing his name large across the top of the page, each letter made out of small *x*'s that pieced together his name. He ran his finger over the *CHASE* made out of kisses and read on.

> *I know I'm not supposed to pick favorites. And of course you know I love and adore all three of you boys, but, dear Chase, you know you have always had a special place in my heart, sweet thing. There is something about you, beyond your devotion—your phone calls, flowers for my birthdays, or notes for no reason. It's that you have a depth and a soul that goes beyond your generation. Like your late grandfather, whom I cherished, you care deeply about the world and helping people, making everything better. But, darling, do me this one last favor: Live a little. You're so serious. The line in your brow is too creased for your tender age. Take the wind in your sails and go places, anywhere, head off the rails Brookie has laid down*

for you so carefully. Jump the tracks, boy! Break a rule! You've been the good one all your life, taking your marching orders from every which way, and I beg you, for me, to let go.

Mr. Taft is giving you a key. It's for a safety deposit box at The Bank of New York on Madison and Sixty-second Street. Mr. Leroy Jones there will assist you. In it is my engagement ring from your grandfather, designed for us in Paris. If you love Liesel, who is a nice girl, then by all means, put it on her finger. But, sweetheart, if you're in doubt, even the tiniest bit, then please do not. I know she fits just perfectly with Brookie's wishes for you, the dream addition to the Lydon family portrait, but I suspect she won't release you the way you need to be set free. By her side, you'll continue to march those set paces, to follow the same road you always have, to repeat your pristine record all over again. And so I say this: Breathe deeply. Fill your lungs with possibilities. We only go around once, dear boy, and for you, Chase, so rich with emotion in your heart, you must uncork to be truly be happy. If it's Liesel that can do this, then you have my blessing. But there may be someone out there to help you soar. To help you see the world in new colors, brighter and bolder than before. Someone who sees in you what I see. The saddest part for me of leaving this life is leaving you. You are beyond my pride and joy. You are the light in my life and I know that in your future you will grow to shine with even more radiance. With all the love in the world as I depart, I send you my kisses, and your name will be inscribed in little x's forever in my heart.

Chase was not wired to cry. He simply couldn't. Always the stoic, he was used to being everyone's rock, and he wasn't about to collapse now. He locked his emotions even deeper and swallowed the horse pill of grief, dry and choking.

24

Life begins at forty.

—W. B. Pitkin

"Honey, tilt your head a bit to the left, would you?" asked Otto. Eden obliged, though she felt a tiny hint of annoyance; he was micromanaging her more than normal. "The light there is fantastic. You are aglow, lamb."

Eden was posed with her back to the canvas, looking over her shoulder *Odalisque*-style, minus the fatness.

"So when is this show due?" Eden asked, looking out the enormous studio windows at the rooftops dotted with water towers.

"Lyle needs only this last one, but I think it could be the image for all the press and marketing, so I need to finish it soon, like three or four weeks. You're coming to Venice, of course?"

This was the first she was hearing of it. "Oh, I . . . didn't know you wanted me there."

"Honey, you are the magnet! They want you, you're the star! We are still a team, no?"

"But this would be our first opening since we've split up. I mean, you don't really need me there, do you?"

"Are you suggesting that I need you there any less because we don't share a bed? We still are partners, we still talk, we still go out to parties," he scoffed.

"I'll think about it," Eden said casually, counting the water towers in the distance, which she'd always done from her post in the studio, the same spot where she had posed in various states of undress for the better part of twenty years.

"You'll *think* about it? No. Eden, you're coming. You're part of the package, honey!"

Eden remained quiet, drifting into her thoughts as Otto painted her. *Honey, honey, honey.* Suddenly the faintest of memories, like tracks of a cirrus cloud, blew across her brain. She smiled to herself as she posed, remembering how Wes used to call her Maple or sometimes Mapes. Over time, Otto's commonplace nickname grew sickly sweet. Since their split, it had become like aspartame—you can taste the fakeness.

"What are you thinking with that twinkle in your eye?" Otto probed.

"Oh, nothing," Eden said. "Just daydreaming."

The door opened and in walked Mary, Otto's gal pal. She was so Iowan, you could smell the corn on her.

"Hi there, Mary," Eden said. She was barely two years older than their son, Cole. "I got some great stuff, from Kipp," Mary told Otto, excitedly. "It's insane, so pure."

The sweet Midwesterner proceeded to cut perfect lines of coke with her Metrocard, the white-line-maker of choice for nose-candy-happy New Yorkers. Credit cards were so *Less Than Zero.* Otto stared at Eden's silhouetted breast as he mixed just the right ivory to paint the teardrop slope, then casually put down his brush, walked over to Mary, patted her ass, then bent down for a line. Barf. Otto obviously would never grow up. Eden was so glad she was the hell out of there. Her perpetual Peter Pan ex had found his new fairy-dust partner to keep him flying, Hugh Hefner–style, until Social Security kicked in.

"Kipp always gets the best shit. Oh, this is great. Eden?"

"No, thanks, I'm okay."

"No, you have to, it's insane. You can't turn down amazing shit like this."

Eden ignored the offer.

As she watched Otto lasciviously watch a bent-over Mary, Eden realized that despite rumors that women's sexual peak was their late thirties, she strangely felt her libido turned off since her split. Which terrified her. And as she got older, like Matthew Mc-Conaughey in *Dazed and Confused* said, Otto's young off-the-Greyhound hard-bodied sycophants and suck-o-phants seemed to eerily "stay the same age, yes they do."

Eden decided to get dressed. "I think your work is clearly done for today, so I'm off."

"So soon?" Otto asked, mildly alarmed at her eagerness to leave.

"I have to finish my care package for Cole's birthday."

"Okay, then . . . ," Otto said, not wanting her to leave.

Eden opened the large steel industrial door onto the street and breathed in the fresh air. In that gulp of oxygen she realized just how happy she was to get the hell out of there, the place she once upon a time drooled over. She had been euphoric to unpack her belongings in there, to be the mistress of that killer domain. It was New York real estate heaven, full of exaggerated broker superlatives, but now it seemed like Hades. Somehow, even though the cubic footage of the large looming loft was gargantuan, Eden was growing claustro despite its gleaming massive white walls. And oddly, in her snug and cozy one bedroom, devoid of massive floor-to-ceiling windows, skylights, and space, she felt sublimely released, like her snug living room was an airy field, wide-open and free.

25

Success is like reaching an important birthday and finding you're exactly the same.

—Audrey Hepburn

It was in Trevi Nails on Lexington that Eden connected the social dots. Allison was leafing through *Gotham* magazine, perusing the hottest bachelors in the city, when her finger landed on a candid shot of Wills Fine, the überstudly buff best pal of Chase Lydon.

"Oh, spread me some of that on toast points!" cooed Allison. "Yummy. I love the Eligible Bachelors issue. I read it in bed at night during Jon Stewart."

"You're too funny," replied Eden, checking out the nail polish hues. "What does Andrew say?"

"He doesn't care! He knows I am mad for him."

Min-Wah Kwang, known in this nation as Roseanna (selected because of the song by Toto), filed Eden's perfect nails to a smooth clean finish. "Whacala?" she asked.

"Let's see," said Eden, studying the names of the tiny bottles of pinks, peaches, and reds. "These nail polish names are hilarious. I mean, *Vampire Bite? Vegas Quickie?* What's next, *Gstaad Roadwhore?*"

"How bout *Back Seat B.J.*," laughed Allison.

"Okay," said Eden, handing Roseanna two bottles. "I'll do one coat of *Limousine Lovin'* and one coat of *Hamptons Orgy.*"

Allison turned the page of the magazine to find a huge photo of Wills's best friend, Chase Lydon, ranked as the Number One bachelor in New York City.

"Holy shit," Eden said. She jerked mid–top coat, causing Roseanna to paint her skin.

"Whoops, sorry!" Eden said.

"I fix, I fix," said Roseanna, dipping her stick into the acetone.

"Alli, *that's* the guy—the guy Chase I met on the street who I saw at that benefit," Eden explained. "He's in this magazine? Who is he?"

"Wait a minute—Eden, he's only the HOTTEST guy in town. You didn't know who he was?"

"No, why would I? I've been living downtown for twenty years. I don't know the Upper East Side from Minsk."

"Oh my gosh, he is so fine. I bet you he is, like, in love with you already."

"No. He has a girlfriend. I saw them at that benefit. She's pretty."

"So? You are foxier than all those girls."

"*Really* pretty. Blond Muffy type. Betty Draper."

"I bet she's completely asexual! Those socialites are all the same. You think she shags him rotten? Hell to the No. She's probably some cold fish country club matron who would rather do TV than KY, if you know what I mean. They know *Grey's Anatomy* better than their husband's anatomy."

"It's weird, I'm so much older, but we did have this bizarre flicker of chemistry."

"See? Toldja. You know with these things! When I met Andrew I knew right away!"

Allison tilted the magazine toward Eden, revealing a photo of Chase with his brothers at a sailing regatta looking J. Crew–ready and so sexily outdoorsy you could practically smell the salt air. Whale pants central. Ribbon belts galore. Cough and a Teva might fly out.

"Look! It's from a new coffee table book of photos by Patrick McMullan all about the good life. See?" Allison said.

"Whatever. He doesn't need an almost-forty-year-old hag when he has that young blondie with the pearls," Eden said.

"Let me guess, you saw Mary?" Allison ventured. "I've never seen you threatened by blondes, or any woman for that matter."

"I did see Mary. Damn, she's young. She's, like, half my age!"

"Eden. You have got to get over this. If you are going to get depressed about the inevitable, then you will be inevitably depressed."

"I know. I hate myself like this."

"Come on, E. You know you still got it."

"Trust me, I might have 'it' for some guys, but not some cute prep type like him," Eden said, gesturing to Chase's photo with her chin as her polished nails were drying to a shine.

"You never know," said Allison. "You can't tell about people from the outside. Look, everyone thought you and Otto were the perfect duo. Every paper in town wrote you were the It Couple. And then what? Maybe Chase is bored with her. Maybe he's itching inside that bespoke suit. Maybe someone like you is just what he needs."

Maybe. Eden exhaled with a shrug. She didn't know. But she did know one thing: whether she was feeling up to it or not, it was time to get back out there.

26

*Women are most fascinating between the ages of 35 and 40
after they have won a few races and know how to pace themselves. Since few women ever pass 40, maximum fascination
can continue indefinitely.*

—Christian Dior

The Lydons sat down to dinner in their grand dining room, the low chandelier light glistening off the crystal and china.

"Sorry I'm late," Price said, waltzing in wearing a T-shirt and messenger bag. "I was out with Fitz."

"Dude, I hear Duke lost his job again. What's he gonna fucking do now, go ski in Aspen for two years like last time?" asked Pierce between mouthfuls of food.

"Pierce DuPree Lydon!" his father said furiously, restrained by his impeccable manners. "Mind your mouth."

"Sorry, Dad," Pierce replied sheepishly. He was thirty-one, but if you reversed the digits you would find his actual maturity level.

"Nah, he's gonna go be a gardener again. Remember he spent

some winter in Palm Beach doing that? Slept with half the married women on Ocean Boulevard!"

"Nice, he's going from hedge fund to trimming hedges."

"Yeah, I wonder if the ladies' hedges are trimmed down there!" he joked, raising his arm up for a high five. "Awww, yeah!"

"Guys," Chase interrupted, out of respect for his mother, despite the fact that she hadn't a clue that her sons were discussing pubic landscaping at her dinner table. I mean, please. As Prince once crooned, *Act your age, not your shoe size.*

"Yeah, wasn't he banging Cooper's mom after the divorce?" Price gave a mischievous grin.

"Who wasn't?" Pierce replied.

"BOYS! Knock it off. This instant!" Mr. Lydon fumed. He looked at his son Chase, dutiful and calm, eating in silence. At least he had one son he could count on.

In an effort to change the subject, Chase asked about his parents' previous weekend at Lyford for a wedding.

"Oh, it was so lovely," Brooke said, dreaming of wedding bells for her own family. "Actually," she said, looking to her husband carefully, "we bumped into Skip and Bitsey van Delft down there. And I know it's none of my beeswax—"

"Darling, don't," interrupted Chase's father.

"No, dear, I won't restrain myself this time. I've had enough. Chase, I was embarrassed. It's humiliating to see them! With nearly three years gone by, it's—it's time. You can just tell Patricia is simply chomping at the bit for a wedding. Chomping! She always uses Ron Wendt and it would be simply stunning. It's what everyone wants! I can't keep running into them at the Colony; it's awkward!"

"Mother, I know," Chase replied, feeling the back of his neck grow hot as his brow perspired under the nuclear rays of his mother's hot gaze. "I just . . . I'm not sure if Liesel is The One."

Brooke dropped her sterling fork with a thud onto her Baccarat plate. "The *One*? Please. What is this, a Disney movie? Are you expecting bluebirds and bunny rabbits to sing on a hollow log? What a positively pedestrian notion! Be realistic, Chasie. I mean, honestly. You're looking for a partner here."

"Mother, it's not a business merger. It's a marriage."

"What do you think marriage is?" She laughed.

"Well, that's sad," Chase replied.

"This is preposterous. Grant, knock some sense into him, please. This is insane! Of course you and Liesel are getting married. This was never a question of *if*. It was about *when*, you said! Now you're telling me you're not sure? What are you waiting for, some lightning bolt?"

"Maybe."

"I can't listen to this nonsense!" Brooke said, shaking her head and looking as though she might weep. "How am I supposed to see the Van Delfts? HOW?"

"Son, take your time. If you're not sure, then you're not sure," offered Grant with a pat on the back.

"You've got to be kidding me!" Brooke said, almost tearing up. "Grant, you LOVE Liesel!"

"Well, of course I do, dear, but I'm not the one marrying her."

"SHE'S GIVEN YOU THREE YEARS!" she screamed at Chase. "FOR GOD'S SAKE, THIS IS RIDICULOUS!" Brooke fumed and stormed out. As a woman, on behalf of all women, she was horrified that her son would be one of those men who strings along a poor doting girl forever, stealing away childbearing years and tossing her aside to start over as her friends are walking down the aisle.

Chase and Grant sat quietly after Brooke's emotional departure.

Grant pierced the silence. "Son, I meant what I said. You know we love Liesel, but you have to be the one who's sure, not us."

"Thanks, Dad."

Chase appreciated his father's gesture, but they both knew Brooke was as determined as Liesel to seal the deal. The problem was, anything that felt like a *deal* probably wasn't what Chase wanted in the long run. But one thing he did know for sure. As his crass brother Price would so gracefully put it, it was time to "shit or get off the pot."

27

Life begins on your 40th birthday. But so do fallen arches,
rheumatism, faulty eyesight, and the tendency to tell a story to
the same person, three or four times.

—Helen Rowland

"With all due respect, Bro, they're right, what the fuck are you thinking? What are you waiting for?" asked an incredulous Wills Fine on the Rover Club squash court when Chase reported the heated exchange with his mother. "Most guys would kill for a girl like Liesel. Hell, I would! She's got it all."

"I guess."

"You *guess*? Dude, you oughta have your fucking head examined! When she started at Sotheby's, every guy who wasn't gay was falling all over himself. I remember I was the auctioneer for this contemporary sale and she walked in the gallery with her boss, and I almost fucked up the bids."

"I remember you telling me that," Chase said, serving the ball.

"I don't know what crack pipe you're on, man. She's hot, she's nice, she's totally wife material."

"I know," Chase said, feeling foolish taking for granted someone it seemed everyone would kill to wed, including Wills. "I'm
just . . . not a hundred percent sure. It's all there, everything you
listed and more. I don't know what my problem is."

"Hey, your problem is called cold feet. All men get that before
taking the plunge. That's why there's a name for it, dude. It's
common."

"I guess," Chase said, whacking the ball as hard as he could. As
it bounced and ricocheted in the cube of their court, he felt his
life was as out of control and zigzagged as that little black ball.

After a steam and a shower, Wills and Chase decided to get
some pasta at Sette Mezzo. The place was packed with people,
flooding out onto Lexington, but Chase knew the owner, who
waved them through, offering a table in five minutes. As Wills
scanned the crowd for familiar faces (there always was one. Or
ten), Chase was stunned to spot Eden. As crisp and clean as he felt
post-workout, sweat started to form on his brow. His heart raced
and he looked away before she could look up.

Eden was at a table of six women, two still-married uptown
mommy pals, Hannah and Maggie, Allison of course, plus single
moms Sara and Callie, who were flipping through their mental
black books of who they could hook up with. While Eden was
like sisters with Allison, she was not a girls' girl. She never had a
Sex and the City pussy posse, and the idea of group dinner, Chardonnay, and chat about young bucks' asses was fun once in a while
but not about to become a weekly habit. Still, on a night when
she would have been doing nothing but sitting around watching
Mad Men reruns, it was nice to get a phone call inviting her out
for a spontaneous moms' dinner with Sara, Callie, Allison, and a
few other friends from their school. They were not at all the
nightmare uptown yummy mummies Eden had envisioned. In

fact, she was surprised to find that they were all very cool, relaxed, and not afraid to lose the edit button.

"Oh my God, I can't believe I just snarfed all that gnocchi," said Allison to her empty plate. "I am Shamu."

"Speaking of whales, did you guys see Chip Krakower out front?" asked Sara. "He has ballooned!"

"Dewars is his water," said Allison, shrugging. "Morbid obesity is the least of his worries. His son has more problems than a math book."

"He's a biter," said Callie, filling Eden in. "He has a constant shadow at nursery school. The class filed a petition to have him booted 'cause so many kids came home with teeth marks on their thighs. He breaks the skin every time."

"No!" gasped Hannah. "You lie."

"I wish I were," said Allison. "You've heard of Teen Wolf? This is Tot Wolf."

"So, Eden, where should we go after this?" Callie asked, her eyes twinkling with estrogen. "Cipriani again?"

"No. Too much competition. It's C.C.S.," said Sara, conspiratorially to the table. "Cougar Central Station."

"Wait, I thought that was Aspen?" asked Hannah, laughing.

"Well, sure, Aspen is our mecca," proclaimed Callie the self-professed cougar-in-chief. "All those hot ski instructors looking to get out of their parkas!"

"You are killing me," cackled Eden.

"Oh, I swear, they are dumb as the rocks they ski on, but they sure know how to make you melt off the slopes," said Sara.

"They put the *mount* in *mountain*," said Callie.

"And the ass in Aspen!" added Sara with a mascara'd wink.

"Yeah, and sure know how to punch my lift ticket," Callie added, as the girls wailed.

"Anyway, since we can't troll for tail in Colorado tonight, we can do the next best thing and hit Bar & Books or the Lenox

Room," said Callie. "I met this hot, stressed-out Goldman analyst who never gets away from his desk, and I blew his mind. I gave him my card and said anytime they let you outta that cage, call me up! He couldn't be cuter!"

"Hotter than the Harvard Tutors guy who's helping Kayleigh with math?" asked Hannah.

"Yes, even hotter," pronounced Callie.

"Wait," interrupted Maggie, horrified. "Are you seriously banging your kid's math tutor?"

"Oh yeah. He teaches her times tables, then after she goes to bed, he gives me some long division."

"Are you kidding? Every uptown divorcée does it!" Sara laughed. "Where have you been?"

"Oh, Mags, everyone knows Harvard Tutors offer full service help," concurred Sara. "I don't even wait for the kids to hit the hay. They fill in the blanks on the quiz while he fills me in upstairs!"

"EW! SHUT UP!" Maggie commanded, putting her hands over her ears, as Allison, Hannah, and Eden pounded the table with laughter.

Just then, Allison abruptly stopped mid-guffaw with a sharp gasp. She threw down her wineglass and grabbed Eden's tiny wrist.

"Holyshitholyshitholyshitholyshit," she whispered, prompting the others to lean inward.

"Eden, it's HIM. Wait, don't turn around."

Eden turned around. She locked eyes with Chase and smiled, turning back to the henfest.

"He's cute, isn't he?" she wondered aloud.

"Wait, isn't that Chase Lydon?" asked Hannah.

"Uh, yeah! Is he a fox or what?" Allison asked. "He and Eden had a *moment*. So sexy."

"Gorgeous," added Maggie. "But super young."

"Come on. It's a new decade! We're hot women here; we're not our mothers and grandmothers," said Allison indignantly. "Forty is the new thirty! Sixty is the new forty!"

"Yeah, and didn't you guys hear?" asked Eden, rolling her eyes. "Dead is the new sixty! Rotting corpse is the new seventy!"

"Shut up, I'm serious," said Allison. "If any of us were single we'd hop on that for shizzle."

"You're so pretty, Eden, you could seriously get any guy," said Hannah. "Allison confirmed that one-hit wonder by Desperate Measures was about you, after all!"

"That was about YOU?" Sara beamed. "I loved that song!"

"Yeah, if anyone can get him, you can," echoed Maggie.

"Thanks for the pep talk, people." Eden ran a hand through her glossy brown hair. "I have to go to the Ladies." She got up and walked downstairs, looking back at her table, who watched as she passed by the empty table Chase and Wills were being led to.

Upon her return, there was no way to not cross their path. The jammed restaurant was like social bumper cars.

"Hello," said Eden as she looked at Chase. "Seems I'm running into you in all the chicest places."

"Hi! Yes, um, nice to see you again," Chase stammered. "This is my friend Wills."

As Eden and Wills shook hands, the waiter brought their drinks.

"Stoli tonic," he said, placing the goblet in front of Wills. "And ginger ale for Mr. Lydon."

"Slow down there, Trouble," deadpanned Eden.

"I, uh, have to get up early for work," offered Chase nervously.

Eden lit up the table with her huge smile. "Okay, then. Enjoy."

As she turned back to her table she realized that not only her gang but also others in the restaurant were staring. She had only just moved uptown and was a new quasi-celeb in these parts, and it was almost surreal to see her interacting with one of their own when she hung on so many cavernous living room walls on Fifth Avenue. One private equity partner slash major art collector had lent his large-scale portrait of her to the Tate Modern for a solo show and missed the work so much that upon its return he and his wife threw a massive welcome-home party for it, complete with Glorious Food catering and coverage on New York Social Diary.

But Eden had never cared about any of those boring 10021 dudes, whether they collected her image or not. Until now. There was a palpable chemistry with Chase that could no longer be denied. And when she looked over her shoulder before sitting back down, she knew he felt it, too.

28

*The first sign of maturity is the discovery that the volume knob
also turns to the left.*

—Jerry M. Wright

After the checks had been paid, both tables got up to leave at the same time. Allison's friends peeled off in their various directions, citing high school babysitter time bombs. After all the gals hugged good-bye, Allison kissed Eden good night and saw Chase and Wills through the glass door, heading up the two stairs to exit onto Lexington.

"There's your lover boy," teased Allison with a whisper into Eden's ear.

"Shut up," replied Eden. "What are we, back in sixth grade?"

"Want me to pass him a note to meet you by the bleachers?"

"Ha-ha."

The two waved and walked in separate directions, just as Wills bumped into an old college chum whom he bear-hugged.

"Wills, I gotta get home," said Chase, quickly greeting Wills's friend before bolting to catch up with Eden, who was slowly striding toward Seventieth Street.

"Hey again," Chase said as he caught up beside her.

"Hi there," Eden said, staring into his eyes.

"Where are you walking?" he asked. His whole body felt swollen. His cheeks reddened, his legs tingled, and his brow began to perspire. "It's such a nice night."

"Home. Sixty-eighth Street between Madison and Park."

"Oh yeah? That's a really nice block." They walked side by side down Lexington.

"It is. I'm right in the middle of those three wide fabulous old walk-ups. I'm on the second floor with these great high ceilings and century-old moldings. It feels very European."

"Sounds beautiful" was all he could muster.

"Yeah, it really is. It was so hard for me to move up here, but I wanted a fresh start and distance from my ex. And the walk-up feels more, I don't know, accessible somehow. More me."

"How do you like it so far?" Chase asked. "Must not be quite as exciting."

"I'm into it . . . ," she trailed off.

"You don't sound so convinced." Chase smiled.

"No, no, I like it, I do, it's very Old World graceful, and my best friend, Alli, lives up here, so it was a natural choice. It's weird, though, how quiet it is. It's practically suburbia compared with downtown."

"Yeah, it's definitely sleepier here," said Chase, who grew more nervous each time he looked at her. "But it has its merits."

"So I see," she said, looking him over.

Chase wasn't used to women who were so outwardly flirtatious. Eden's eyes flashed right at him, penetrating his gentlemanly façade.

"So, I didn't realize when we first met that your husband, or I guess, um, ex-boyfriend, uh, is Otto Clyde," Chase stammered, recalling the artist's sold-out lecture at MoMA that Ruthie attended.

"Mm-hmm, that's him. We're still friends so it's all fine, but I just needed some room."

"I'm a big fan of his."

"Really?" Eden mused. "Funny, I don't take you for an art guy."

"Why not?" Chase asked, almost defensively. The fact was, he loved art and knew a lot about the contemporary and modern markets, thanks to Ruth.

"I'm sorry, I didn't mean to offend you. I just meant you seem like . . . Mr. Serious."

"People aren't always what they seem to be," Chase said, half-smiling. "I'm not so serious."

"Really? Do you ever break loose, Dow Jones?"

Chase shifted and ran a hand through his hair as they waited at a stoplight. "Sure. I guess."

"You guess, huh?" Eden said, penetrating the space between them with a small step toward him and knocking on his head of caramel-colored hair. "I bet in there, there's someone who is just itching to break out." Her words teasingly tripped over his ears lightly. "Come on, Nasdaq," she whispered in his ear. "Live a little."

"I try to; I mean, I'm so busy with work that I just kind of forgot how." He shrugged innocently. "I always want to, but I just have . . . so much stuff I have to do."

"You know, Chase, we're all going to be dead in eighty years. Life's too short for too much *stuff.*"

She stared straight into his eyes. As he gulped back the nervous energy coursing through his blue-blooded veins, Eden turned to him, right on that windy street corner. She lightly picked up the bottom of his elephant-covered navy blue Hermès tie, pulled him into her, and kissed him, infusing his body with a zap he'd never known before. He kissed back in a way that engulfed his whole being, enlivening his arms to encircle her waist and his breath to quicken. Their mouths made his brain short-circuit—but after a few seconds, his conscience caught up to his body and he pulled back abruptly.

"Who says you don't know how to have fun? That was fun, right?"

"I'm sorry, Eden, I can't," Chase said, stepping back farther. "I-I'm seeing someone," he stammered through blushed cheeks and sweaty brow.

"I'm so sorry," Eden said apologetically. "There's just . . ." She made a motion with her hand from his chest to hers, like a swift spoon swatting the energy between them.

"I know," Chase said.

" . . . something here," she finished.

"I . . . can't act on it. I . . . apologize," Chase stuttered. "I really should be going." Instantly he snapped back, like a preppy Gumby, into his original upright composure.

"Good night, nice to see you again," he said politely from his stoic stance two feet away.

His body, lithe and liquid like boiled spaghetti only moments before in Eden's arms, had returned to its mechanical, hard, uncooked state. He walked away at a brisk pace, part dutiful toy soldier, part Ken Doll, part moral Robocop, all impenetrable.

29

It's sad to grow old, but nice to ripen.

—Brigitte Bardot

"How was it at the studio today?" Allison asked as she talked to Eden on the phone. Allison was making grilled cheeses for her kids while Eden was lying down on her couch, legs up on the wall, like a fourteen-year-old. Loath to ever buy a cordless phone, Eden twisted the old-fashioned curly cord in her fingers.

"Weird."

"How so?"

"Otto told me I seemed distracted. And then I realized, I was."

"By what?"

"Fuck. I'm too embarrassed to even tell you."

"I'm so insulted! It's *me*, E."

"Okay, okay. I've been thinking about that guy Chase."

"Chase Lydon. *Thinking* about him, thinking about him?"

"It's stupid, anyway. Useless, in fact. He fully rebuffed me."

"Huh, that's new for you, isn't it?" Allison teased.

She was right. Eden went through her life like a flip book and couldn't think of a single man who had ever turned her down.

"I barely know him. I mean, we're strangers and couldn't be more different. But there was definitely something intense there. Sparks."

"Interesting."

"We were walking and talking and I just had this sensation that I wanted to bring him home with me, but he pushed me off and said he had a girlfriend. Which I knew. I'm such a schmuck, I walked right into a land mine."

"God, you are ballsy," Allison marveled. She didn't know many women who could do that.

"And delusional, obviously. I've lost it. That hold I used to have on guys."

"Not true."

"Yes, it is! I'm old."

"No, you're not.

"Two words: Crypt Keeper."

"E, it has nothing to do with that. Don't think of it as rejection. He's taken!"

"I guess."

"I thought you said you wanted to be alone so you could figure out what you really wanted," Allison reminded her. Deep down, though, she knew Eden never could fly solo for long.

"I do, I really do," Eden claimed. "I just liked him. I don't even know why, I found him very sweet. He has this innocence; he's so *earnest*, you know? You can just tell he's a good person."

"Sounds like someone has a crush."

"Oh gosh, don't make me sound like a tween."

"Maybe it's good for you. Get the motor running. Also, E, in the real world, most people experience rejection, regret, all that fun stuff. It keeps things in perspective."

Eden felt engulfed by fear that her winning streak of power over men had come to an end. "I'm just so lonely," Eden confessed. "I don't know what's worse, being so lonely with Otto that I sometimes used to cry myself to sleep, or actually being alone all the time."

"Being with Otto was worse," Allison explained. "Because even though you're lonely now, you have the promise of someone coming in to fill that void."

"Ugh, I feel so . . . desperate."

"You're not desperate. The desperate ones are the ones looking to get those cobwebs out of their uteri. You have Cole. You don't have to worry about your eggs passing their sell-by date. You have time to really look and find someone amazing."

"Okay, so maybe I'm not freaking out. There's no race. There's not even a finish line. I'm just thinking about knowing someone again. Having someone know me."

"Hey, breaking news: That's what everyone wants! You were seeking all this other stuff, and you got it, and then you realized what was missing. I'm telling you, Eden, it will come. But not until you rebuild yourself first."

"I know. You're right as always, Alli," Eden said, thinking about her best friend's knowing smile. "How did you get so smart?"

"Thirty-nine years of practice."

30

Middle age is when your age starts to show around your middle.

—Bob Hope

A full fifty-six hours elapsed in which Chase was positively besieged by guilt. Gut-crunching, headache-inducing, soul-stirring guilt. A strong-headed, fiercely principled do-gooder, Chase had never once cheated on a quiz, tax form, or girlfriend. His business dealings never ventured into shady territory, and his record was always sterling—scholastically, professionally, socially. And now he felt like a schizo.

He was tormented by that kiss—in two ways: He was stung by the prickly thorn of his transgression but also still lured by the petals' bewitching pleasures. He was sick he succumbed to an impulse behind Liesel's back. And yet he was also sick it was over so quickly. He oscillated between wanting to press rewind so he could record over it with a more chaste departure. But then in his mind he was rewinding it only to replay it over and over. It was such a fleeting miracle of passion he didn't know he could feel, his four ventricles finally pumping in overdrive. And he also knew it was proof that there was more to life than the safe love Liesel offered him, that his mother so prized, the perfect union that their platinum petri dish wanted to see in the *New York Times* Weddings section.

But perhaps his mother and father were onto something. Maybe marital bliss isn't about fiery passion. Maybe he owed it to Liesel, after all their time together, to pretend that moment with Eden, no matter how incredible, had never even happened.

Refreshed after a shower that Chase vowed would wash away his lingering thoughts of Eden forever, he met Liesel for a romantic dinner at Amaranth. She was waiting for him at their normal table, looking radiant. Her hair was coiffed to perfection in a straight blowout with a thin headband, and she was the picture of elegance and poise, her gumball-sized pearls glowing in the candlelight as she sipped a glass of rosé by the window.

"Hello, darling," she said, rising to kiss him hello. She straightened her black shift dress beneath her as she sat back down while Chase ordered a drink of his own. After ordering appetizers and greeting streams of fellow diners, Liesel began to tell him about what she had been working on that day at the auction house.

"Do you think you'll get that promotion?" Chase asked. "You clearly deserve it at this point."

"Well, actually," she said. "I'm trying to get a different job. At Doyle Galleries. It would be a huge career move for me."

Chase scratched his head. "I didn't know you were even looking."

"I know, I wasn't, but I heard about this position yesterday and I've always wanted to be there, so I'm interviewing next week."

"That's great," said Chase, surprised but happy for her. They sat in silence for a moment as he looked at her delicate, ringless left hand. He took a deep breath and felt his pulse quicken as he recalled his indiscretion. He knew they say it's never good to tell of an infidelity. While it would rid him of the burden of remorse, it would also pass the burden of knowledge on to her small shoulders. But he felt so awful about it. The deed had thrust him into a prison of regret, and he needed to break free. It was as if *Law & Order*'s constant *cling-clang* sound was playing on a loop in the tinny speakers of his brain. As the seconds passed, he couldn't take it any longer. His courage mounted. He opened his mouth to speak.

He drew a long guilty breath to let the words flow out. But just before his confession could spill from his lips, Chase noticed huge tears welling up in his girlfriend's eyes. Oh no. Poor thing. She'd had it. She was at her wit's end. She was through watching her friends get married after only a year of dating while she had been with Chase for three. She was done with dinners and trips and romance all by rote, each with the reverie of a ring at the other end, and no such luck. Shit, he couldn't tell her now. Instead he took her hand, which was freezing.

"Liesel—"

She blinked a hot tear down her cheek, which she casually brushed away, as the spear of shame gutted Chase's side. He had put her through all of this waiting, only to cheat on her with an illicit kiss with a complete stranger. And now, ever reserved and ladylike, she withheld her emotion as best she could, with all her strength summoned to let out only one solitary tear. The dam of her self-control held back emotional floods as he caressed her hand in his across the table.

Chase knew for sure now, seeing her distressed face, that he couldn't come clean. It would kill her. Instead he picked up her hand and kissed it.

"I'm so sorry," Liesel gushed, more tears seeping past their emotional levee.

"Sorry?" Chase asked, confused. "What for?"

Liesel looked down at the white table linens, straightened an askew fork.

"I slept with Wills."

Her long lashes lifted from the silver cutlery up to meet his dumbfounded gaze.

Chase's universe was put on instant mute. One could have dropped a risotto grain and it would have sounded like a deafening boulder. The rest of the crowded café was suddenly a blur as he sat thunderstruck.

"Chasie, say something. I'm so, so sorry!" Liesel said, dabbing at her eyes with her cloth napkin. "I have been so sick about this. I'm ill. I feel so awful. I'm so sorry."

"Wait . . . *Wills*? My best friend?"

"We both feel just terrible." She wept.

"You and Wills. You had sex?"

"Chase, I am so sorry. I've been wracked with guilt."

"When did this happen? How?" He couldn't possibly imagine them together. It was too surreal, too bizarre: his girlfriend of three years and the guy who would have been best man in their wedding.

"I bumped into him on the way out of work yesterday and we started walking home. We got to talking about how Shelly just got engaged and I kind of insinuated that I prayed I was next, and then he said he didn't know what you were waiting for, that I was such a catch, and then I guess I was so flattered. I just . . . didn't know if you would ever step up, and I can't wait forever. I was feeling like I had a safe place to vent with Wills; I've been feeling like my life was on hold. And the next thing I knew, he invited me up to his apartment and I saw this montage of pictures of all of us, and I realized that he cared for me quite deeply."

Chase stared at his plate of prosciutto, silent.

"And I've been patient, Chase, so patient, and then in that moment I knew Wills would never have kept me waiting three long years; he has more photographs of me in his apartment than you do and I feel so terrible because I wanted it to be *you* nursing this crush for me, but I realized: You aren't."

Chase looked up at her. Her face, her confession, even her sudden honestly about what she had been going through rendered her a total stranger across from him. As the votive light flickered on her pretty face, Chase found her virtually unrecognizable.

"When he saw me looking at his bulletin board of all those pictures—from our trip to Little Compton and then Susie's wedding at Mill Reef, Wills looked at me in a way that you never do. With longing. And so he kissed me. And I realized I have a history with him, too, and he always wanted me. And I need to feel wanted like that. So we kissed more. And one thing led to another. We both feel terrible about it but agreed I should be the one to tell you. I'm so sorry, Chase."

Liesel's eyes glistened with tears as she blinked a stream down her pink cheek. Her polished index finger wiped it away as she stared at him, waiting for his response. She exuded a strange mix of guilt and strength, a sudden confidence Chase didn't recognize, but that clearly Wills gave her. She was apologizing but not asking for forgiveness. She was there to confess and then obviously go back to the guy who "made her feel wanted." Chase just sat in silence. He didn't know what to say. Especially because, as emotions swirled in his head, he didn't really know what he thought.

Liesel braced herself for a lashing. Would he scream at her? Would he pop like a whistling kettle, jealous steam coming out his ears? Would he go shithouse and throw something? Anything, even smashing porcelain or hurling fish forks, would be better than this reserved silence. What could he be thinking? He simply sat silently, his jaw clenching periodically, Tom Cruise–style.

Inside Chase's head, he visualized two distinct colors swirling together. One was bilious green, a sickened hue of shocked envy and bitter betrayal. He couldn't believe this was actually happening. But then, in that poisoned sea, in the distance, there appeared a patch of glowing, pulsating red that slowly intruded more and more in thick foaming waves: a tide of juicy, deliciously red *relief.*

31

Forty is the old age of youth; fifty is the youth of old age.

—Victor Hugo

After a long and solemn hug good-bye, Liesel left Chase on Madison Avenue with one final "I'm sorry." There was nothing else to be said.

"It's okay, Buttercup," he said calmly. "I wasn't giving you what you needed."

"Oh gosh, don't make me cry," she said, welling up again. "And please don't blame Wills. It was probably my fault. I do think, in the end, though, it will all be for the best."

"I don't blame either of you, I promise," Chase responded in all sincerity, as thunder clapped and drizzle started to sprinkle their mutually culpable heads.

"Bye, then," she said, turning to hail a cab, no doubt to Wills's apartment.

"Bye," Chase said through the cab window, which she started to roll up as the rain sprinkled her face. "Take care."

He closed the door and watched her cab turn the corner. He stood in the light rain, looking for another taxi. He found one quickly, climbed in, greeted the driver, and gave his address in his usual proper manner, as if he'd just come from a business meeting or doctor's appointment. He sat there, still, looking out the window as the cab wheels spun him off up the avenue and another set spun in his brain. He sat jostled in the pleather backseat, like a wobbly Weeble, rocked from side to side by the driver's shitty driving. It was a physical echo of his emotional state; his world was rocked but he was somehow stable. Nothing ever knocked Chase Lydon down.

When he got home, the sound of the door closing behind him sounded like a bank vault slamming, heavy and leaded, trapping him in his solitude. He stood in front of the mirror, loosened his tie, and took off each cuff link and pulled out his collar stays. He looked at his reflection. It seemed different. He saw not only his surroundings but also himself in a new way. But he couldn't label the blistering emotion welling within him. Was it rage? Anguish? Resentment? No . . . it was nothing like that. It was none of those. Or all of those. He didn't quite know.

He didn't quite know what to do with himself, either, post-emotional-apocalypse. He couldn't watch TV. He started pacing. Maybe he could call one of his brothers. He looked down at his vintage Rolex. Ten thirty. Both were no doubt out carousing at Dorian's. Maybe other friends? But in that moment, not one popped to mind. The thing about Chase was that everyone always came to him. New school? Kids lined up to be his buddy. Girls? There was always one who was in hot pursuit of him. Everyone in his life would initiate plans and call him, invite him drinking, sailing, to every event, but he never would unload a problem or open up to anyone, bromance-style. So while he had had many *buddies*, Chase realized in the solitude of his apartment, he had no friends. The one person he had ever spilled his guts to gutted him with the blade of betrayal. He certainly didn't feel up to calling or even confronting his so-called best friend.

But even more shocking than Liesel's amorous revelation was

that Chase wasn't nearly as pissed as one would imagine he'd be. And not only that, he even had the sensation of having been released, unmetered, magically freed. Now it wasn't on his shoulders when he told Brooke that Liesel would not be her daughter-in-law; it was Liesel's own doing, even though deep down, Chase knew he had been pushing her away and having doubts about their relationship all along. Wills, meanwhile, always lusted after Liesel in ways that Chase didn't. So perhaps, despite the shadowy origins of their kindled sparks, this burgeoning relationship made sense. Suddenly, Chase realized with perfect clarity that in fact Wills and Liesel would be very happy together. And that was that.

It began to rain harder. Lightning crashed outside, and drops spattered his window in pelts so strong it was like Mother Nature was drumming her nails against the thick glass. He sat in his father's old cognac leather club chair, worn and weathered, staring at the sheets of water on the pane. His now ex-girlfriend's tearful exodus didn't even make him feel heavy with sadness, just . . . blank. He didn't know whether to call someone or read a book or continue to stare at the chaos outside. It was strange, he thought, that the gray clouds were more in an uproar than he was, given the evening's revelations. The clouds were thrashing and crying in a way he couldn't.

He felt so drained that he barely moved for over an hour. And then, before he could figure out what to do next and without even consciously thinking about it, he very casually got up and walked out.

"Mr. Lydon, don't you need an umbrella?" the doorman asked as Chase headed for the torrents of rain in his jeans and button-down shirt. "It's really coming down, sir. I have a spare here—"

"That's all right, Tony, thank you," Chase replied robotically, walking straight out into the flood.

The thick raindrops were so big, they bounced off the pavement, heavy enough to wash away the confusion and the past. He was soaked through instantly without a care in the world. Maybe he thought he would feel something if he steeped himself in the wild tempest he had watched through his window. He stepped through the torrents of rain as if it were any old sunny day, impermeable to chill or discomfort. Sloshing through puddles he strode, five blocks down, two blocks east, until he was there, right in front of the town house in which Eden lived.

32

With mirth and laughter let old wrinkles come.

—William Shakespeare

An orange light glowed from the parlor floor. Chase searched the window for her perfect silhouette, but she wasn't sitting by the window. He looked for a shadow on an adjacent wall or even the ceiling; just a hazy swath of light cast on an elbow would do. But there was nothing, no sense of her presence within. He backed up a few steps to crane his neck in case she wandered by the French window. He'd been obsessed; thinking about her body, her long hair, her unbridled confidence and outwardly sexy yet still mysterious vibe. In the previous days, he had forced himself to flush all those thoughts out of his mind, but they burst forth, released by his now-vanished remorse. Thoughts of her flickered on the movie screen of his brain. Her thighs in that short dress. Her skin, her green eyes.

The rain flooded down on him as he stared into the window for what seemed like an hour. His blue shirt was a drenched second skin, the angles of his face like little slides for water to pour down. He shivered a bit, bewitched by the glowing light of the window. And then . . .

"Chase?" he heard behind him.

He turned to find Eden, walking toward him, holding an umbrella she had bought at the MoMA Design Store. It was all black on top but underneath was a bright Magritte blue sky with a few clouds on it. He didn't know what to say. He had hoped to see her, but didn't have a plan hatched out. He just looked at her, breathing as the heavy raindrops pelted him.

"You know, stalking is very underrated," Eden said, stepping toward her soaked suitor and covering him with the umbrella, a shared haven of sunny azure.

Without speaking, Chase grabbed Eden as if in slow motion. He engulfed her under the umbrella and kissed her madly, his wet hand running through her long hair, his eyes closed, blinded by his own passionate attack. It was what he had longed to do at their last encounter. The light on that street corner and the light in his heart both said GO, but in his head, bound to Liesel, it had been flashing red instead. But now in the rain he was no longer linked to another and was bursting to return the kiss he had so abruptly broken off.

As Eden returned his breathless embrace, the umbrella fell to the ground beside them. The blue sky under her umbrella now turned upward as the people it once shielded became waterlogged by the merciless storm. They didn't care. Chase's hands searched her warm neck, the soft hot skin of her back beneath her cashmere sweater, as he drenched her with his own wet body. Their clothes were soon soaked through, but each felt the heat of the other through the sopping fibers and the drumbeat of each other's chest.

There was a deafening smack of thunder. Eden gasped and pulled their lips apart and looked at him with wild eyes.

"Should we go inside?" he asked nervously.

"Sure," she said, putting her arms back around him. "My place or . . . mine?"

"Your place." Chase smiled. He followed her through the double doors of her grand but semi-broken-down town house. He bounded up the stairs of her small building's once-elegant lobby as if the rust-carpeted path were the yellow brick road, minus the midgets. Chase gazed up at Eden; she was rain splattered and smiling, and couldn't have looked more bewitching. Even if she had primped for hours, she couldn't have looked more gorgeous to Chase as he entered her apartment. She held his wet hand, leading him excitedly down the hallway and through the living room. It was as if the apartment were hot water and she was the tea: Everything around them was infused with her style, her scent, her magnetic draw; it was an eclectic extension of the woman he was following to the bedroom. There were random bowls of beaded jewelry, ethnic knickknacks, small frames, small frameless paintings leaning on book-covered shelves, old wood-block letters, cashmere throws, pillows galore, chic woven rugs, treasures from around the globe. It was like Eden had the whole world inside her apartment walls: Her spiced sachets and sweet perfumes indulged his senses more than any four-star chef's, the jingles of her thin arm full of bangle bracelets better than any symphony's. The walls and upholstery were covered in warm fabrics with cozy details, from tassels to toasty blankets to the velvet ribbon with which she tied back her long disheveled hair.

As she turned around to face him, his damp cheeks flushed, Eden reached back and pulled the ribbon out, letting her hair down. Chase lunged for her, free and wild, bathed in the warm dim light. He pawed her so fiercely they almost toppled down several times as they staggered to the bed. They rolled into each other on the cloud of her downy comforter, leaving person-shaped rain stains on the coverlet. Chase's breath was hot and fevered as their kiss deepened. His eyes were closed, his hands grasping her like he would never let go. He had never felt more electrified, and while there had been more than a few pretty girls in his arms, there had never been a real woman. The vixen beside him was a tigress, and with her it was like he had finally come alive, charged in every finger, every hair. For the first time in his entire life he felt out of control, drunk on Eden's sultriness. He was in the sexual passenger seat, unsure of the slick wet road's exciting twists and turns.

Eden was happy to drive. Again. After two decades of being Clyde's sexual pawn, she was in charge. She could feel in Chase's desperate grasp that familiar sensation of being not just wanted but needed, *craved*. It was endearing how Chase kissed her so many times all over her body, as if to mark her every pore with his lips, as he lifted her black sweater over her head. She took off her lace bra and tossed it aside, reaching back to him. He was at once burning for her but incredibly tender in his touch, and as he held each of her hands in his and breathlessly interlocked their twenty fingers, she suspended all her worries about their chasm in age. She closed her eyes, threading her hands through Chase's hair, then tripping down each vertebrae.

She stood up and pulled off her skirt and panties as Chase pulled back to marvel at her naked body. She transcended all fantasy and eclipsed his wildest notions of what it meant to be truly engulfed by another being. He would sign his life away in that moment just to spend his last minutes entangled with her limbs.

"Come on," Eden whispered, reaching down his pants. He lunged for her with a force so intense, he didn't recognize himself. He cupped her breasts and ravaged her neck as she unbuttoned his shirt and pulled off his pants. He was in ecstatic shock when she pushed him down on the bed and climbed on him. She arched her back, moving over him. He thought he would finish in a nanosecond but she stopped and teased him, coaxing, as he watched her body above him, reaching up to hold her breasts as she guided him to a fit of fireworks that grew to a culmination of such bodily delirium, Chase almost blacked out and thought for a moment he may have died.

The two collapsed in a heap of dewy bliss, both aglow with patchy apple hues of flushed skin, scratched backs, love bites, and lust bruises that would appear at sunrise. Not bad for a night that began with a dinner seated across from someone else. A sweet girl diametrically opposed to the sexy, iconic woman Chase woke up with. He had dined with Betty Draper but slept with Bettie Page.

33

At 20 years of age the will reigns; at 30 the wit; at 40 the judgment.

—Benjamin Franklin

"OH NO, YOU DI-IN!" Allison squealed.

"Guilty as charged," admitted Eden, fuchsia with abashment.

"I'm in shock. SHOCK! You totally cougared out!" Allison said, laughing.

"Puma," corrected Eden, twisting the phone wire in her fingers.

"Oh well, I beg your pardon."

"Don't. It's splitting hairs. It's all the same. We both know I am a disgusting molester. I'm gross, right?"

"NO! Not at all—this is major! He is *to-die-for* gorgeous."

"Yeah, gorgeous and barely legal!"

"Oh, please. Look, you were every guy's arm candy for years and years. Now you've earned the right to be the arm. And enjoy that tasty candy!"

"He is cute, isn't he?" Eden blushed.

"Um-hmmm."

"And sweet. And warm. And—"

"Look at you! You never do this! I'm freaking OUT!" Allison said giddily. "Tell me more."

"I mean, yes, okay, obviously he's stunning. But he's also so kind and good," she mused, picturing his earnest face. "God, he's also just so wound up. Remember I told you he seemed to have this pent-up passion ready to explode? Well, I was right."

"He did, didn't he."

"Yup. And not just physically. I mean, sure, that was incredible. I just felt like there was this charming sweetness in him, that innocence. Maybe it's his youth?"

"Come on, he's twenty-eight, not eighteen! He can't be that naïve."

"It's not that, it's just a general . . . *goodness,* I guess. Does that sound so *Little House on the Prairie?*"

"Guess what: After everything you've been through with chucky Otto you could use a little Ma and Pa goodness. And a solid butter-churning, if you know what I mean."

"ALLI!"

Allison's eyes flashed with girlish mischief. "The great maestro Otto Clyde would simply die. Just keel over."

"I know," Eden said solemnly, the wind suddenly out of her sails. "That's why I want to keep this all a secret. He's not ready, I'm not ready. Plus, Chase literally just split up with his girlfriend. And Cole . . . oh my God, he would die, too."

"He would totally freak."

"Poor Cole. As much as I miss him, it's so for the best that he's in school far away right now," Eden said, remembering how she had fought him tooth and nail to stay on the East Coast. It was a good thing he was headstrong like his parents and moved west, anyway.

"Oh, I love that adorable Cole. Is he still painting?"

"No, unfortunately," Eden said, missing her son. "He knows

he's talented, gifted really, but he doesn't want Julian Lennon syndrome."

"I hear ya. All those fucking critics . . ."

"Otto always said critics were the Horsemen of the Apocalypse. They never create; they just tear down."

"Please. I never read a bad review of an Otto Clyde show in my life."

"Yeah, well . . . he's their darling. Tamed those wild horses, I guess."

"Listen to me: I know he's your friend, but fuck Otto," instructed Allison between sips from her green Starbucks straw. "This is the dawn of the era of Eden. You have to live for you now. You lived for Otto and for Cole and now you have to live for you, for your moment."

"I realize that. It's just that I still work with him, you know. We have a huge show coming up soon. We're a team, and he's always taken care of me."

"As he should! You made him!"

"Or he made me, depending on how you look at it," Eden said, rolling up the purple sleeve of her cowl-neck sweater to see her watch. "Oh shit, I have to bolt and get down to the studio."

On the number 6 train, Eden swayed from side to side as the underground engine powered the rocking cars. The occasional hipster with messenger bag or uptown lady heading to Soho to shop each saw her and knew immediately it was Eden Clyde. But the giddy inamorata was too adrift in her own world of post-Chase high to realize they were staring. Everything at that moment was dazzling. Even the rainbow-covered ads for Dr. Z, curer of anal fissures, didn't gross her out. Spanish ads for lawyers, night school posters, dating Web sites—all seemed colorful and made her smile. Eden breathed in the air of a new lover, a feeling she had known previously but hadn't felt in eons.

She barely knew Chase at all, really, but there was something so familiar about him. Something comforting. She put her arms around herself as a chill traced its way up her back. She smiled, knowing she would see him again soon. She breathed deeply as the subway car bustled south along the track. Meanwhile, the mental train in her head skidded off the tracks she'd known for so long, headed off into a strange, exciting new direction.

34

What most persons consider as virtue, after the age of 40 is simply a loss of energy.

—Voltaire

The Lydons ate dinner together every Sunday night come hell, high water, or *Sopranos* series finale. Nothing—not even pneumonia (from which Pierce once suffered after surfing in Costa Rica for a month)—would relieve these aristocrats from Brooke's Chippendale table. Luigi and Clemenza, the couple the Lydons employed, who resided in a one bedroom in the same building (back elevator), served each family member as napkins were put on laps. Luigi poured wine from a Saint-Émilion vineyard owned by the DuPrees. Chase had shared many a bottle with his grandmother Ruth, sitting on the front porch of the family summer home. There had been many late nights during which he had nursed his one glass while Ruth slammed back several. Vinyl Billie Holiday records played, and Ruth's jokes got dirtier as the hours passed and more wine was decanted. But now the family sipped the same wine without revelry, the sound of awkwardly clanking dinner silver their only soundtrack. Price pounded the fine vintage as if it were Colt 45, not a care in the world about the rare grapes and their pressing, bottling, and aging. It was booze, dude.

Chase took a deep breath. "So I have some news," he said as The Family looked at him. "Liesel and I have parted ways."

"NO! Oh no. NO!" Brooke screamed in a tone normally reserved for Hiroshima-level news. "I simply cannot BELIEVE you did this," Brooke seethed. "This is all your fault. It is because you did not step up to the plate! I knew this would happen!"

Chase hadn't wanted to tell his mother about Liesel and Wills—it would only send her into orbits of rage, vilifying Liesel when he was also to blame.

"Mother, it simply wasn't meant to be. I'm sorry if I've upset you, but—"

"THREE YEARS! There was good stuff there, my God! Three years, for Christ sakes! I mean, really Chase. It's time to be a grown-up."

Chase inhaled deeply, trying not to exude the anger he felt boiling inside.

"Mother. With all due respect, I *am* a grown-up. If anything . . . I believe I'm too grown up. Grandma even said on her deathbed that I should loosen up and live for once."

"Please. What garbage. Ruth was a perpetual Peter Pan," fumed Brooke. "Of course she told you to loosen up, she was OLD! She was on her way out. You're in a different place."

A different place indeed. Despite his mother's ferocious rantings, Chase was in heaven. Cloud nine. As his mother droned on about facing Liesel's parents at so-and-so's annual party or at the River Club, his mind wandered back to Eden; just the memory of her was intoxicating. He replayed their thunderous night in a stop-and-rewind delirium. It was close to torture, then, to be trapped in the austere surroundings of his family home—prim, proper, and pulled to perfection, but held together with sharp pins.

"I'm simply mortified to see the Van Delfts. They'll be at the opera gala; they always take a table. Always." Brooke steamed.

"Too bad it's not like that Save Venice ball with those masks," Pierce said with a laugh.

"Yeah, you could wear one of those huge headdress things and totally avoid them!" chimed Price.

"I'M SERIOUS!" Brooke said, shaking her head.

"I wouldn't worry, dear, these things happen," Grant said calmly. The patriarch was just like his youngest son, ever calm, rarely riled. He sipped his whiskey on the rocks from a mono-grammed tumbler. "The Van Delfts won't blame you for Chase's wrongdoings."

Chase wanted to pull the rip cord and get the hell out of there.

"Should I call them, you think? This is really going to be so awkward. I cannot believe you put me in this position, Chase! What on earth do I say when I see them at the event?"

Chase inhaled sharply, not wanting to cause a rift. He wanted to get up and storm out, rebel, finally, but of course, he couldn't. Chase was the good son, reliable and stable. But the burden of the so-called righteous path was getting to be simply too much to shoulder.

"I'm sorry, Mother. That's all I can say. Father, I'm going to work early tomorrow and should go. Clemenza, delicious dinner, thank you."

The truth was, Chase would rather be alone than with these people. In that moment, Chase could not relate to his family at all. In fact, he almost loathed them.

On his walk home, while he may have donned a suit and tie and dutifully marched with steady pace up Fifth Avenue, his heart was doing the moonwalk backward. His libido was doing mental back handsprings Béla Károlyi would freak for. And when he passed the rowdy crowd in front of the Plaza cheering the ol' school break-dancers, rigid, wooden Chase Lydon wished he could join them in a rollicking sidewalk spin. He wanted to get down on the ground, feel the beat box that echoed in his bursting cocoon, and twirl until his body was as dizzy as his thoughts.

Social Swans Bid Adieu

The Upper East Side's Ken and Barbie have sailed off into the sunset—in two separate yachts. Rumor has it the oft-snapped boldfacers of the Junior Committee set, **Chase DuPree Lydon** and **Liesel van Delft**, have called it quits, and all the clubs—from the Colony to the Knick—are abuzz with shocked whispers. No word whether the comely twosome, who courted for three years, parted ways amicably or who was to blame. But sources in Camp Van Delft say the leggy Liesel had long been eagerly awaiting a rock. And now, friends of the family, whose vast fortune hails from the paper clip patent, say they are ready to throw stones. "He took so much time from her!" one socialite wailed, hoping for a big wedding. "Don't worry about Liesel," quipped a second. "She'll be on her feet in no time." One wonders who will land each of these former lovers—both the ultimate catches for the pedigreed pearls and poodles set.

35

To be 70 years young is sometimes far more cheerful and hopeful than to be 40 years old.

—Oliver Wendell Holmes, Jr.

"My God, have you met someone?" Otto asked as he studied Eden's blushing cheeks. He knew her face so well. After two decades of capturing her every expression, each gleam and twinkle, the famed artist instantly decoded the distinct glint that was now present in Eden's green eyes. Someone had had her last night.

"What?" asked Eden, alarmed and suddenly feeling naked, though in the series Otto had just started, she was wearing a long, billowy white dress.

Otto left his easel and walked slowly toward her, paintbrush in hand. As he moved closer to her, he never broke eye contact.

"There's no *what*. The question is who? *Who is he?*" His tone was teasing, as if he didn't care, but naturally he did. Deeply, in fact. "I knew there would be someone in the picture soon enough. How long have you ever gone without a man doting on you? You couldn't survive long out there unattached, right? The attention is like a lung, no?"

"No one, okay?"

"Whatever you say."

Otto walked back to the easel as Eden reclined on an antique chaise. As her ex returned to his canvas, Eden became lost in her thoughts of Chase. At one point, feeling the warmth in her chest, recalling how Chase kissed her clavicle and breast, she accidentally smirked. Shit.

"Aha!" quipped Otto, as if uncovering a forensic clue that cracked his case. "I knew it. Who is he?"

"Otto. I don't want to talk about this."

"You *don't want to talk about this*. That's an admission; now it's out there! You see, I got you. I *knew* it." Otto was the type of person whose affectations caused him to pronounce the word "knew" like *nyoo*.

"I just *knew* it." He was very satisfied with himself. "It's some big collector, right? I know! Henry Kincaid Sanderson. He's lusted after you forever! He has two private jets. A staff. Homes all over the world. You'll be living the high life, no?"

"No, Otto."

"Hmmm," Otto said, staring at her, walking around the chaise slowly, inhaling a joint, which he then handed to Eden. "Ah, I know. Lucas McGillicuddy. And he's what, sixty-nine, right? Well, you'd be earning every penny with that one. And really, who wants to be wife number four?"

"I'm not playing this game," responded Eden.

"So it *is* him."

"No."

"I'll find out at some point. I really don't care, to be honest, so you might as well be open about it. I know you too well, don't you see that, honey? I'm your closest friend; you can't get anything past me."

The truth was, he was right. She hated that he was right. And she didn't have many friends at all. The camaraderie of the busy studio was a built-in circle, and instant party, a gang. The rapports had been so strong that she never felt the need to cultivate relationships outside the studio other than with Allison. But now that she was on the other side, Eden knew that all those people—the other models, hangers-on, assistants, publicists, gallerinas, *everyone*—was on Team Otto since the split. After all, he was the one paying their bills.

"You can't be 'best friends' with someone you're paying," Eden explained.

"Why the hell not, that's so ridiculous!" Otto had fumed.

"Because then it's what I call an Agenting Friendship—they are profiting ten percent from the friendship. Look at Jennifer Aniston and her hairdresser! Clearly he needs her more than she needs him, so there's an imbalance. There's no cold, hard truth."

"Well, I sure know *you* never bit your tongue," he scoffed. It was true. Despite all his controlling and manipulations, Otto had been Eden's truest confidant apart from Allison. She wondered how long she could keep something like this from him. And she hoped that there would be a "something" to speak of.

As she sat perfectly still, eyes out the window, she dipped into that sweet vat of memory. A chill shivered her gut where Chase's arms had once encircled her. There was something special about this guy, about Eden when she was with him. Something different. Something *nyoo*.

36

At middle age the soul should be opening up like a rose, not closing up like a cabbage.

—John Andrew Holmes

Over plates of pasta with grilled eggplant and a plum tomato sauce, above the flickering glow of eight mercury glass votives, Chase watched Eden relish the food she'd labored over. They sat on two sides of an enormous antique Vuitton trunk Eden and Otto had happened to discover at Clignancourt flea market in Paris, hand-stenciled with the initials *EC*. They lounged on big pillows on the floor beside it as Eden's impromptu table setting was covered with diagonal-swirled goblets, small bud vases filled with blush pink ranunculus, and plates of hot, delicious food.

"It's so good," Chase complimented. "I'm so impressed. My mother never cooked a thing, so I am always blown away when people can make meals like this at home. I'm a big reheater," he confessed.

"My mom never cooked, either. But I'm guessing in your situation it's because you had a four-star chef," she said sarcastically. "My mother could sure boil a mean hot water, though!"

"I've never met anyone like you," Chase said, his eyes on the angel hair spinning in his spoon. Eden felt a small rush, a warmth in her chest. She wanted to take care of him. She got up and walked around the trunk and plopped down next to him. She put her hand on his cheek and slid it down his neck, just looking at him. She leaned in to kiss him. His fork fell as he reached for her. He had been dreaming about this moment since he had left her side and as they tumbled on her Moroccan rug, he realized he had never been this taken with any girl. After they made love, they meandered to the bed, where they lay for hours, talking about their lives, their recent breakups, all while Chase held Eden's hand and traced each finger over the top, as if outlining her dainty skeleton within.

"It's funny, I traveled a lot of the world with Liesel, we stayed in every four-star hotel, dined in every Michelin restaurant, and I'm happier with you just lying here and doing nothing." Chase laughed. His arms and legs were intertwined with Eden's, her long shiny hair draped across the pillows as Chase stroked it away from her forehead.

Eden curled up closer to Chase. "Otto and I were the same. Always jetting around to this or that fabulous event, having a party full of people over. If we had even one night with no plans, he would say, 'Who should we ring for dinner'! It was like he needed to have a crowd around him to make him feel as though he existed—he had to be the center. I don't know." She shrugged. "I guess you know you're happy when you don't need any outside stimulation."

She got up to get a bottle of red wine off the trunk, walking stark naked through the bedroom without a care in the world. Chase realized that in three years with Liesel he never once saw her walk around like that. The closest she came was self-consciously darting to the bathroom, naked except for her pearls around her neck.

She plopped back in bed, poured the Bordeaux, and handed Chase a glass. He looked at her with wonder.

"What, you never drank red wine in bed, either?" she asked him, brow arched.

"No," he smiled bashfully. "Not once."

"Why not?"

"I don't know. It could spill and stain the sheets."

Eden looked at him with a cat-that-ate-the-canary look. She took a long sip, drinking most of her glass except for one little sip, which she then splashed on him.

"What are you doing?" he asked, astonished, with burgundy droplets covering his face and chest.

She threw her head back and laughed.

"Here, I'll mop it up for you." She climbed on top of him and kissed him.

His body collapsed in her embrace as she pinned him down, kissing him as she slid him inside her. She moved on top of him as their mounting breaths grew in hyperventilated sync. He looked up at her, wet with wine from his chest. With the sweet smell of the grapes emulsifying their tangled limbs as they rolled on her sheets, Chase felt his head pounding. "You know, I've got news for you," she said, sitting up and crawling back onto him, getting right in his face, her lips a millimeter from his. "You are the oldest twenty-eight-year-old on the fucking planet."

Chase looked down. It was true.

"Well, you're the youngest . . . thirtysomething—," he stammered.

"Thirty-nine. What do you think of that? That's almost forty, you know."

"Thanks. You know I learned all my numbers by my twenty-fifth birthday," Chase teased.

She certainly seemed generations younger than Liesel, not just in her spirit but in the way she carried herself. But beneath the saucy exterior was a girl who was worried that her youth—and all the attention her looks brought her—was officially over.

"So you don't care? That I'm old?"

Chase smiled and shook his bed head.

"You're not old. Your age never crossed my mind."

"How is that possible? I mean, they say age doesn't matter but . . . it kind of does. I think about my age on a daily basis. No, hourly."

"I don't. I never think about it." Chase shrugged. "Or yours."

"That's 'cause you're a man. You keep getting riper while we wither on the vine."

"Come here, you rotting fruit," he jested, grabbing her.

She let out a ticklish laugh. "I'm serious! We're practically *Harold and Maude*," she semi-joked.

"Who are they?"

Holy shit, he hadn't even heard of one of the great movies of all time. Damn, he was young.

"Never mind."

As she lay down beside him again, holding his hand, she looked at a growing crack in the ceiling.

"I should get that repainted," she mused casually. "This place seems so quaint and cute, but if you look closely, it's kind of falling apart."

"I don't see that," Chase said. "It's perfect as it is."

37

Middle age is having a choice between two temptations and choosing the one that'll get you home earlier.

—Dan Bennett

The next day, at her recon lunch with Allison at Fred's, Eden picked at her French fries, oscillating between two poles of exhilaration and nonchalance.

"So what are you going to do about this? This is such a reversal. I thought you said the cougar thing was gross. . . ."

"It is! But this doesn't quite feel like that. I mean, I'm not in Callie and Sara's league of ordering beefsteak sandwiches."

"It's so weird you're with Chase Lydon. Talk about the *opposite* of Otto."

"I'm not *with* anyone."

"What's he like?" Allison beamed.

"He is so anal, God love him. It's like he's been tied up in gold twine his whole life. He's just so . . . burning to open up, you know? He has this pent-up energy. He's practically ready to burst. Sure, he's been to the requisite New York institutional galas, but he's living in this little Limoges box. But God, is he sweet. Just the most doting, kind, amazing guy. And gorgeous. And entirely too young for me. Otto would die of shock if he saw that this was who I'm shacking up with. That's why I want to keep it under wraps."

"I love it. Clandestine romance. Hot."

"Well, it would be even worse with regard to *his* family. Can you imagine if his fancy parents saw my apartment with that nude portrait of me hanging in the living room?"

"I heard his mother, Brooke, really puts the 'cunt' in 'country club.'"

"Great, see what I mean?" Eden said, throwing her hands up.

"Yeah, but so what? What are you going to do, sneak around because his momma and Otto wouldn't approve?"

"I've got news for you: *I* don't approve! I could be his mother."

"Eleven-year-olds don't usually menstruate," Allison assured her.

"They do now because of all the hormones in milk and stuff. I swear. They go bra shopping now at, like, age nine."

"Oh God, I hope not. Please tell me my little Kate won't have hooters in four years. Not possible. Anyway, we eat mostly organics," Allison told herself.

"The point is, I can't go gallivanting around with this young guy on my arm! It's wrong."

"Says who?"

"Says me. I must look ridiculous."

"He's not so young that you're, like, tasting Similac on his breath, he's twenty-fucking-eight! That's old enough," attested Allison. "And furthermore, since when do you give a shit about what people think? You're the last person to worry about gossip. You've led a fantastic, unconventional life, raised a brilliant, fabulous son, so what the fuck do you care what people say?"

"You're right. Plus, I have no clue where it's going, if anywhere," Eden said, thinking about her night with Chase. "I just know I love the way he makes me feel. I feel great. For the first time in a while, I'm . . . young again. He's like a fucking time machine."

"And like a fucking machine, clearly," said Allison with a wink.

"You know, yes the sex is amazing, but it's different. He's not one of those guys who could unhook a bra with one hand in pitch-black. He's not a player; he's almost timid, a truly good person, gentle and kind. He's got to loosen up a bit, but I see in there a spark locked inside."

"Just wait," said Allison knowingly. "Sooner or later, like everything else, it will have to come out."

38

I'm at an age when my back goes out more than I do.

—Phyllis Diller

"I can't stop thinking about you, I mean, literally I can't stop," Chase whispered on the phone to Eden from work. While he sat lit by the glow of his computer screen, Eden lay on her couch covered with cashmere throws from India, resting on pillows still smelling of the lavender sachets she had packed them with for her move.

"Is that so?" she asked seductively.

"It is."

"I'm flattered. I miss you, too." Eden giggled. She was not a giggler. Her schoolgirl chortle surprised even her. "But you have to do what you have to do! Whatever that is. Numbers stuff."

"Eden, let me take you out to dinner tonight. You can choose the place."

Eden didn't think that would be such a good idea. "Let's just stay in, no? I can cook something. I'll head down to the farmer's market—"

"Please. I don't want you to lift a finger. Let's just go out."

"Great. Then everyone in the restaurant will remark what a

nice mother-son dinner we are having. Until we start making out."

"We both know you are not old enough to be my mother, Eden."

"Okay, fine, but I am still most definitely a brown leaf next to your green one."

"Golden brown," he teased. "Come on, you're being ridiculous."

Eden paused. He was right. In this day and age, it shouldn't matter. But Eden knew the world enough to know that it wasn't as open-minded as she was. If she was spotted at a restaurant with him, news of their pairing would get out. Everyone would laugh that she, nearly four decades old, thought she could have Chase Lydon. It was setting herself up for humiliation. But then she thought of her old self. The stronger, more secure person who simply wouldn't give a shit. Somehow, along the way, bouncing through the calendar year after year, Eden realized she had lost her shield. Had it been chipped away or did it vanish overnight? She didn't quite know but she realized that it was time to get it the hell back. Allison was right: Fuck it. Since when did she feel like she wasn't worthy of someone?

"Where should we meet?"

Eden wrote down the Second Avenue address and shook off her paranoia. It was all in her head; everyone else was too involved with their own lives to care about Eden's, right? They have their own stuff to deal with, so why would they even notice her and Chase?

Elio's was aghast.

Eden felt like a rotisserie chicken spinning before the heated gaze of the well-to-do onlookers.

"Isn't that Chase Lydon?" one blond, shoulder-padded matron

whispered to her husband, who drank his straight vodka and could barely divert his gaze from Eden's endless legs in her hip, strapless minidress.

"Who's that?" the hubby asked, watching as Eden moved her long hair to one side of her bare shoulder. Eden sat down at the bar and began reading a cocktail menu as Chase greeted the maître d'.

"That's Eden Clyde, the former *lover* of Otto Clyde, the painter. Took his name but had their kid out of wedlock! Carriage without marriage," the patrician matron whispered back, brow arched. She knew Brooke Lydon casually from around the Colony Club and surmised her acquaintance would be . . . unthrilled.

"Wait a second, hasn't he been going with Bitsey van Delft's daughter?" her friend asked, a polished finger tinkering with her pearls as she glanced at Chase and Eden, coral lips pursed in disapproval.

"Oh, you didn't hear?" the other Hermès-scarfed lady whispered loudly. "They split recently. Guess he's not wasting any time."

Ralph Lauren and Matt Lauer both entered separately with their wives, and still all eyes were on Eden and Chase. Chase reached over and took her hand, sensing her awareness of the crowd of onlookers. His warm touch softened her discomfort about being plunged into the Upper East Side social center. She was certainly used to people noticing her, but in the downtown restaurants, where often Clyde's drawings hung on the walls, where those who knew her sent over desserts and wine. Here all she was getting was ice. She felt like she was in another galaxy. A judgey one. The Chanel suits and MAC lipsticks may as well have been black robes and gavels.

A young couple walked in holding a cherubic baby girl.

"Oh, how delicious," Eden cooed. She was so happy to see such an innocent face in what she suspected (rightly so) was a room full of vipers. "What's her name?"

"Piper," the beaming mom replied. "She's six months."

"What a cool name," Eden said, looking at Chase. "You can't not be happy with a name like Piper. I love it!"

"Mr. Lydon, your table, sir. Follow me." Eden waved good-bye to baby Piper, who smiled for her, and as Eden started to walk away hand in hand with Chase, little Piper lunged forward. Eden stopped to hold her tiny hands.

"I just love babies," Eden said wistfully. Otto had never let her have a second child, and in that moment, as Piper linked her cute fat fingers with hers, she secretly regretted giving up her campaign.

"She likes you!" the young mother said, smiling. She turned toward her husband, who also needed a drool bib. "Gee, just like Daddy!" she joked in a whisper after Eden and Chase walked off.

As the two gabbed the hours away, Eden grew more and more comfortable with the fact that people were blatantly watching their table. *Let 'em stare*, she knew Allison would say to her, *live your life*. And so she did, happily. Chase watched as Eden relished a mile-high pile of spaghetti, a dish he loved but that Liesel would never touch for fear of carbobesity come morning. And as the new couple held hands across the table, the cacophony of the restaurant faded away behind their doting glances, and the crowd, unsubtle in their conspicuous gazes, didn't deter them, rosy with wine and *amore*, from feeling they were all alone.

"RRREAR! Move over, **Ashton** and **Demi**! New York has its own pair of May-December stunners in eligible finance heir **Chase Lydon** and famed model/muse **Eden Clyde**. Just weeks after Lydon's own breakup, both lookers turned heads at Elio's last night when crowds beheld the pair canoodling at a corner table. Clyde, 39, and Lydon, 28, did not stop holding hands through the whole meal, sources say. No word on whether his socialite mom, **Brooke DuPree Lydon**, approves of his much older gal pal, or whether Eden's ex, **Otto Clyde**, knows of his favorite subject's new boy toy, but both got tongues wagging uptown and down after their cozy caresses. And from the look on their flirty faces, the crowd surmised, the new duo would be devouring more than penne pasta that night.

39

When you are forty, half of you belongs to the past.

—Jean Anouilh

The city went shithouse. Eden didn't ever read the gossip columns. But they were Allison's bible, taken before her daily bread (a croissant), with café au lait, skim milk.

"Holy shit!" Allison said as she scanned the tabloid over the phone. Eden heard rustling tabloid papers and heavy breathing. "Okay, here it is—"

"Ugh, I don't even want to hear it, Alli, really," said Eden, still bleary-eyed, as Chase had only just left her bed for work. "Really, I barely slept a wink last night, and it'll only stress me out and make me feel gross."

"Fine," Allison said. "But you better call Otto. Lyle Spence reads the news before he even drinks his three espressos. Call him."

"News? For real? This isn't *news,* Alli. There is a whole world out there. This is ridiculous!" Eden protested, amazed anyone would care.

"Maybe it's a slow news day. Regardless, people want some spice in their lives. Everyone reads this!"

"Oh, please."

"Seriously, Eden, you have to call Otto before he hears through everyone else. Fasten your seat belt. I bet you he freaks."

"He won't freak. Why would he care? He's seeing someone. We're through, and he knew this was bound to happen."

"Just call him," instructed Allison, suspecting Otto might not be so thrilled to see the woman he "created" out and about with a younger man. "Bye."

Eden hung up the phone and looked at it. Lyle, Otto's gallerist, knew anyone and everyone and breathed in the tabloids like air, exhaling newsy gossip to all his friends. Okay, damage control. She reached for the receiver. But before she could lift it from its cradle, it rang. Great, here he was. She braced herself.

"Otto?" Eden answered, heart pounding.

"Mom, it's Cole."

Shit. The blood ran from Eden's cheeks. "Hi, Cole—"

"Tell me it's not true."

Eden started shaking silently, trying to find the words she was looking for.

"A girl in my dorm, a friend of mine just saw online you're dating some young guy?" he asked, incredulous. "It's bullshit, right?"

Eden didn't know what to say. And in that five-second pause, Cole knew it wasn't.

"Mom! Seriously? You're joking," he said, clearly disturbed. "Are you nuts?"

"Cole, it's not what it seems—"

"This guy is like MY AGE!"

"He's not your age. He's older."

"He's closer to my age than yours."

Eden quickly calculated in her head. Shit.

"I thought these kinds of people were everything you and Dad detest."

"Cole, listen to me." Eden thought she would drown in her desperation to get him to understand her side. But she paused. She couldn't set the record straight without spilling all the stories of his father's countless infidelities, some with girls way younger than Chase was. But she didn't want to throw stones at her son's father, so she tried to proceed calmly.

"Your father has moved on. I have a right—"

"Mom, I love you but you're gonna be a laughingstock."

She sat silent on the phone, calmly trying not to cry.

"Are you finished?"

"Yes."

Eden could still sense his anger and discomfort with the situation.

"May I speak now, please?"

"Fine."

Eden felt tears well up in her eyes as her torments mounted. She was so angry at the double standard. Geezers had banged young girls since toga time and now she was a social leper, a pariah for simply being with a guy eleven years younger. Eden took a deep breath and tried to be strong.

"Cole, did I ever as a mother judge you? Did I ever try to control you? Did I ride you to do your homework, brush your teeth, cut your hair, clean your room? No. I gave you more freedom than any other mother. I knew you were a mature, independent person, with a great mind and perfect grades, so I let you be. I didn't ask where you were going, or give you fucking curfews or smell your breath or any of that shit. I trusted you. Now you have to trust me."

Her words were greeted with silence.

She was right. Cole knew it. All his friends had naggy moms who rode them on everything, from who to date to what to wear, and Cole never had anything like that. His mom was different. She was young and his friend, and he loved her for it, but he felt threatened and protective now that this bombshell was in the press.

"I'm sorry," Cole said, and Eden exhaled in relief. She knew she hadn't raised a judgmental son, but she privately acknowledged that it must be difficult for him to have such unorthodox parents, especially since their split.

"I'm so sorry you had to find out that way, sweetheart, and I'm sorry this is uncomfortable for you. But, Cole, love, you are out west, finding yourself. And frankly, I'm doing the very same thing here on my own. I don't even know what this is, where it's going, if it will last. But for now . . . it's good for me."

"Sorry," he said quietly. "I'm just upset to have people thinking you're like some—"

"Cougar? Some hag preying on a younger man? Well, I've got news for you, it happens all the time in reverse. I'm not hurting anyone. Why does anyone even care?"

"Because . . . they do."

"So what, I'm supposed to live my life by what complete strangers think?"

It did seem silly once she said it so matter-of-factly. Cole didn't really care what people thought. He just loved his mother and wanted the best for her.

"You deserve to be happy, Mom." And then he added, in a quieter, softer voice, "I know it hasn't been easy. Dad is Dad. And that must have been hard for you. . . ."

He knew. He knew his father had been a cheater. Eden blinked a tear down her cheek.

"You remember, Cole, when you were little and we'd go out to dinner just you and me, while Daddy was traveling, you remember what I'd say to you?"

"You said . . . we were growing up together."

"That's right. I said that. But it wasn't true," Eden said, wiping another tear. "You passed me by a long time ago. You had such a good head on your shoulders and you sprinted right ahead. And now I have to try to figure this all out on my own. I don't know if this will last with Chase. But relationships are like experiments, really, or one of your math problems that now I have to work out. I mean, I'm trying to follow my instincts and see where the paths take me. I promise you, I'm a strong, centered person. I'm not just screwing around for the sake of it," Eden confessed to her son, who listened guiltily, hearing her out.

"I know, Mom. I trust you. You did a great job, and I'm sorry for freaking out. I just want you to be happy."

After they said their good-byes, Eden exhaled, wondering what that phantom desire was welling within her. She had checked off all those unattainable elements on her mental F List—family, fortune, fame—and now, while she didn't know what she wanted next, she would have to do something anathema to her lifelong ambitious nature: Stop looking to the future, and take each day one at a time.

40

A diplomat is a man who always remembers a woman's birthday but never remembers her age.

—Robert Frost

Meanwhile, on Fifth Avenue, Brooke DuPree Lydon raged with an ire that made velociraptors look like fluffy kittens.

"What is the meaning of this?" a steaming Brooke hissed into the phone in an attempted controlled whisper that echoed louder than a yelp.

"Mother, I'm working, I don't have—"

"WHAT, you don't have *time*? For your mother? After all I've done for you, this is how you repay me? By *humiliating* us? By parading around with some trollop not a month after you broke up with Liesel? This is BEYOND embarrassing. Are you trying to make me miserable? Because allow me to inform you: You've succeeded."

Chase paused to take a deep breath.

"I'm sorry. But it's not about you or anyone else," he replied blithely. "And, Mother, she is not a trollop," he corrected, wincing at his mother's harsh, antiquated insult. "She's an amazing woman."

"Oh really? *Amaaaazing*, really? Mm-hmm. I get it. So this *person* is the reason you ended things with Liesel. You were sneaking around with this *amazing woman* and now you're flaunting this relationship to scorn me. What, because she's somehow attractive to you? Because she's 'cool' in some way?" She vamped, complete with finger quotes in her gilded study.

"Mother. I have a lot of work to do."

"Terrific! That's just grand. Here are some numbers you can crunch! Here's a bottom line for you: her birth date and your birth date.

"Mother, PLEASE."

"Perhaps I'm not being clear enough: She is too OLD for you."

"I don't care," Chase responded with a shrug.

"Ohhh, *you* don't care, okay. How nice for you! That's just fine, just dandy. Never mind that we are a family and that your embarrassing actions reflect upon all of us."

Chase's annoyance was morphing into sheer anger.

"If that were really the case, why would you have excused Price's DUI?" he demanded. "Or Pierce's little dalliance with that count's underage daughter?"

"Please."

"So you're saying it's better Pierce chased that sixteen-year-old girl? Better that he broke the law than for me to be with someone older?"

"You have been the one who . . . doesn't do these things, Chase. You've been—"

"The good son. The one with the halo, right?" he shouted. "Well, I'm making it clear that I am a grown-up and while I love you, I need to make choices for myself right now."

"That's just great, then. Just sit back and relax and enjoy watching your life go up in smoke," she huffed. "But when you realize the perfect life we handed you on a silver platter has been engulfed by flames, don't come running to me to put them out."

Click.

Across town, the news was met with the same venom, if with a diametrically opposite tone. The bitter pill had simply been deep-fried and dipped in powdered sugar.

"I think it's great, marvelous, *truly!*" feigned Otto with a beaming smile. While he may have been a genius painter, Daniel Day-Lewis he was not.

"Great. Because I'm happy with him. It's . . . been really good for me, I think."

"Wonderful news!" cooed Otto. "I just hope the age difference doesn't . . . you know, affect things."

"Well, it didn't seem to between us," retorted Eden. "You and I have a much bigger gap in years."

"Yes, my dear, but usually the female is the May and not the December in the equation," he jabbed, which was of course the truth. "Aristotle did say that males are best married in their late thirties and women in their late teens."

"Aristotle didn't know women who used sunblock or worked out."

"Touché, darling. And of course no woman is as beautiful as you, so I'm certain he would have amended his views were he to see your gorgeous face, honey. I'm thrilled for you, just thrilled. Truly."

41

*The best years of a woman's life—the ten years between 39
and 40.*

—Anonymous

The next night, spurred even more by the world's thumbs-down and upturned noses, Chase and Eden attacked each other with such ferocity there were Billy Bob and Angelina—era bruises on each other's bodies, though they skipped the blood vials and tats. It was torture for both to separate in the morning, and their good-bye kiss lingered so long that finally Chase disrobed and made love to Eden again. Then he really did have to go.

A few hours later, the buzzer rang, piercing the sound of the SUMMER '90 cassette tape Eden was playing. Unable to trash her old mix tapes, the late adopter of CDs and even later user of MP3s couldn't bear to chuck the audible gems she had so loved through her young life. Even if she iTunesed the exact songs, the well-worn wheels turning, the handcrafted liner notes from friends and lovers, and the time infused in each laborious mix tape was a treasure she cherished.

"Hello?" she said into the ancient intercom.

"Flowers, ma'am."

She buzzed in the mystery flower delivery, thinking only afterward it could be some scary predator like Chevy Chase's Land Shark on *Saturday Night Live*. *Caaaaandygram!*

She opened the door a crack to find, in fact, the single most gorgeous blossoms she had ever beheld. Seventy-five pink peonies. She knew from her early mornings cruising the flower market for buds for Otto's paintings that the blooms retailed for about ten dollars a stem, making the arrangement north of seven-fifty with tax and delivery.

Chocolate grosgrain ribbons encircled the chic vase, and fastened by a pearl pin was a vellum envelope and card.

"Don't bother picking off each petal," the small card read. "The answer is, he loves me. Chase."

Eden smiled and flopped on the couch and moved her finger over his words on the vellum. As she breathed a contented sigh, she just hoped their unusual pairing wasn't a Kenny Loggins–style highway to the danger zone.

42

Women deserve to have more than twelve years between the ages of twenty-eight and forty.

—James Thurber

"Trust me," Eden consoled, "the art world is way more accepting than the Upper East Side. If any one of my tattooed friends entered Swifty's, half the matrons would collapse into their frisée. It's not like that downtown. Just come with me . . . I need you. Please."

"How can I go to an Otto Clyde opening with Eden Clyde? Won't he be upset?"

"Chase, you were the one who told me not to care, so now I'm telling you: It's fine. Otto is going to have to get over it, and so is everyone else."

"Okay," said Chase, exhaling as he leaned to kiss Eden. "I'm almost convinced I'd do anything for you."

"Great. Then in that case, we're going shopping."

"Now?"

"This instant. Cue the *Pretty Woman* makeover montage music. I may be the one who's eleven years older, but you, my dear, dress like you should be collecting Social Security."

Chase looked down at his gray suit and looked up, clueless. "Okay, I'm all yours."

Holding hands the duo boarded—gasp!—rapid transit.

"Amazing, right? A train that goes underground!" Eden teased.

Chase laughed at the jab but knew deep down she was onto something. He only ever took a town car and driver and couldn't actually tell the green line from the red from the yellow.

He looked at the passengers throttled side to side at each halt, at the thicket of bodies pouring in and out to the musical ding-dong of the opening doors, and at the profile of Eden reading the advertisements. He knew then and there that he'd give up all the town cars and tree-lined avenues of his childhood just to ride the subway by her side forever.

On the Lower East Side, the duo walked in and out of several boutiques with hipster sales folk and sleek shoppers. Little by little, the oxford was replaced by a tight tee and the crisp trousers turned to relaxed pants, and Chase went from uptight banker to chilled-out downtowner.

"Wow, I feel like I've shaved off ten years already," he said, kissing her.

"Great, then that makes me two decades older."

He didn't go overboard with the messenger bag and sleeved tats, but he definitely blended better than he had with his Thomas Pink and Paul Stuart ensemble. Still, Chase was haunted by his mother's cruel words about Eden's reinvention: You can take the girl out of the trailer park but you can't take the trailer park out of the girl. What if it was the same with him? You could take the boy out of the country club but could you take the country club out of the boy? Would his edgier ensemble fool anyone?

With a shopping bag in one hand and a crêpe from a street vendor in the other, Eden drank in her new creation and then threw her arms around him for a kiss.

"Thanks for the new me," he said, looking himself over. It was just as Ruthie had written; he'd been fighting to break out, and he just needed someone to unlock those steel gates that took years to fashion. And busting out of them felt better than he'd ever imagined.

43

My Birthday! what a different sound That word had in my youthful ears; And how each time the day comes round, Less and less white its mark appears.

—Thomas Moore

"Please tell me you're joking," Allison scoffed.

"Why? Why shouldn't he come with me?"

"Are you mad, girlfren? Otto is so not ready for that. Neither is anyone else, for that matter. I mean, I know I told you to go out and live your lives, but the *gallery*? Why do you need to flaunt it? Keep the relationships separate," Allison instructed while braiding her daughter Kate's hair on a park bench.

"Auntie Eden, do you have a boyfriend?"

Allison's jaw dropped as Eden laughed.

"Where did you get that, miss?" her mother asked.

"Mommy told Daddy that you're in loooove . . . ," Eden's god-daughter cooed.

"Maybe I am," Eden said with a smile, patting Kate's hair. "I don't know yet."

"Don't you just *know*?" little Kate responded, conjuring frothy fantasies of Aurora, Ariel, and Cinderella struck at first sight. "That's what they always say. You just know."

"Not really. It takes time," replied Allison. "You don't just dance in a meadow with some bunny rabbits and bluebirds and fall in love because you can sing well together."

"You can't?" Kate said, looking depressed.

"Yes, you can," Eden corrected, looking at her goddaughter. She then whispered to Allison. "Gee, way to ruin her dreams, you B-I-T-C-H!"

"What does B-I-T-C-H spell?" Kate asked.

"Nothing, honey. Look, E, what do I know? Do what you want, I guess."

"I need to bring him, Alli. It's not to show him off or anything even remotely close to that. Otto gets to have his whole swooning entourage; why can't I just have my one companion?"

"You can. You're right. You've certainly earned it."

The snap, snap, snap of camera lenses lit up the wet, cobblestoned street outside Otto's gallery. Hordes of fashion victims swarmed, abuzz with words like "breakthrough," "stunning," and "seminal" as they looked in through the huge window at bodies and crisp canvas squares. From the outside, Eden beheld the muted frenzy of sycophants and fancy pants, and squeezed Chase's hand with a deep breath as they crossed the street. The outside throng of press were facing the cars that pulled up to the curb, guessing who would open the door and step out.

As each door opened, the wide eyes and long lenses were poised to observe the newest connoisseur—would it be an actress? Socialite? Wall Street tycoon? Or another artist who worshipped at the altar of Clyde? Or, ugh, the worst: a Nobody. When some poor anonymous schnook stepped out of an arriving car, there was a disappointed silence. But then, as all the shutterbugs were clicking away at some young heiress who fancied herself a collector, one lone firefly with his black beret spied the Queen Bee crossing over.

"EDEN! EDEN! EDEN!"

The heiress was cast aside instantly as the hordes vied to capture Eden. And who was the good-looking young man on her arm? COULD IT BE? Patrick McMullan, the Kevin Bacon center dot through which all degrees of separation pass, nailed it.

"CHASE LYDON? Chase! Chase! Over here! Chase!"

As the crunch of paparazzi went ballistic, inside the Lyle Spence Gallery, people enraptured by the languid images of reclining Edens caught wind of the fact that the real creature was just outside. The mutters and cacophonous streams filled the cavernous loft space and suddenly died down to a muted murmur as the crowd looked through the window onto the scene on the street. Otto Clyde, who was at the center of the action, realized little by little that the deafening compliments and gaping stares at his work had slowed as more and more heads turned away from the walls and out to the street. His head was the last to turn. And when he saw his former flame leaning on the young and gorgeous scion, he was not pleased.

Eden posed for a moment, clearly a pro, as Chase gave a tight-lipped smile, just as his mother always had. He realized suddenly that this barrage of images of the new couple would instantly be everywhere, and that Brooke's BlackBerry would be abuzz with bad, bad, bad vibrations beamed from her magpies. And the only thing that surprised him was the fact that he didn't care at all. He had the sexiest woman alive by his side. He felt the ninety-block-long leash disintegrate into the night as he freely inhaled the damp air and got ready to enter the packed gallery.

"Thank you," said Eden sweetly to the photographers, signaling her posing had come to an end. As cries for one more echoed behind them, Chase and Eden took deep breaths and entered the cavernous space. All four hundred eyes were on them, but they squeezed hands and walked in, ready to face the music.

44

Growing old is mandatory; growing up is optional.

—Chili Davis

Their nerves dulled a bit as they entered and were instantly engulfed by well-wishing collectors who reveled in the new works.

"Eden, you're bewitching as always," Rock McGhee said. "I just bought the one of you by the window."

As they made their way through the space, more and more people came up to Eden, so Chase took a moment to duck away and fully drink in the images hanging in the packed gallery. He didn't want to cling to her. Though she had asked him to stay by her side, he wanted to give her space and allow the myriad hangers-on to have their air-kiss moment. He knew the drill from his family, so he filed off quietly to look at the paintings.

Each one was more spectacular than the next. In one, Eden wore a bright red flamenco dress, leaning up against a window frame; in another, she reclined on a shrink's couch in profile, as if discussing her fantasies. Chase wandered into a small alcove off the large space and found what he instantly believed to be the crown jewel of the show. There was Eden, lying on her stomach, nude, her head dreamily looking at the viewer with a twinkle in her eye, as if she just had sex and was about to fall blissfully asleep with no alarm clock to worry about in the morning. It captured a perfect moment, at once intimate and life-size. He got lost in the folds of the sheets, her leg casually peeking out, her soft back carefully il-luminated by a glowing lamplight. It was the most magical paint-ing he had ever beheld. He looked for the label to the lower right of the work. It read, appropriately, BESIDE EDEN. And no sooner had he read the title, a black-clad, waiflike gallerina in a black shift dress strode by in her spike-heeled Brian Atwoods.

"Excuse me, sir," she said apologetically, batting her lashes as she leaned down in front of the tag. As she rose and smiled at Chase, he caught her flirtatious eye, then looked back at the tag. And beside *Beside Eden* she had placed a small red dot. Sold.

Meanwhile, across the large crowded space, Otto was furious as he felt his control over the woman he "created" was slipping away.

"What do you mean, you're not coming to the dinner?" Otto asked her in shock. "Darling, don't be ridiculous! Of course you're coming. Lyle and Kiki are throwing an amazing party for us in a private room at the Greenwich Hotel. You must come. Bring the boyfriend. Chance or whatever."

"It's Chase," she corrected, annoyed.

"Chance, Chase."

"I think we're just going to let you guys have fun. We'll grab something uptown—"

"Please. Eden, sweetheart, let's be adults here. Surely I'm not going to get jealous of this boy toy! Trust me, I have a sold-out show. I can handle it."

Eden fumed. "He's not a boy toy. And you know his name isn't Chance. I know what you're doing, Otto, now cut it out," she seethed.

"Okay, fine, I'm sorry," he said. "It's just you are part of this studio. You haven't missed an opening-night dinner in twenty years. Why start now?"

"If you promise to be kind," she said, looking for Chase over Otto's shoulder. "Then I'll think about it."

"Okay, I'm sorry, all right? I apologize. I'm just stressed with opening nights, you know that," he said, running his hand through his gray mane. "Please, Eden? Please come . . ."

She couldn't stand to see him beg and felt she owed it to him to at least make an appearance.

"Fine," she conceded with a huff. "Great."

The scene in the penthouse ballroom was about as chic as a New York fête can get. Lyle Spence toasted the sold-out show in front of the celebrities, boldfacers, and tastemakers who had purchased the works. Champagne flowed in a current of bubbly bliss and glasses clinked, sycophants oohed and Eden giggled as Chase held and kissed her hand.

"You look so exquisite tonight," Chase said.

"Thanks. You, too." She leaned in and kissed him sweetly. "Thanks for coming with me."

"Are you kidding? It's my pleasure. It's such a different kind of crowd than I'm used to. It's like a whole other world. The people, the vibe, the music—"

"How does it feel to have all these eyes boring into you?"

"I don't feel a thing." He smiled, squeezing her hand. "You make me feel impenetrable."

"Me, too. Spartan army. We're soldiers three hundred one and three hundred two!"

Chase smiled. "How did I get so lucky?" he asked, almost transfixed.

Eden's red lips sipped her champagne and she leaned into him, her bare shoulder silky and tantalizing. "How about we leave in a few so we can go home and you can really get lucky?"

Across the buzzing salon, Otto couldn't help but notice Eden whispering to Chase. Normally the center of a wheel from which all of the social spokes extended, Eden was off to the side, causing necks to crane. When a famed DJ mixed vintage Michael Jackson with the newest technobeats from Paris, not a soul was left sitting down save Eden and Chase, who cooed as if they were in a small café in a winding street.

Otto danced with the young and sexy hangers-on, including a very scantily clad Mary, who was wagging her ass on the dance floor, hands in the air like she-don't-care. Eden didn't even notice her, she was so engrossed in Chase. But Otto noticed. Mary thought she was so cool and sexy doing that Raise Da Roof crap, but in truth she was embarrassing herself. Suddenly, Otto acutely felt the sting of Chase, the pedigreed interloper. He walked away from Mary and interrupted his celebrated dealer, Lyle Spence, dancing with his wife, Kiki.

"Spence, tell me something."

"Sure, what is it?"

"That Chase Lydon. Was he the one who bought *Beside Eden*?"

"Nope. Some lawyer in Midtown, partner in a big firm."

"Okay, good," Otto said, relieved. "I was worried that little trust fund shit got the prize of the show."

"Well, they are big collectors. It never hurts to be on a Lydon's wall. They have enough of them, and a couple of your early pieces, I might add."

"Fucking brat," said Otto, who pounded his scotch, his gaze never leaving Eden conversing with Chase in the corner cabaret table. "As long as he didn't get that one. That's my best piece."

"I agree," added Lyle. "You keep getting better and better."

Otto ignored the compliment, he was so seized by jealousy. His rage was emboldened by Chase's loving gaze in his ex's direction. He stormed across the space to the bar, his eyes fixed on Eden and Chase in the corner.

"Sheesh, someone's just a tad jalouse," said Lyle's wife, Kiki, as she watched Otto's unsubtle surveillance.

"Well, even though they've split up, she'll always be his inspiration," Lyle said with a shrug. "When he started painting her, that's when he really took off. She's his muse."

"More like his doll," she replied, staring as Otto tilted back another shot, then violently plunked the empty glass down on the bar. "Clearly he does not want to share his toys."

After pounding two more shots, a wasted Otto approached Eden and Chase in their amorous corner perch.

"Eden," Otto interjected, woozy with blurred vision and a blood alcohol level that would horrify a Hilton sister, "you deserve more than this little Swiss bank account piece of crap!" He muttered, the vapor of his scotch knocking the couple out.

"I know what it's like, tapping that sweet ass," he taunted Chase. "Does she throw you down on the floor, huh? What does she whisper in your ear?"

"SHUT UP, OTTO!" Eden fumed, spinning around to grab her bag with the fury of a Fujita Scale F5 tornado.

"Wait—I'm sorry," Otto slurred. "I'm drunk—"

"I'M DONE!" she blazed. "In vino veritas."

"No, Eden—wait," he slurred, reaching for her.

She pushed his hand away.

"I tried to take the high road, work with you, stay 'friends.' But friends sure as hell don't treat each other this way. You don't even know what real friendship is. Actually, I take that back—you have two true friends: your ego and your dick. And I don't get along with either of them."

Eden stormed out toward the exit, Chase following her. Her face was flushed with wrath and embarrassment. Over his shoulder, Chase looked back at Otto, as the wasted artist got enough grasp of his waning motor skills to give Chase an evil laugh, muted by the blaring bass—and flip him off.

HEY, OTTO, TREAT HER RIGHT!

DING, DING, DING! Ladies and Gentlemen of the Art World, the heavyweight fight of the year! Put down the paintbrushes and pick up the boxing gloves! In one corner: famed artist **Otto Clyde**. In the other corner: his ex-lover and baby mama, **Eden Clyde**, model, muse, and current flame of uptown hottie **Chase DuPree Lydon**, scion of the famed political family. Otto and Eden, who have up until now remained "on close, friendly terms," according to one insider, went from frames to fisticuffs at the after-party for his sold-out opening at the Lyle Spence Gallery. Otto was pounding shots while a source says Eden and Chase "were practically doing the lambada" on the dance floor. Says the snitch, "He was on her like hair on a weasel." In a jealous rage, the off-kilter Clyde verbally attacked the lovebirds, who flew off for greener pastures—not before the inebriated Picasso gave Lydon another kind of bird: the finger.

45

When you were born, you cried and the world rejoiced. Live
your life so that when you die, the world cries and you
rejoice.

—Cherokee proverb

B rooke Lydon fainted.

"Oh Lord! Mr. Lydon!" Clemenza screamed, hand on heart as she knelt beside the woman she had simply called "Meesus" for close to thirty years.

In fact it was Clemenza who did much of the raising of Chase and his brothers when their parents were off at Davos, Sun Valley, or Paris, or taking on the slopes during an impromptu trip to Aspen. Clemenza loved the family and was treated as part of it, with access to the inner sanctum of their secrets and dreams.

"MEESTER LYYYYDON!!!"

Grabbing the *New York Post* from the ring-covered clutch of the unconscious Brooke, Clemenza began to fan her mistress. But the back-and-forth motions of the tabloid came to a sudden stop as Clemenza beheld the headline on the subway paper teasing the gossip item inside: TROUBLE IN PARADISE: LYDON SCION

STROLLS EDEN'S COUGARIFIC GARDEN CAUSING SNAKEBITES FROM OTTO CLYDE. Beneath the screaming bold font was a candid photo of Chase kissing Eden's cheek at the packed gallery opening.

"Clemenza! Oh dear God. Brooke! Brooke, can you hear me?" Grant yelled. He lifted her head onto his lap and clapped loudly as he instructed Clemenza to dial 911.

"Meester, she sees this photograph, I think."

She handed him the paper. His eyes widened as he beheld their son on the front page. Within minutes the sirens rang out on Fifth Avenue. Paramedics were able to resuscitate Mrs. Lydon, but for precautionary measures they brought her to Weill Cornell.

When Chase got the call, he had been sound asleep in Eden's arms. Stunned out of the reverie by Nokia chimes, Chase jerked into consciousness and saw his father's cell phone number.

"Dad?"

"Your poor mother's nerves are now mincemeat thanks to your shenanigans. We're in an ambulance. You have a lot of explaining to do. Meet us in the family wing."

Click.

"What is it, Chase?" Eden purred, kissing his upper arm. "Want to cook a fabulous breakfast together? Why don't you blow off work and play hookie with me. Let's see a matinee."

"I . . . can't. My mother is not well."

"Oh gosh, sorry—is everything okay?"

"I'm not sure. I'll be back tonight, though. Can I see you tonight?"

"Yeah, I'm having some friends over. We're going to cook and drink a shitload of wine and play parlor games."

"Okay." He smiled. "I miss you already."

He kissed her forehead, and she flopped back down in the sheets like a weary teenager happily remembering it was Saturday, ready to snooze till noon.

In the DuPree Pavilion of the hospital, Chase charged through the grand halls of the brand-new glass lobby, pressing the up button nonstop until the green arrow lit and the bell dinged. On his mother's floor he sprinted down the hall and found his mother in a huge suite near where his beloved grandmother had died. The room overlooked the East River, quiet with serene views of sailboats and the soft light of a cloud-obscured sun. She faced the window blankly and didn't turn her head as he walked in.

"Romping and cavorting with trash is not what I imagined for my sons, whom I poured everything into," she whispered from a stone face. "And this, in the papers, your grandmother is rolling in her new grave," she said, stabbing her son with her venom-spiked words.

"Mother. She's not trash, she's—"

"Defending your trollop to your sick mother who lies in her hospital bed, that's rich."

"I love her."

Brooke's eyes rolled as she limply lifted a hand to her heart. It was as if her frail aorta were scarred by the scratch of the cougar's claw.

"Mother, Mother! This is not fair."

"I can't breathe," Brooke muttered as Grant fanned her devotedly from the bedside.

"Mother, I love you. I respect you, but I haven't been able to breathe my whole life! I feel like . . . someone has somehow lifted the top off the shoe box I have been living in!"

"A shoe box. Really?" Grant said, anger mounting. "Of all the things to say! For everything we have done for you!"

"All of it, Father, has been much appreciated. But it was all to service the world's perfect perception of me. I was laced up, packaged, and shipped off to the right schools. I dated the right girls, like Liesel, all for you. For what? To have little perfect children and send them to the same schools and start this all over again?"

"Really! This is not the time for this discussion," Grant stammered. "Look at your mother's state!"

"It gives me zero pleasure, truly. But I need to get out of here."

"The hospital? Why?"

"No. Yes, the hospital, but everything. The job. The scene, the world. I just can't be the picture-perfect son anymore."

And with that, as tears streamed from Brooke's closed eyes and Grant grasped her tiny hand, shaking his head, Chase exited their flower-laden suite without looking back.

46

Youth would be an ideal state if it came a little later in life.

—Herbert Asquith

"Where are you?" Otto demanded on the phone to Eden. "I need to get to work."

"What do you mean, where am I? I'm not coming. After the way you treated us, I quit."

"Really? You *quit*. Over this . . . what do the papers call him? This modern-day JFK Junior?" Otto asked from his studio as he applied gesso to a huge canvas. "You can't do this. I have the Paris show less than two months away."

"I don't care."

"Clearly. You're probably deriving joy from my humiliation. The tabloids are just loving this. Rupert Murdoch should send you dividends! So indiscreet, the two of you! I thought he was supposed to have some class, no? He couldn't keep his signet-ringed paws off you."

"Nor could you, once upon a time, I recall. And he does not wear a signet ring."

Carmina Burana blared on the speakers behind Otto as he felt sick. As the music rose to more and more violent tones, Otto recalled how he had once painted Eden with such passionate vigor, his brushstrokes zigzagging wildly, re-creating her flesh in ecstatic blots of beige. And now she was defending her new puerile paramour. Sometimes when he looked at his collection of drawings of her that filled his walls, Otto longed to make love to her again. But it wasn't *she* who lit his fire; it was the image he created and re-created of her. It was his narcissism. It made him fucking sick that that Lucky Sperm Club shithead got to bed her now. He knew he couldn't ever get her back—not that he really wanted to.

"So you're really done posing for me."

"Yes."

The two sat in silence, the emptiness on the phone receivers sad and heavy.

"So, have you spoken with Cole?" Otto asked, piercing his thick regret.

"We e-mail every day but it's not the same. I miss him."

"Me, too. I miss us all," Otto admitted. "You know, Eden, Mary is nothing to me."

"Otto. It's too late. I'm not coming back. To your bed or to your canvases. It's over. Too much has gone down. I'm a different person now."

"Really? In a mere few months you are a *different person*," he sneered, his nostalgia switching on a dime back into anger. "Wait till Cole meets Chase. He'll be just as disgusted as I am."

"Please don't say anything to Cole about Chase, okay?" Eden asked, feeling vulnerable. "I don't want you to poison him by stoking the fire."

"You don't think he would understand. Hmmm. Now that's interesting. If you are trying to hide this relationship from your own son, don't you think perhaps you should examine it a bit more and whether it's even worth it to see this boy?"

Otto touched a nerve, reminding her of Callie and Sara, and she shuddered.

"He's not a boy. And I'm not hiding it. Cole knows all about Chase. And you're in no position to talk. Hello, you've been banging barely legals and you don't ever get shit for it," she fumed at the double standard.

"Because, unlike you, my dear, I am discreet."

"So, what, I'm supposed to dart in the shadows and hide whom I'm seeing?" she asked, starting to see the clear difference in Otto sleeping with a younger girl versus her sleeping with a younger guy.

"You are part of this studio. Whether you like it or not. This studio is a family, a business, a house," he said, reddening.

"Otto, I don't think you understand: I'm not part of the studio anymore."

"You always will be. The oeuvre is out there! You are part of the body of work and synonymous with me. He's beneath you, against everything we've stood for, with these lowlifes with their compounds in Maine and crests on their silverware. It pulls the studio down, too. I mean, this is everything we have always loathed!"

"Speak for yourself. I don't have nearly as much class anxiety as you! And by the way, don't pretend to not be elite with your town house and trips around the world. Why are you no different?"

"Because I create things. These robots move money around. They live high on the hog while people's pensions swirl down the shitter!"

"You're so high and mighty. Did you ever stop to think what one of your million-dollar canvases could do for a village in Africa? Huh? I mean, seriously, it's a few damn dabs of paint, and you get a boatload of money!"

"I never heard you complaining."

"I don't complain. Unlike some people."

"Let's not have these quarrels. They're so tedious. You used to

be fun. Maybe those stiffs got to you. Your little schoolboy's boring ways are rubbing off on you."

"Actually, funny you should say that . . . ," Eden trailed off,
smiling out the window. "In this weird way I feel like I'm the
young one in the relationship."

"Oh?" probed Otto, calmer now and intrigued. He was like a
tempestuous roller coaster, slow and steady or plunging with
speedy screams.

"His family is so conservative and old-line but he's almost
roaring to break out of it and I guess I help him do that."

"No doubt they are not pleased, my dear, about you."

"I'm sure they aren't. But I think we make each other better.
He's an old, old soul and I make him feel younger. I've always
been a free spirit and he makes me feel grounded and more mature. I don't know why I'm telling you this. You obviously have
such disdain for him. For this relationship." Eden shook her head
and looked at her watch.

"No, I'm sorry. Eden, honey, I . . . can't lie to you. Naturally I
always suspected that perhaps you might leave me for a younger
man. You were my model who revered me, but of course I knew
one day I'd wake up from my reverie to find that the student had
outshined the master."

"Otto, don't be so dramatic. You did the leaving, might I remind you. You're the one porking every hot piece of ass that
comes through there."

"It is what it is." He shrugged matter-of-factly. "You know I
love you more than anything. Always."

They were bound together, forever, and they would have to
get over this hurdle, not just for her future with Chase but because of their lifelong tether through Cole.

"I apologize for my shallow jealousies. They are foolish," he
admitted. "Tell me more about him."

"I don't know, I just . . . his devotion is so full, so persistent. Actually, he kind of reminds me . . ."

Her voice trailed off as it broke a bit. She could never utter Wes's name to Otto. In that moment, on the phone with Otto, of all people, Eden realized something. That familiarity she loved in Chase? It wasn't him. It was *her*. Her old self. Chase didn't so much remind her of Wes—they were incredibly different. It was that Chase reminded her of *her, back then*.

"Yes," Otto probed. "Who does he remind you of?"

"Nobody. Just my old self, that's all."

"I remember that girl. She was effervescent and beguiling and tempting and sparkling, and she still is."

Eden sat quietly, wondering if Chase saw those qualities or thought of her as old and wise, *experienced*-sexy versus *hot*-sexy.

Otto continued, "I want you to know I love you still and want you to come over to talk, to sketch. Will you consider forgiving me and posing tomorrow? Working through this together?"

"No. I'm sorry, but no."

"No? That's it?"

"I can't, Otto. I have to move on. Of course we'll still be friends for Cole but as for spending time working together, I just can't do it. Why torture each other with this feeding-tube crap? It's better for everyone this way."

"So that's it? You're just going to burn this bridge?" he sneered, surprised. "All this work we create together?"

"Yes, I guess I am. I'm all for burning bridges," Eden said matter-of-factly. "If a bridge is rickety and wobbly and can hurt people, burn that shit down! You'll build another with someone else. But as for me, I'm thumbing it to the next one."

47

*About the only thing that comes to us without effort
is old age.*

—Anonymous

I t was over lunch at Swifty's that Eden realized she had gone
from art world and gossip sensation to full-blown celeb. She
had arrived five minutes early to meet Allison, who had just
finished parent-teacher conferences at Carnegie. While she waited
at the teeny bar area, she first heard the general whispers she had
long grown accustomed to: " . . . Otto Clyde's girlfriend . . .
split . . . muse," and the like, but then she heard bits and pieces of
words like "Brooke DuPree . . . suicidal . . . what is Chase thinking . . . trouble." Self-conscious, Eden pulled her soft scarf closer
to her neck as if to insulate her not only from the draft coming
from the vent above but also the raised silver forks ready to stab
her.

"Sorry I'm late." Allison sighed, bursting in, shawl aflutter,
heels clacking. She double-kissed Eden, oblivious to the scores of
mascara'd eyes upon them. "Apparently Kate has H.R."

"What's that?" Eden asked, noticing a Hitchcock blonde with
a crisp pale bob staring at her over a glass of Chardonnay.

"*Homework Resistance.* Like it's a syndrome now. Uh, hell yeah, I resisted homework, who doesn't?"

Eden looked to the maître'd. "Hi, we're both here now," she said, glancing back at the table of ladies whose eyes were Krazy Glued to them. "Is there anything in the back?"

As the two followed the man to their table, Allison walked up alongside Eden.

"What's wrong?"

"Nothing. Just these women are all staring at me."

"Yeah, well, big shocker, Brooke Lydon is like the Kevin Bacon of the Upper East Side. Except everyone is only two degrees away from her, not six. Ignore these wrinkly hags! They're jealous, trust me! You think they really want to bang their crusty old billionaire husbands? You think they would put up with their gnarled asses if they didn't have a trill in the bank? Fuck no. They're not in love like you and Chase are. It's all acting! They *play* the *Penthouse* Pet to *get* the penthouse! Got it?"

"I guess," said Eden, putting down her wine.

"Speaking of which, I just saw that collector who has, like, four of your paintings, the one who lost everything with that Ponzi schemer guy? Anyway, that fab duplex we partied in a few years ago? On the market. Naturally the fuckers at Brown Harris wouldn't print for how much. So annoying! You know my three least favorite words in the English language? Price Upon Request."

Eden smiled weakly, sipping her water. Allison knew all was not well.

"I'm curious, Eden. Since when the hell did you ever care what anyone thought, anyway?" asked Allison. "I feel like in your old age you're starting to obsess. It's like you're going through now what most women dealt with during adolescence and their twenties."

"I know. It's not like me. I'm so . . . . off."

"Well, of course you are! You and Otto were together for—"

"It's not that," Eden said, shaking her head.

"What, then?" Allison probed.

"The big you-know-what," Eden said, arching her brows as she looked at the tablecloth.

"No. What?"

"Four-oh."

"Not this garbage again. Please. I'm forty! I told you, I was freaking and then it came and went and it was, like, who the fuck cares?" Allison laughed. "It's because all your life you were praised for your looks and you feel all that slipping away. But that's all bullshit! It's sexier in a way, to be older. Experience is hot!"

"Oh, come on, Alli. That's ridiculous. What man leaves his wife for an older woman?"

"I can't think of one, but I'm sure it's been done."

"Yeah, once. Somewhere. Think about it, when a woman actually still looks good, they say she looks good 'for her age.' But implicit in that so-called compliment is that a younger, firmer, fresher woman is still hotter."

"That's not true. Sometimes older woman are gorgeous without qualification of her age. Rene Russo in *Thomas Crown. En fuego!*"

"I don't know. I'm used to . . . being—"

"Young and perfect and the *muse*," Allison finished. "So get over it! Welcome to planet Earth, looks don't matter that much! And hey, if you're still obsessing and being vain, well, at least you know you're still foxy enough that *Gotham*'s most eligible bachelor wants you. Thirty-nine is the new twenty-nine."

"I feel like I have parentheses around my mouth," Eden lamented, ashamed of her sudden vanity. "My nasolabial folds are getting worse."

"Are you talking about your vagina or your face?" Allison teased.

"Shut up."

"Listen to me, Eden. I'm your best friend and I'm starting to get annoyed with you: Stop being crazy."

"You know, I see those guys on the subway who wear their vintage Clash tees and suspenders and hipster pants and messenger bags. And they're my age but they're—"

"Rejuveniles." Allison nodded. "I read about them in *New York* magazine."

"Exactly," said Eden. "And I read that article and thought, no, no, that's not me because I have a kid. But I think I'm both. I'm this mature mom but I'm also the wild child, like the people in that article. I think a big step is leaving Otto, like for real," Eden said.

"I think that's healthy. It's time. A clean break is much better for both of you."

"We talked for a long time and I know it's sad but for the best. I just feel like under Otto's watchful and judgmental eye, I'll always doubt myself. Especially my relationship with Chase."

"You just need to take one day at a time, E. Don't overanalyze this; just enjoy what you guys have in your bubble. Forget these matrons or Otto or 'the future.'"

"Well, that's hard! Especially given my age. I mean what am I doing? Do I want to marry this guy? What am I searching for?"

"Why do you need the answers now?" Allison asked. "Fuck all these losers; just live your life! Give yourself a break."

"I'm so confused. I have zero clarity about my life."

"Hey, I've got news for you: You're in the deli line at Zabar's— take a number. *Everyone* hates getting older, but guess what?"

"What?"

"It sure is better than the alternative."

48

For all the advances in medicine, there is still no cure for the common birthday.

—John Glenn

"Hey, man, it's Wills." Chase heard his (former) best friend's voice, slow and cautious over the phone. He had run to grab it after entering his apartment, hoping it was Eden, and instantly regretted his fourth-ring dash when it wasn't her.

"Hey," replied Chase, surprised. "It's been a while. How have you been?"

"Yeah, it has, man. It's actually really good to hear your voice . . . ," Wills trailed off.

Chase was happy to hear from him as well, realizing only in that second how much he had moved on from his past life since he'd been seeing Eden.

"Yeah, you, too."

"Look, Chase, I feel really bad about how everything went down. I'm sorry, you know, for everything—"

"Don't even worry. It's all in the past. I'm happy. You're happy and I'm happy, and I'm glad everything worked out this way," Chase said in all sincerity.

"I'm, uh, also calling to tell you something," Wills said sheepishly. "I, uh, *we* have some news."

Eden came home to find Chase outside her door with a dozen peonies.

"Well, you are a terrific sight this chilly night," she said, beaming, wrapping her arms around him and kissing him. "Let's go up!"

They walked in through the double doors and up the stairs. "You're awfully quiet. Is everything okay?"

"Yeah, I just . . . ," his voice trailed off. "I actually just heard from my friend Wills. He and Liesel are getting married."

Eden stopped in her tracks and turned to him.

"What? Are you joking? It's been what, four or five months?"

"Well, I guess they were so close as friends already—through me—that they just got out the gate pretty quickly. It's kind of surprising."

They walked into Eden's apartment and flicked on the lights.

"Are you okay?" she asked, taking his hand.

"Completely. Honestly, it's strange, but I don't feel anything other than total happiness for them. I think because I'm happy for myself, being with you."

"Why is everyone getting married so young? I read the Styles section and I feel like they are getting younger and younger!"

"Life is short." Chase shrugged. "Why not settle down? My parents got married at twenty-five."

"Well, that's totally different. That was another generation," Eden said, rolling her eyes.

"Why?" Chase asked, confused. "In the scope of thousands and thousands of years, why should we get married later all of a sudden? It worked for millennia to marry young. Relative to the history of man, we practically just started marrying older two seconds ago."

"Yeah, because they used to croak at forty!" Eden explained. "And if they didn't, they were fucking miserable, at least most of them were. Wake up, Chase, it was about the dowry, not the pitter-patter of their beating hearts! It was about finding someone who had the most cattle and sheep or allowance per year, not the most in common."

"You really think that?" Chase's innocent cerulean eyes looked crushed.

Boy, was he ever young. Eden started to casually straighten up the living room, fluffing pillows and picking up wineglasses and bringing them to the kitchenette as Chase stood in the small foyer, waiting for an answer.

"It's not my opinion, Chase. It's fact." Eden shrugged as she flurried around the house. "Marriages throughout history, across cultures, were often created by matchmakers, not chemistry. It wasn't about love with angels singing and trumpets and shit. People were torn apart all the time because of what was advantageous. And they did what people do: They move on with their lives."

Chase suddenly felt very far away from her, seeing up close Eden's jaded side. While she was so loving and affectionate in bed, doting on and taking care of him, there was a side that seemed to fear real tenderness or emotion. Perhaps it was because she was scarred by Otto, or maybe she always just had to look out for herself and could never get too attached? Chase wasn't sure what propelled her, or even what she wanted from life, but he knew one thing for certain: He was falling more and more madly in love with her.

Chase knew deep down he could get any girl he wanted, but he wanted Eden. In her he chose someone more sophisticated, more eloquent, sexier, worldlier. Not just a pretty girl looking to snag a husband, get prego, and push their blond tot up Madison in a Bugaboo. Chase knew that a life beside Eden was his dream— her sass, her edge, her independence, her badassness, all made her more alluring to him.

Chase watched her cut the stems of the flowers and arrange them in a vintage vase. The chasm between them, he realized, was far more than just years. Sadly, he sensed that her mind was beginning to wander to other places. In that moment, watching her fill her red teakettle with water, Chase began to worry that she would one day slip away from him, traveling away somewhere in that head of hers to a tableau far away. He wondered what she saw for herself, what future paintings of her life would look like. And if he would be in them beside her.

49

The older the fiddler, the sweeter the tune.

—English proverb

E den hardly fixated on Chase the way he did on her, but when they weren't together for a night or two, she missed him. She missed his companionship, his passion for her, and the way he lovingly helped put the Humpty Dumpty of her shattered ego back together again. The truth was, while he made her feel more confident than ever, she also wondered what the fuck he was doing with her. During their days apart, she felt like an old aging hag, and when she saw him across a packed restaurant or theater or park path, Eden was struck all over again by his young skin, his smile, the charm that captivated every debutante up Fifth Avenue. He made her feel young again.

"Hi, gorgeous," she said to him across the glowing hurricane lamp in an intimate café.

"Sorry I'm late," he said, kissing her cheek. "I was so excited to come and see you, I ran out of the office without my briefcase and had to go back."

She reached over and took his hand in hers, tracing the tops of his fingers delicately.

"Chase, I don't think I've ever seen this hand not clutching that tan case."

"I know. It's been intense lately," he said, taking a breath, shaking his head. "Maybe I need a vacation. I mean, I go away with my family, but that's not . . . really a break, you know? In a way it's harder than work! I realized the other day that I haven't taken a *real* vacation in forever."

"What's forever?" she wondered.

"Oh gosh, I don't know. About four years."

"Are you kidding me?" Eden asked, aghast.

"No, I wish I were," he said, shrugging. He watched delightedly as Eden delved into her food with relish. "So many girls I've met are so self-conscious, they push around some sad salad and nurse a Diet Coke. You just dig right in and I love it," Chase said lovingly, watching as she snarfed a generous plate of gnocchi. "You can tell just by watching you eat how much you love life."

"Yeah, all that celery stick bullshit is for the rich," she said, grinning as she stabbed a soft potato dumpling. "If you saw what I grew up eating, you'd get it. All these people? They have private chefs. I had Chef Boyardee."

Chase looked at her across the hurricane-lamplit table.

"You know what I love about you? You appreciate everything," he observed. "You're not like these jaded women who've done it all, seen it all. You could have gotten sucked into your life with Otto but you're still so grounded."

"What's not to appreciate? I mean, look at this! Delicious wine, delicious food—can you try this gnocchi, by the way? I swear, I'm ruined for this dish anywhere else. They may as well serve up a pile of pebbles with tomato sauce. These are so light and fluffy!"

Chase smiled to himself; her enthusiasm was almost childlike.

He stared at her starry-eyed and held her hand across the table. "Eden, I am crazy about you," he said slowly.

Eden shifted in her seat. "I can't thank you enough for catching me when I jumped ship from Otto," she said, trying to steer away from the intensity in his gaze. "Really. You have saved me, in a way."

"I have never felt like this before," he said, ratcheting it up a notch.

The truth was, while she wanted to reciprocate his enthusiasm in that romantic moment, she really couldn't say the same thing back. But she didn't want to complicate the situation by thinking about her past or her future, so she simply put her hands on the table and pushed herself up to kiss him over the wine bottle and bread basket, as people looked on, charmed and jealous. She remembered Allison's instructions to her. *Be happy right now.*

The glittering duo lived in a glorious ménage à trois with New York City: restaurants, operas, theater, indie film houses, out-of-the-way galleries. Chase showed Eden more of *his* New York, taking her to the Botanical Garden Ball, antiques shows on Park Avenue. And she took Chase to photo exhibits in Brooklyn, hole-in-the-wall theaters with unknown playwright friends, and dinner parties hosted by downtown actors who had collected Otto's work and known her for years. Rolodexes shuffled like Vegas cards: Eden met Philippe de Montebello and Lee Radziwill and Chase met Liv Tyler and Sarah Jessica. Eden heard the philharmonic for the first time, and Chase heard the Scissor Sisters. She dined at Le Cirque, he at a dumpy hibachi Japanese restaurant where you sit on the floor next to NYU students doing sake bombs (Brooke would die). It was a thrilling time, for both, with months full of adventure and new discoveries and cinematic film-still moments. But Eden tried not to think of the future; she wanted to just stay in the moment.

One night, the pair stood in the freezing cold after dinner, deciding whether to hail a cab home or go for a drink. The night was so beautiful, it felt a shame to retire so early.

"I have a random idea," Chase said. "Would you ever want to

get some coffee or hot chocolate and walk across the Brooklyn Bridge? I haven't done that since I was a kid and it looks so cool tonight with the lights and the moon like that."

"Okay, sure, great idea!" Eden responded, happy he was so spontaneous; she didn't know he had it in him. "Look at the moon! It looks so orange tonight, it's almost like Mars."

"I've never seen it like that," Chase marveled, transfixed. "Though, honestly, nothing shocks me when I'm with you."

They started walking under the patterned cables and cross-hatched steel web that felt grander than any portal she had ever walked through. They clutched coffee cups with their outside hands and held the inside ones, fingers interlaced. But while Eden was fully relishing the moment with Chase, she slowed down, the brakes put on her feet by a sudden flood of crystal clear memories that charged forth like rushing, whitecapped waves washing over her brain. It was déjà vu times ten.

The scenic image she beheld felt so close and recent to her, she could almost see Wes on that very bridge, when she had looked forever in the face and so callously dismissed it. Half a lifetime ago. A chill rushed through her body and Chase held her close, thinking mistakenly that it was the night wind that made her shudder. But in fact it was the sudden and overwhelming recollection that she had walked this bridge before, also in the throes of young love, on the same chilly kind of night, under the same bright stars, on the same exact path, but in an altogether radically different place.

50

Sooner or later we all discover that the important moments in life are not the advertised ones, not the birthdays, the graduations, the weddings, not the great goals achieved. The real milestones are less prepossessing. They come to the door of memory unannounced, stray dogs that amble in, sniff around a bit and simply never leave. Our lives are measured by these.

—Susan B. Anthony

After a post-dinner stroll home under the stars and another blissful night of curling up in Eden's pillow-covered bed, the duo parted ways the next morning. Chase kissed her good-bye and hurried off to work.

"See you tonight." He waved and she blew him a kiss.

Now that she was out of Otto's business, she had the burden of having to figure out what to do with herself all day. She still had enough money from Otto, at least for now, and she wasn't much of a shopper, so she faced the blank road of hours ahead of her like ticking lines on a highway, outstretched, infinite and loaded with exits. What to do? Ah, the problems of a lady of leisure.

Eden decided that she would spend the day at the Metropolitan

Museum. To her own shock, she realized she hadn't once been there since her move uptown, despite her proximity.

She bought herself a coffee at E★A★T and walked up the many steps of the majestic building at 1000 Fifth Avenue. After giving her donation and pinning that day's bright orange MMA circular metal tag to her lapel, Eden gazed up at the awe-inspiring ceiling, overwhelmed by the scope and choices. There were so many different artistic avenues she could wander—Etruscan vases or French paintings? Dead shark or dead Egyptians? Something about the grandiose, magnificent building gave her chills; it made her feel so small, the scale and scope of the architecture, the history of art before her. In fact while the enormous campuslike museum held sculptural busts and portraits of pharaohs and presidents, it also displayed Eden. Her portrait hung in the Lila Acheson Wallace Wing, the modern arm of the museum; she had gone several times when the museum first acquired the piece, a grand, ethereal, haunting masterpiece of Otto's from fifteen years back. She was sealed in, part of the canon. Like Dora Maar. Or Whistler's mom. Or the dead shark.

Most people in Eden's position would want to revisit their painting, to experience anew the thrill of being immortalized on such a spectacular skylit wall. But not her. The picture represented a time long ago lost. So she blithely decided to go in the opposite direction: toward the tombs.

She leaned over sarcophagi, looking at the gilded stenciling and imagining the lives of the people who lay beneath. They probably bit it by forty. Or if not, by her age, they'd certainly be the village elders. Ye olde wise one. She meandered on, admiring a lapis pendant, checking out a headless statue with huge boobs (some things never change), and scanning the hieroglyphs. Why were the people always drawn sideways? They could build huge fucking pyramids but couldn't render humans without profiles?

Eden was happy to let her brain float to outer space as her eyes gazed at the myriad earthly treasures. Even the architecture itself was art. In the vast and serene Temple of Dendur, she walked along the gleaming, windowed wall, the muted light washing the mammoth but quiet room, as she watched kids throw coins in the shallow fountain and make whispered wishes. She smiled to herself watching the sweet-faced teachers hush the giggling kindergarteners on a field trip. As they gleefully tossed their shiny nickels, she felt a pang; she missed small children.

"Eden?!" a voice beside her asked with surprise. "Is that you, my dear?"

She turned to see a beautiful older woman, long graying hair pulled back in a chic bun, wearing a black dress and boots. "It's Penelope Bennett! Do you remember me? Wes's mother—my Lord, I haven't seen you in twenty years, my girl, and you look exactly the same!"

"Oh my goodness!" Eden squealed, hugging her. "Of course I remember, YOU look the same! Gosh, how are you?"

"I'm fine, just terrific," she said.

"What a coincidence running into you," Eden marveled. "I was just recently thinking of Wes. It has been so long! And you really do look the same," Eden squealed. "What are you doing here?"

"Well, I'm in from Memphis for a few weeks. I'm . . . settling Wes in, actually. He's moving back from London."

"Oh," Eden said, surprised. "That's great!"

Eden shivered, recalling a dark rainy night a couple years earlier, when Otto was missing in action, God knows where. She had pulled a huge charcoal cashmere sweater over her knees and found herself tinkering around on the computer, looking up Wes.

"So he's been in London?" she asked, knowing damn well from Internet write-ups on his work that he had been there for years.

"Yes, yes! He's been doing such great work there. He won several awards, in fact," she said, beaming, then caught herself. "Ugh, sorry, am I the braggart mom? I'm just so proud of him, he's really done beautiful designs."

"Office buildings?" Eden asked.

"Well, yes, initially, but he actually stopped designing new buildings and now specializes in restorations of old ones," Penelope explained. "He refashions old homes, dilapidated factories, schoolhouses. He totally revamps them and breathes new life into them. It's painstaking work, but he has restored some incredible places."

"That's amazing. That's exactly what he was meant to do, beyond his wildest dream," Eden said, impressed. Wow, Wes was really doing it.

"So, now he's launching his own firm in New York, specializing in that niche. He actually is doing a huge project in Red Hook and one on the Lower East Side and another Brooklyn condo building that used to be a chocolate factory during the Depression."

"You must be really proud of him," Eden guessed.

"We are. So proud, in case you couldn't tell! But most of all, we're so thrilled to have him back in the New World, as I'm sure you can appreciate."

"Absolutely," said Eden, her heart heavy, thinking of Cole. "I have a son, actually."

"Oh, lovely."

"Cole. He moved to California for college, and it's hard," Eden confessed. "I hate having him so far away."

"Don't I know it," Penelope commiserated, noticing a somewhat sad flicker in Eden's eye.

A beat went by as Eden gathered the courage to inquire further about Penelope's son, whom she had once so adored.

"Does . . . Wes have kids?" Eden inquired carefully.

"No, no children, never married."

"Really?" Eden blinked in mildly relieved surprise.

"He came close," Penelope explained. "He lived with one woman, a very nice British girl, a surgeon, and he was thinking about proposing. They were in Florence and they strolled the whole day through with the ring in his pocket."

"Why didn't he do it?" Eden asked, trying to casually mask her curiosity.

"Well, it's a long story, I suppose. . . ." Penelope caught sight of Eden's badly masked inquisitive look. "But the long and short of it is . . . well . . . *you.*"

"Me?" Eden's heart started to race. "How?"

"It's a crazy story, actually," Penelope said, shaking her head with a smile. "He took her to a museum he loved—that he had helped restore, actually—and he was planning on finally asking her there," Penelope said. "And there they were, in the center of this huge room, and in walks the curator with a team of handymen. They were carrying one of your portraits that the museum had just acquired and was hanging up, right then and there!"

"No." Eden was stunned.

"Wes is not one to take things as silly signs or anything like that, but he just knew that he couldn't go through with it."

"Oh gosh, I feel awful," Eden confessed, putting a hand to her chest. "Does he hate me, Penelope?"

"Oh Lord, no, not at all! He's so happy. He's incredibly successful—he's redone huge buildings in London, two in Hong Kong, and is jammed with projects and commissions here now. It's incredible." Penelope tried to rein in her filial pride. "On the other hand, how are you doing?" Penelope asked Eden, patting her arm.

"I'm okay . . . ," Eden said. "You know, turning forty soon, kind of strange how time goes by."

Penelope sensed a muted pain in Eden's green eyes.

The two women looked at each other.

"Eden, would you like to go sit in the café downstairs and get a cup of tea?"

Just what the doctor ordered. Eden exhaled.

"I would love it."

The two women, reunited after two decades, walked to an intimate, sunlit dining area in the American Wing. At a cozy corner table they sat with their warm mugs, and Eden felt a strange comfort from being in Wes's mom's presence. She recalled how, on her visits, laden with groceries and various house gifts from sweet-smelling candles to curtains she'd sewn, Eden had thought, *So this is what having a really doting mother feels like.*

"You know I have to tell you, Penelope, I don't know if you remember, but your visits to our old apartment really stuck with me. This might sound crazy, but I feel like in those two or three weekends you showed me how to be a mother to Cole, in a way. You were always so warm and affectionate and I . . . never had that."

"You know, Eden, I always had such a wonderful feeling about you," said Penelope. "I loved those visits. I knew there was something larger than life about you. You were special."

Eden smiled with a pang.

"And I hate to say this," Penelope continued, "but when I looked at the sparkle in my son's eyes, I knew that you would smash his heart."

"I'm so, so sorry," Eden replied, starting to get nervous. She thought she would choke on her guilt. What she did to him, her abrupt good-bye, her scatterbrained apologies clouded by her own excitement of impending fame, made her sick with remorse. She felt a knot in her throat as she pictured Wes's floppy brown hair in their chipping-plaster doorway, his blue eyes shining through his little gold glasses. "I just feel so awful, Penelope. I think in truth I have never forgiven myself."

"No—don't worry, sweetheart, please. You see, I didn't finish. What I was going to say was, I knew, knew to the core of my soul, that instead of feeling sorry for Wes, I felt sorry for *you*."

"Me?" Eden felt her tenuous link to her past growing clearer as her emotions welled.

"Even after you split and you went off and became famous, I still felt for you because I knew something that you didn't: that you would regret it more than anything in the world."

Eden blinked and wiped a tear from her eye. Penelope took her hand.

"Was I right?" Penelope gently asked.

"I'm so . . . confused, I—." Eden felt more hot tears stream down her face. "My life has taken so many twists. So many things went according to plan, but then so many things were unexpected. Otto and I broke up last year. I'm happy but I'm also a bit lost, I suppose. He's now with a woman who was my age when I met him. I think to myself, of course she is with him, how could I fault her? He can make her a star. But gosh, you are right, Penelope. I have had moments where I've looked back at that crossroads and dreamed of what that other path would have been like. I'm so sorry." Eden put her hands under her eyes and washed away the streams of salty water.

"Dear, life is all about those crossroads. But just because you've moved on doesn't mean you can't go back to the past. Just take the next exit and double back . . . like I did."

"How? What do you mean?"

"It's never too late for anything," Penelope said. "That's how I got back together with Wes's father."

"Back together? Had you split up?"

"You never heard the story?" Penelope asked.

"All I knew was that Wes was conceived at Woodstock."

"So you never knew our whole saga?"

"No," Eden said, wiping the last of her tears as she shook her head. "Would you tell me?"

"How much time do you have?"

"All day," Eden said blithely through her tears. "All week."

51

You can be gorgeous at 20, charming at 40 and irresistible for the rest of your life.

—Coco Chanel

Wes Bennett, Eden's first love, was indeed conceived in Bethel, New York, at the famed music festival. It was the summer of 1969, and during the opening chords of Jimi Hendrix's legendary set, a slim, soft flower of a woman named Penelope meandered with a friend to sit with a group of shaggy, stoned, southern guys. Wes's father, Wesley, was immediately struck by her, and by the concert's end they were in the grass, moving on each other in a kaleidoscopic collage of acid, blaring guitar chords, and the fabulous perk of outdoor make-outs: the delicious contrast of chilly skin and warm mouths.

Wesley and Penelope held hands for three days straight, slept under the gleaming stars, and made love among the masses, but felt as if they were on a desert island. Dizzy in a swirling sea of colors and music, and each other, they shouted, "I love you," over deafening metallic riffs and whispered it again into each other's cold ears at night. Theirs was a generation about freedom and raising a fist to convention and institutions of all kind, including marriage. So both young lovers, though thoroughly smitten, assumed this glorious cometlike time together, burning and bright, would fizzle into the darkness of the past when amps were unplugged and the crowds parted. Still high from both acid and the opiate of the dreamiest sex of their lives, Penelope and Wesley scribbled phone numbers and hugged good-bye, each swept up in the tides of their friends and the harsh wind of sobriety. Slowly, both looking back over their shoulders, they moved like cattle away from each other. As Wesley met Penelope's tearful gaze, he almost ran back to her, until she turned around to face the path ahead.

In the days that followed, both pressed rewind on the static-filled hazy film of their fleeting union, and the highs continued long after the pharms wore off. But when a rainstorm drenched Wesley's skin, smearing the digits of Penelope's 415 number, and when she misplaced Wesley's ticket stub with his Tennessee address, the two were parted for what would probably be forever. So Penelope and Wesley were set adrift with only their memories of that fateful night.

And a little something else.

After the party of the decade came the ultimate party favor: that September, Penelope was coming out of a café on the Haight when a sudden tsunami of nausea engulfed her. *Oh my God.* Even before her friend Susan teased, "Whoa, Penny, you knocked up?" she knew. Shit.

Her well-to-do Pac Heights parents were, ahem, *displeased*. To say the least. Her Woodstock cross-country odyssey was a whim that they had frowned upon. And that was just for a few days. This would be for life. Penelope paced. She puked. She knew what she had to do.

She announced she would keep the baby; the impending stork flight caused shrieks of dismay from her parents. When her mother and father told her she could either say bye-bye baby or bye-bye inheritance, she instantly bid adieu to the dough, moved in with Susan, and seven months later gave birth to baby Wes. With no way to track his father's whereabouts, and convinced he would be horrified even if she were able to contact him, she simply did what women have done forever: went at it alone as best she could.

Penelope poured all her love into her son. She and his god-mother, Susan, doted on him constantly, rearing a sensitive, kind, loving boy who chose cuddly animals over trucks, blocks over guns, hugging over hitting. Wes had the sweetest soul of anyone she had ever met. And by his second birthday, brown hair floppy and eyes ablaze with cheer, little Wes was the spitting image of his father, full of hope and promise, with a heart so big it must have been crowded in the tiny bones of his rib cage.

A few months later, Susan announced she had fallen in love. Her new boyfriend, Jonathan, had just moved to San Francisco from Washington, DC, where he had worked for "The Government" (translation: the CIA). Disenchanted, he had moved out west to start a new life using his skills as a private investigator.

"Well, do I have a job for you," Penelope said over a candlelit table of Napa wines and Susan's vegetarian cooking. "Any chance you could help me find Wes's daddy?"

"Absolutely," Jonathan said, fist on the table. "I fucking hate deadbeat dads."

"Oh no, no, no, it's not like that." Penelope laughed, catching Susan's eye. "See, Wesley doesn't even know he was born."

52

Middle age is when you've met so many people that every new person you meet reminds you of someone else.

—Anonymous

Chase asked Eden if she would accompany him to the opening night of the New York City Ballet. Le tout New York was there, gilded in their glittering gowns and jewels, reluctant tuxedo-wearing husbands in tow as society shutterbugs captured the affair, one of the most glamorous in the city.

While most dresses grazed the marble steps of the New York State Theater, Eden's hem was blush-inducingly high.

"Is that Paris Hilton's cousin?" one society matron sniffed within earshot of Chase. "Brooke Lydon must be beside herself!"

Chase, overhearing, kissed Eden's hand and apologized. "I'm so sorry," he whispered. "We can leave if you want."

"Leave, are you nuts? This is beautiful. Plus, Allison made me swear not to think about what a couple of embalmed uptown hags think of me," Eden said. "Her exact words were 'these crusty matrons haven't been laid in two decades, so who cares what they think?'"

"Allison is a smart lady," Chase said, squeezing Eden's hand. He liked her short dress. He felt the ripple of rebellion in his stomach, knowing his mom would wince. And he dug it. Shit, after all his crazy brothers had done to bend (or even snap and break) the rules, Chase thought if the most insane thing he had done was to love an older woman, well, then screw his family.

In the glowing light of the auditorium, the Who's Who of the city's art patrons scanned the crowd, searching for friends and famous people, eyes almost always landing on Chase and Eden, who held hands and flipped through the evening's program. Eden reveled in the artistic choreography of the three acts of *Jewels*. But as the ethereal dancers glided and spun against the glowing scrim, Eden's thoughts wandered in the darkness to Penelope and her story.

As the thunderous applause rang out at the end of the act, Chase led Eden outside during the second intermission.

"It was so stunning, beyond my expectation. Thank you so much."

"I'm really glad you liked it," Chase said, beaming, proud he had taken her. He kissed her cheek as they looked out at the Lincoln Center fountain all lit up. "I enjoyed it more than ever tonight," he said.

Just then the glass doors to the outside balcony opened. It was Wills and Liesel, holding hands. The confrontation was unavoidable.

"Hello, Chase," Liesel said politely. "Nice to see you. Hello, I'm Liesel," she said, extending her hand to Eden.

"And this is Eden Clyde," Chase replied. "Eden, this is Wills."

"Beautiful dress," Eden said, admiring Liesel's long, flowing, pale pink J. Mendel gown. She realized she was the only one in a short hem, a fact all of the drooling men and their jealous wives had already noticed.

"Thanks," said Liesel.

The four stood in silence.

"Well, it's a bit cold out here," Liesel shivered. "I think I'm going to go inside and get a glass of wine before the last act."

"Nice to see you both," said Wills with a crisp nod, following his fiancée back inside.

"She's really pretty," Eden said, unfazed. While many girls would dread a run-in with their lover's ex, particularly one over a decade younger, Eden didn't bristle. "She looks like your mom. But younger."

"I think that's why my family liked her so much." Chase smiled.

"Well, then," Eden teased, "I am dead meat."

After the performance, the crowd streamed to festively adorned tables designed by Antony Todd with floating votives and fragrant gardenias. The room glistened as candlelight reflected off the crystal, and ballroom chairs were pulled out from the silk-cloth-covered tables so the ladies could take their seats with ball gowns fluffed and prepare to demonstrate their own well-honed craft: the art of fake eating. Push the frisée to the left, cut a slice of salmon, take a mock bite, and move garniture off to the side.

Brooke, the queen of this special talent, approached the table with a tight smile, wearing head-to-toe Oscar. The Family had been sitting separately in the theater (Brooke was with the rest of the Board), and now Chase's whole family would be dining together at the best table in the vaulted atrium (center table on the dance floor), as tradition had it.

Eden, while hardly shy or nervous, was the guest of this esteemed family and knew she had to be polite. She stood up as Brooke approached.

"Hello, Mrs. Lydon," Eden said. "I'm Eden."

"Yes, dear, I know," she said, forcing a smile.

"Thank you so much for having me here tonight. It was just amazing!" Eden said.

"Well, Chase insisted you come along, so I didn't want to disappoint him," Brooke replied coldly.

Eden looked at Chase, who nervously bolted up to introduce Eden to his father, who was scanning the crowd for young hot socialites. Hey, he was married, not dead!

"Grant, darling," Brooke summoned him. "We're starting, please take your seat."

Pierce stumbled over, already hammered. "Mom and Dad are fucking shitting bricks. They said you were with some hag, but she is SMOKIN' hot. For an old chick!" He thought he was whispering but wasn't.

"Pierce, please," Chase harshly whispered. Eden pretended to ignore it as she perused the bread basket.

"The older ones probably do *anything*, too, man. Liesel never did anything but missionary, am I right, bro? This one's got the experience, you can just tell."

"Pierce"—Chase leaned in—"shut up. Now."

"Whoa, bro, chillax. It's a compliment! Dazzamn."

Chase exhaled, thoroughly mortified by his family's behavior. For a clan so allegedly refined, they sure were a bunch of boors. It could not get worse. And then, it did.

"Hey, hey, hey," Price, the eldest Lydon son, said approaching the table, his hand up Raise-Da-Roof style. "Guys, this is Olga." He presented with pride a tall, striking, twenty-year-old model, his date.

"Hallo," Olga said, taking off her fur wrap (a gift from Price). "Nice to meetchu."

"Charmed," said Grant, giving Price a surreptitious wink.

Even Brooke thawed momentarily. While she was not happy to have her son dating a fashion model from rural Latvia (one step above courtesan, really), her tender age made her an instant improvement over Eden.

Olga sat one down from Eden, next to Pierce.

"Hallo, Mees Clyde, I am SUCH huge fan. My grandparents in Riga have two of your portraits."

"Oh, thank you," Eden said.

"Oh? They're collectors?" Brooke thawed further, emboldened by Olga's obvious wealth.

"Yes, they have many, many peectures. They lof Otto Clyde. Eden, you are beautiful."

"Isn't she?" Chase asked as Eden smiled gratefully.

"My mudder, Katia, ees your same age—you will be forty soon, no?" Olga asked innocently.

"Uh." Eden cracked into laughter at the awkward fact so vociferously highlighted by the doe-eyed girl. "Yes, I am thirty-nine."

"My mudder sess you geev her hope dat when she feel old she see you and you luke so bootiful and comFORTable with your age, no surgery. She ees inspired," she said in a Slavic-meets-British accent (her English tutors were always from London).

Eden smiled kindly and leaned into Chase. "Gee, that was lemon juice on my wrinkles," she murmured.

"I have an idea," Chase said, leaning in with a whisper. "Wanna get out of here after they serve the main course?"

"Is the Pope Catholic?"

As her fellow tablemates conversed about subjects ranging from observations of Wendy Whelan's unmistakable style (Brooke) to the new hooters on the Chock Full o' Nuts coffee heiress (Price), Eden quietly pushed her frisée around the plate. Her fork moved like waves, just as her thoughts did. From the din of lipstick-marked greetings and cocktail rings against glass, Eden's mind swam upward, into a daydream in the vast atrium. She wandered away to her long talk with Penelope, her body politely immersed at the table, but her thoughts up in the sky, doing frothy, dream-like pirouettes.

53

Thirty-five is a very attractive age. London society is full of women of the very highest birth who have, of their own free choice, remained thirty-five for years.

—Oscar Wilde

Standing by Susan's side, Penelope wiped a tear from her eye as the soft tulle of Susan's veil flowed in the Bay breeze. Jonathan stepped on the glass, and the rabbi pronounced them man and wife, and Wes at age four marched happily up the aisle, holding an empty velvet ring pillow in front of the married couple—his beloved godparents. While Penelope was an outside-the-box girl who always had rocked the boat of her parents' traditions, she felt surprisingly misty over Susan's white wedding ceremony, the flying pale pink petals, the dance as bride and groom. But most of all, she was emotional when she saw the look in Jonathan's eye as he watched his new wife glide toward him after a twirl that had taken her all of three feet away. As he pulled her back into his arms, Penelope knew she was now officially losing her best friend.

The four of them had been like a family, cooking dinner and

setting the table with three wineglasses and a plastic cup. And now their little unit was moving on. Just down the street, but still. Then, a few weeks post-honeymoon down the California coast, Susan and Jonathan came by for dinner.

They had news.

After two years of juggling his other (paying) cases, Jonathan had a crack in his search for Wesley. He handed Penelope a small index card with an address in Tennessee and a phone number. She stared at it as she cleared the table and cleaned the dishes. She looked at it as she sewed a patch in Wes's pants. She folded and unfolded it as she sat alone at the table with a bottle of Merlot Susan had brought. Penelope had a huge glass of wine and dialed the area code on her rotary phone. As the little finger-sized circles spun counterclockwise, her pulse pounded so hard she thought she would register on the Richter scale. She hung up. She calmed herself down and tried again. And again. Finally, a day later, she was able to dial all ten digits. Wes slept on the bed beside her as she heard his father's voice answer the phone.

"Hello?"

She cleared her throat to speak but no sound came out. It was like that bad dream in which the murderer is over your head avec machete but no scream can emerge from your paralyzed larynx.

"Hello? Is someone there?"

She struggled to speak but couldn't.

Click.

Shaking, Penelope hung up. She was seized by a surge of panic. That night, she woke up and lay staring at the ceiling, watching the headlights from passing cars move across the beams and white paint. Finally, just as the sun began to rise and Wes rubbed his blue eyes with his little fist, Penelope did something borderline insane: She tossed his T-shirts in a bag, zipped up some toys and dresses and toothbrushes, buckled him in the car, and climbed in the driver's seat. She unfurled a poorly folded map of the United States and started driving. And driving. And as the twisty colored lines of the map's roads crisscrossed and swirled like veins, Penelope just pressed the pedal and headed east.

54

In the midst of winter, I finally learned that there was in me an invincible summer.

—Albert Camus

Tires of a black sedan screeched Nascar-style the hizzell out of Lincoln Center as Eden and Chase told the driver for the evening to gun it. Rubber burned, along with Eden's unpleasant memories of an evening laden with heavy gazes, ugly judgments coated with mascara. But as the numbers on the green-and-white street signs declined, so did Chase and Eden's inhibitions, as they kissed in the backseat, like horny teens after prom.

Downtown on Grove Street, Eden strode into Marie's Crisis holding the hand of the guy whom every man in the mostly gay bar would turn away from the piano to scope.

"Oh. My. God. That's Eden Clyde and Chase Lydon," one sexy young crooner whispered to his friend.

"Love her! So fierce. Her black-and-white Marc Jacobs campaign was on my wall as a teen," the other said. "But who's the man candy?"

"Chase Lydon? You know that family in *Wedding Crashers*? He's that."

"Great! I can be the little brother who ties him up!"

The famed haunt was a gem amidst the West Village's crazed collage of winding streets. Everyone from drunken NYU students to sexily androgynous theater queens to old-timer performers sang their blues away or celebrated living in New York City here.

Eden loved singing. With pipes usually reserved for the shower, she belted along with the crowd, which had styles ranging from American Idol to Billy Idol.

"Where are we?" Chase asked, surveying the tiny Christmas lights (a year-round decoration) and the throngs of people singing along happily, while Dexter, the vivacious ivory-tickler at the piano, played and sang.

"I've lived here my entire life and have never even heard of this place," Chase said.

"You're probably the only straight guy here." Eden smiled. "Everyone is jealous of me tonight."

They held hands and stood off to the side, and as Eden sang every lyric out loud, Chase loved how un-self-conscious she was.

"Hey," one cute guy said to Chase. "Why'd you bring your mother?"

By this point many people in the city knew of Chase and Eden's pairing, and while she was older, she obviously wasn't his mom.

"She's not my mom, she's my girlfriend," Chase said politely. Eden didn't fume or even feel a small sting; she simply sang on. She didn't give a shit. She had Chase's hand in hers and music banging from the piano. *Tits and asssss, bought myself a fancy pair, tightened up the derrière . . .*"

She danced as Chase stood behind her, arms around her waist. She loved that he was there to catch her, to hold her as she crooned her lungs out. He even chimed in on occasion.

"Shake your new maracas and you'll shiiiiine!!"

Otto never had time for her affection for musicals and often said she was a gay man trapped inside a woman's body. The three weekends Penelope and Wesley came to visit, they had splurged and took Eden and Wes to shows on Broadway, igniting a Broadway binge by Eden from Tower Records's terrific show tunes section. As Wes and Eden sat beside his parents and the lights dimmed and the overture sounded, Eden got a rush like none other. Because of those few heavenly nights out with the Bennetts, Eden took Cole every few months to see a show, just the two of them. It was funny, Eden thought to herself, how people come in and out of your life and leave behind certain little pieces of themselves. Her love of theater only grew because she fostered it with trips to Times Square with Cole, and she realized her son was enriched because of Penelope's generosity. How strange life was, now that she sang those same songs here, in new times.

After an hour of requests, a star turn by Maggie the waitress, and a full dividing of the whole bar into Dannys and Sandys for a spirited rendition of "Tell Me More," Chase was ready to take Eden home.

"You ready?" he whispered.

"I'm never ready. I could stay all night." She then burst into tune. *"I could have daaaaanced all night!"*

"A patron by the bar has offered Miss Eden a round," Maggie said. "What can I getcha?"

"Tell him thank you," Eden declined, pointing at Chase. "But he has work in the morning."

"Will do, see you both soon, I hope!" Maggie hugged Eden good-bye, and Chase looked back at the warm Christmas lights and pumping piano keys. He never would have been inside this jewel box of joy if it weren't for Eden.

"Thank you" he said, kissing her hand. "I think that is the happiest place I have ever been."

"More than my bed?"

"Second happiest."

The night was surprisingly mild, and there was not a cab in sight, so they started strolling.

"Maybe if we start walking east we'll find one," Eden suggested.

The minutes flew by as the duo held hands and navigated the bustling crowds moving through the night on their way to clubs or cafés, performances or parties. Before they knew it, they were by the Bowery and had been walking for almost an hour.

"So much for going home and crashing," Chase said, squeezing Eden. "I don't even care about work anymore. I feel like nothing else matters but spending time together."

Eden smiled in response. She then looked across the street and stared. Chase followed the upward trajectory of her mint eyes.

"What a cool building," Chase marveled, looking up at the perfect symmetry of the redbrick structure and large-scale grids of clean glass windows.

"It's the Bowery Hotel," Eden replied with an imperceptible beat of sadness.

"It's beautiful. Have you been inside?"

"No, I haven't. I was invited to go there for a party a few years back when it opened but I couldn't bring myself to go. I guess it reminded me the neighborhood had officially changed when it opened its doors."

"Yeah but that's a good thing!" Chase said. "You said it was heroin junkies around here when you were younger."

"That's true," Eden dazedly replied, spaced out as she looked at the hotel's clean stylish façade and packed restaurant Gemma on the corner. Young people buzzed in and out, and through the big windows they could see a huge candelabra with Phantom of the Opera–style dripping candles with a hundred flickering wicks. "I know it's better now. Of course it's an improvement. I just . . . sometimes get nostalgic, that's all. I know it's silly."

What Eden didn't want to mention to Chase was that once upon a time, on the very site of the gleaming, chic hotel, with its crowded restaurant of fashionistas eating shaved raw artichoke salad with truffle vinaigrette, there stood a shitty little dive where locals and students, young and hopeful—poor on cash but rich with ambition and ideals—could go to get the best burger in town. Where Eden would scrounge together coins from the bottom of her bag to afford hot oatmeal with raisins, and how nothing in her entire life, before or after, ever tasted so delicious.

55

You're not 40, you're eighteen with 22 years' experience.

—Anonymous

With a creased, unfurled map, empty soda cans, bags of chips, and a sleeping Wes passed out across the backseat, Penelope crossed over the border to Tennessee. A nervous surge moved through her; seeing the Welcome sign made her realize what she was doing. And unlike hanging up a rotary phone after hearing a hello, this time, after two thousand miles, there was no turning back.

She woke up a bleary-eyed Wes at a greasy spoon where they would stop for lunch. Stretching their legs outside the car for the first time in hours, they staggered *Night of the Living Dead*–style into the restaurant. In their pleather booth, nervously fidgeting with the sugar packets, Penelope smoothed her hair and straightened her rumpled blouse as Wes drew on the paper menu with broken crayons from the bottom of his mother's handbag.

"Mommy, what are we doing here?" Wes asked, breaking into a yawn.

"Well, honey," Penelope started slowly. "We're here to try to find an old friend of mine. His name is Wesley."

"Does he live near the restaurant?" he asked.

"I think so," said Penelope as the waitress placed eggs and pan-cakes on the table. Wes began to devour them as she stared into her coffee cup.

"I'll take some more when you get a chance," she said, lifting her mug.

Caffeinated to the point of quivers, Penelope pulled into a small driveway marked with the address Jonathan had given her. She put the car in park, then sprung Wes from his backseat perch and walked slowly toward the white clapboard house. It had a lovely slate-blue-painted front door and a nice front yard.

Please God, don't let a wife open the door, she thought.

She knocked. No answer. She knocked again. Nada.

Hmm . . . it was late afternoon and a gray truck was in the driveway. She took Wes's hand and went around the back to the yard area.

Oh no.

A swing set. An inflatable kiddie pool.

This was a huge mistake.

"Hey, a playground!" Wes said, running to the white picket gate.

"No, no, honey, we—we have to go right away. Mommy is sorry. We're going home."

"Why?" he whined, frustrated and confused.

"We have to go, sweetheart, let's get back in the car."

Penelope took her son's hand and walked quickly back around the side of the house toward the car. She opened the door to the backseat, sweat pouring from her small feminine brow. She thought she might cry.

She buckled in Wes, then went around to the driver's side and opened her door.

"Miss?" she heard a warm voice ask. "Can I help you? Are you lost?"

She stopped still, then slowly turned around.

That 180-degree pivot was the longest second of her entire life. But when she put her feet together and faced Wesley, her reddening eyes could hide her emotions no longer. His handsome face was the same, and as they locked eyes, his fingers opened, and the two grocery bags in his hands fell to the dirt below.

56

Youth had been a habit of hers for so long that she could not part with it.

—Rudyard Kipling

With thoughts of that little diner on the Bowery flooding her mind, Eden brought Chase back to her apartment, where, awash with memories, she kissed Chase more deeply than ever. He was moved by her unbridled affection and held her tightly as she undressed him and they collapsed on her bed.

He made her want to be outlandish, to be young again, to be unburdened by what anyone (including herself) thought. Maybe she could run away with him to some island and never return. Chase grabbed her back as he moved inside her and Eden very suddenly felt a chill down her spine as her breaths grew staccato, as she slowly let her lids fall shut. And against the dark screen of her closed eyes, hazy like a Super 8 film in her mind, recollections played in quick-flashing cinematic frames.

Sexual fantasies had a bizarre habit of making unannounced appearances, and sure enough, in the throes of passion with Chase, her mental movie projector made a jump cut back to Wes. He was so fresh in her mind from a week of thinking about him; her long afternoon with Penelope had popped a cork and now all the bubbly bliss was flooding back. In recent days, Eden realized, she had been thinking about him more and more. The fact that he would be arriving in New York after so long made her sick and excited. What if she ran into him? What would they do if they saw each other? What could she possibly say?

Though she was intertwined with Chase, in her closed eyes, Eden was back at the little diner on the Bowery. She imagined she was not in a lavish designer bed and Pratesi sheets but on the cheap mattress she and Wes shared on the floor, unmade as their sheets swirled soapy wet in the basement washing machine they never seemed to have the quarters for.

As Chase breathed harder and harder, Eden kept her eyes closed. She didn't want to exit her reverie. She couldn't help but envision that it was Wes pushing deep inside her. Chase said her name and she flushed the sound out of her head, as she wanted nothing to bring her back to the present; she found herself enjoying what her mind's eye was offering her so much more. She had a flash of Wes diving onto the mattress as she laughed, an image of him holding a long wooden spoon for her to taste the tomato sauce he had made, how he pressed her against the window, kissing her, running his hands over her. The details flooded back as if the film frames were digitally enhanced in the replay; she saw the large vein in Wes's wrist as he drew sketches, his fishbone boxers and worn-in white T-shirt. She pictured him taking off his gold glasses before he made love to her on his drafting table. Eden was growing more turned on by the fantasy of Wes in her arms. Each push inside her thrust her back deeper into her past until she could barely breathe—she was holding all the air in her lungs as if 1990 were trapped inside her and she didn't want to exhale and let it all flow away from her body. She relived Wes's quickening heartbeat and breaths, imagining he was kissing her neck, and she let out a deep sigh of delirious ecstasy. And when she opened her eyes to see Chase's flushed, happy young face, she couldn't believe she had deceived herself so vividly.

Chase, on the other hand, could not have been more in the moment. After exhaling and collapsing into her, he lay holding her, breathing deeply, inhaling the unique fragrance of her apartment. As Eden silently drew little swirls on his back with her finger, Chase finally felt like he had the life people relished. This woman had literally walked into his life and had altered it forever.

"I think this might be my favorite place on earth," he said.

He looked around the room. This place was Eden, his own version of paradise. Vinyl records played almost constantly. Every surface of her apartment was covered in vases—fresh cut flowers, overflowing plants, everything was in bloom. Eden had imported her very namesake into every place she had ever lived. No matter how cold or rainy it was outside, no matter how bare the branches of the trees were by her window, there was always life within her four walls.

"Thanks, but there's a whole wide world out there, Chase," she said. "I promise you, my apartment is not cloud nine."

"It is to me," he replied.

The next morning Chase walked down the street, toward Park Avenue, beaming with exhilarated glee. He pondered how strange life was, how random it was that one person could cycle into your orbit and change the way you walk down the street, how you carry yourself, how you think, how you spend free time, how you value the little things. As he walked he was in his own world, in a dream state, in his very own Eden. Chase didn't even notice that, at the stoplight at Fifty-eighth Street, his father's town car had pulled up alongside him.

Grant, who was sitting behind Luigi as always on his morning ride to work, suddenly spied his son outside the window. He put down his *Wall Street Journal* and reached for the button to lower his window. But just as he was about to do so, through the thick tinted glass, Grant saw Chase smile to himself. His hand paused above the button as he watched his son. Chase was in his own world, grinning ear to ear. And Grant echoed that smile to himself: His son was happy. Finally.

Cheden's Pub Crawl!

Aging model/muse **Eden Clyde** and her younger beau, **Chase Lydon**, known lovingly by gossip bloggers as *Cheden,* went from Ballanchine to belting out tunes at West Village piano bar Marie's Crisis. Uptown at the NYCB gala, the *crisis* was all **Brooke DuPree Lydon**'s— the high-society swan was spotted shaking her head at her son's date, whose sexy scarlet frock had all the up-town gents drooling, and their jealous wives left to mop it up. But downtown, the drool was for Brooke's son. The bar, filled with gay crooners, allegedly screeched to a halt when the matinée idol–esque, youngest Lydon scion strolled in for a round of drinks and songs with his beloved. Of the comely twosome one observer offered, "They're both hot so who cares how old they are? They only have to answer to themselves, no one else." Added another, "No matter what anyone else says, you could just tell they were totally into each other. And that should be all that matters."

57

Years wrinkle the skin, but to give up enthusiasm wrinkles the soul.

—Douglas MacArthur

"Penelope?" Wesley asked slowly, syllable for syllable, as if saying her name in a foreign language. His blue eyes flashed as he walked slowly toward her, vegetables scattered on the ground behind him. "Is it you?"

"It's me," Penelope replied, blinking back Fiji-style waterfalls. "I-I-I'm sorry to just show up like this—I was just, um, going to go—"

"I've been wondering about you," he said, stunned. "All the time."

"Me, too, for four years," said Penelope.

"Four and a half," said Wesley, shattering any ice with a huge, all-engulfing hug. As she felt his big arms around her—the only ones that had touched her since Wes's conception—she crumbled. She thought she would choke on her sobs and tried with all her might to hold them back.

"Sorry," she said, pulling back, wiping a tear. "I'm so sorry."

"Why? Do you know I've been trying to find you? I've thought about you so much, I even went to San Francisco."

"I saw the swing set—are your kids—"

"No, no kids. Those are for my nieces. I have three, just down the street."

Relief had new meaning as Penelope's entire tightly wound-up body grew limp with the word "nieces."

"Mom?" Wes's muted voice called through the closed car door as he knocked on the window.

Penelope ran to the car and opened the door, unbuckling Wes. She helped him step out of the car. She picked him up, holding him on her hip in his little red T-shirt and blue shorts as her heart sprinted like hoofbeats in a derby dash.

"Wesley," she said in a voice so shaky it was studded with nervous breaths. "This is Wes." She put him down and held his hand.

Wesley bent down on one knee, facing him.

"Hey, buddy," he said, charmingly. But then, his expression changed, his eyes widening. As he looked into Wes's eyes, he knew. He instantly looked up at Penelope. "Is this . . . ?"

Penelope's mouth quivered, and she simply nodded.

To her complete shock, Wesley grabbed Wes and hugged him so tightly she thought the boy's lungs would squeeze out his last gasp of CO_2.

"Wes. Wes, I am your dad!" he said to her son. "I'm your dad."

Streams of tears flowed down Penelope's cheeks. Wes looked confused, but Wesley's warmth and enthusiasm were infectious and softened any apprehensions.

"You're my daddy?" Wes said, looking at Wesley's welling eyes.

"Yes, I have a son!" He engulfed his child in a bear hug, and

Wes's little arms moved from his sides up and around his father's neck, encircling him so tightly that his little hands touched his elbows.

The vision transcended Penelope's wildest hopes. It had been only a few days, so long ago; drugs, music, a blur of rolling in grass, of keeping each other warm, a rainbowy collage of dancing and good-byes. And here they were.

"I was so worried you had a family," she said. "And I didn't want to just show up but I've been trying to find you for so long and I have just thought of this—dreamed of it—for so long."

"Penelope," he said, kissing her cheek and squeezing her hand. "I'm so happy you're here."

Without talking about plans or the future or even the past, the little family cooked dinner. The next night they did the same. And the night after that. For two weeks, as Wesley lay awake in a spare room off the kitchen while Penelope slept upstairs in his bed, he replayed the memories of Woodstock, fresher and more colorful than ever.

One night after Wes went to sleep, Wesley asked Penelope about her life in San Francisco. She spoke of her friends, the familiarity of the rolling hills and winding streets, the place she bought her paper, the café where she sipped her espresso.

He reached over and took her hand.

"I was so terrified we'd come here and ruin your life," Penelope confessed, feeling the spark between them as he ran his fingers over hers.

"*Ruin* it?" Wes laughed, kissing her hand. "Are you kidding, my life is made."

As Penelope's eyes watered, Wesley got up, moved her chair with her in it, bent down and swept her up in his arms. He carried her to his bed and kissed her like he had in the grass, but no magic pills, no dewy damp air, no music. This time, the guitar chords were all in their heads, shared memories they now relived together. Their spines both tingled even without acid, and now to be completely naked together, warm skin on skin, legs intertwined, Wesley and Penelope transcended their former ecstasy by finding it once more, as adults.

"Penelope," Wesley said, holding her trembling soft body. "Can you and Wes stay? I don't have that much, but whatever I have, it's yours."

58

Old age is like a plane flying through a storm. Once you are aboard there is nothing you can do about it.

—Golda Meir

"So the sex is like mind-blowingly sensational, right?" probed Allison.

"I guess, yes," said Eden, stirring four Sugars in the Raw into her cappuccino.

"What do you mean, you *guess*?" asked Allison.

"It is," replied Eden, warming her hands on the scalding mug. "I'm crazy about him. He's such a great guy and I just am so grateful to him, you know? I feel like he picked me up and dusted me off after Otto basically chucked me out with yesterday's news. He made me feel beautiful and special again."

"Uh-oh," said Allison, leaning back in her chair, knowingly. "He's toast."

"What? Wait, why do you say that?" Eden asked.

"I know you. That tone."

"No, no, it's just . . . ," Eden trailed off. "I feel like Chase is so wonderful, he's such a great guy but . . . I have this strange kind of . . . *ache* lately."

"For what? My analyst would say for your youth, maybe," said Allison. "That's not surprising. I was running around with a hundred guys in my twenties! You were bound to Otto and had Cole! Maybe you just miss that era in your life; you weren't shagging a million people like the rest of us."

"It's not about the million people," Eden said, trailing off as she stirred her coffee. She finally got the courage to meet Allison's inquisitive gaze across the table. "It's about one."

"Who?"

This was too embarrassing. Eden could barely admit it to herself, let alone say it aloud, even to her best friend.

"Never mind," said Eden, shaking her head quickly as if to scatter the memories away. "I mean, it's literally Paleozoic. Forget I said anything."

"Eden. Come on, it's totally normal to think about past relationships, about people who were in your life . . ."

"Seriously, not this long ago," Eden said, looking out the window at the busy street. "It's the past. It's foolish to even wonder. It's just that I bumped into Wes's mother, Penelope."

"WHAT? When?"

"A few weeks ago. I can't stop thinking about him now. He never got married. And his mom, God, she was so . . . amazing, Alli. We spent this whole afternoon together—until the museum closed—and I just have had all these memories flooding back. She told me this whole saga of how she got together with Wes's dad, and I'm obsessed with it. I realized that I think I've been, I don't know, haunted by that relationship in a way."

"I can see that. I mean, he was such a great guy. And you totally decimated him."

"Thanks."

"What? You did!"

"Don't remind me. I've been thinking about that, you know, the path not taken or whatever. I can't stop! It's so unproductive and stupid to waste time thinking about it but knowing what I know now . . ."

"You regret it?"

"No, I mean . . . I don't have regrets. I have Cole, I have a life here. It's just Wes was such an amazing person; he never would have treated me like Otto did. He was the type to love each wrinkle and fat roll, you know?"

"I don't see any of either, annoyingly."

"I'm just saying I may not have been starting over at this age, you know?"

"Or you might have. There is no way of knowing."

"Right, as I said, it's foolish to even think about," Eden huffed, clearly wanting to change the subject. Sort of.

Allison caught her drift. "So he never married?"

"No, never."

"Really? Where is he?"

"Moving back here," Eden said, looking cautiously up at Allison.

"Oh, boy."

"But it's irrelevant, anyway. He probably hates me. And there's Chase. I think in this strange way his sweetness reminded me of Wes. I guess in the whole blur of falling for Otto, having Cole running around, I kind of forgot about the purity of that relationship. I don't know, in a weird way I think he's the only man who ever truly loved me."

"Oh, bullshit! Don't make me puke. You had countless guys wrapped around your finger!" Allison shot back, calling Eden's bluff.

"But they didn't love *me*. I was so lonely for years with Otto, and I think I was lonely in the beginning, too, but I just didn't notice because we had so much going on when Cole was a baby, and traveling so much, and I was blinded by all the stuff that I now know is just crap. Wes was my best friend. He was totally devoted and I shat all over him. I didn't break his heart, I trampled it. I obliterated it. I smashed it with a mace."

"Mace? Like that spray you use on rapists?"

"No, the club with a metal orb with spikes on it. He thought we would be together forever. I didn't deserve him."

"Where the fuck is this coming from? Seeing his mom?" wondered Allison, who had never seen her friend pine away over *any* guy.

"I don't know, I'm unglued," Eden marveled, not recognizing herself. "Maybe being with Penelope was the catalyst, but I think because of my big birthday coming up I've been doing all this bizarre emotional reckoning. I also think . . . maybe in a way being with Chase reminded me of my younger self. What I used to be like. Anyway, it's a silly time-suck because you can't go back."

"I remember now that you said Wes's mom was really cool. Didn't she used to visit and take you guys out? You loved her—"

"Yes! She's amazing. She's so self-assured and happy and still in love with her husband. In a way she's what I would love to be like at that age."

"Geez, I never knew this haunted you like this."

"It didn't . . . until now. Somehow Chase reminds me of what Wes wanted to be; the same strength and ideals, but with money. All the money Wes wished he had so he could shower it on me. I was such a greedy piece of shit."

"Listen, give yourself a break," Allison said. "If he was so great, you wouldn't have ended up with Otto."

But in the darkest recesses of Eden's mind, she knew the truth was too embarrassing to admit to even her best friend. She had ended up with Otto because he could make her famous. He would make sure she would never have a return bus ticket home to Shickshinny. Otto made her safe, and then he made her a star.

The older she grew, the less her ego mattered to her, and the more she felt the emptiness in her chest. The first four decades had been scripted, mapped out with a cartographer's precision. She got to the destination she thought she had punched into the satellites of fate above, only to find that X sadly did not mark the spot. Unlike the first forty years, the next forty years were hazy and uncharted. And this time, she wanted to go off road, drop from the grid, not care about where she was going or what she would find. The only thing she wanted to seek was happiness—something, she feared, was more difficult to locate than even the most deeply buried treasure.

59

Time and Tide wait for no man, but time always stands still
for a woman of thirty.

—Anonymous

After Wesley and Penelope tucked young Wes into bed, they sat on the front porch with two glasses of wine, side by side.

"I feel strangely spiritual all of a sudden, and I'm not a religious guy," Wesley said, smiling.

"You are amazing," said Penelope, taking his hand. "Here you are, living your life, and we show up like a tornado, and you take it all in stride. I'm so sorry. I—tried to call, I just didn't have the guts. I had to just be extreme, I guess that's what I do. That's how I got to Woodstock in the first place, it was total impulse!"

Wesley squeezed her hand. "Thank God you did. See? There I go again. I've never believed in God. And in these parts, that is top secret—you're in the Bible Belt, my dear. But I just never connected with the church or even the whole concept of a higher, invisible being. I'm a builder. My work's based on things working, fitting together, making sense. I run my hand over the beams, I can touch the wood, bend the metals. God never has made sense to me."

Penelope nodded, understanding his point.

"And then—I was sitting right here, two, three days ago and I thought to myself, no, I guess it was a prayer, really, that I could fall in love and have a family. Your arrival," he said, looking in her eyes. "It's almost like I was heard."

Penelope leaned in and kissed Wesley, and the kissing, as it turned out, never ended. Six months later, once again in his young life, Wes would serve as ring bearer: but this time to his own parents.

With Wes carrying their thin bands, handmade by a goldsmith friend of Wesley's, Penelope and Wesley got married. The years were good to this one-time fractured family, and they more than made up for lost time. And soon, Wes became a brother.

His parents had three more children, Lila, Hugh, and Eloise. Friends from his old neighborhood in San Francisco would come to visit, reminders of a life Wes could barely recall—a life with his mom that was now eclipsed by the picture-perfect family. It seeded in him a desire to wander; after all, his own parents wouldn't have met had they ignored their insatiable urges to travel, to experiment, to take risks.

So it wasn't a complete shock to his mom and dad when Wes announced, at eighteen, that he wanted to move far away for college. In a quasi-continuation of his father's line of expertise, Wes decided he wanted to study architecture and went to Columbia in New York City.

Naturally the family was crushed, but something inside his mother made her proud—Wes was certainly wired like his parents, following his gut, going for what he wanted, and maybe, she hoped, his path would lead him to a love who deserved him and cherished his enormous heart and those big blue eyes like his father's. She suspected, even when Wes was four, that he would have a loving gaze so powerful that a woman who felt that connection to him could never get over him, just as Penelope could never get over Wesley. Until she found him once again. And she was so happy, so at peace, finally, that she knew if she had never gone after him, he would have haunted her forever.

60

Looking forty is great! If you're fifty.

—Anonymous

Eden got a nervous chill as she clicked through Wes's company Web site. It was crazy to think they were together before the Internet was even a glimmer in Al Gore's eye. So much time had passed. Each aspect of the site was pure Wes. Clean and restrained, cool and laid-back. It was unpretentious, with modest copy and clean lines. As she looked at the images of what he had built abroad, she smiled. How amazing, what he had done. As much as she loved being with an artist all those years, she saw in Wes's portfolio true art fused with science, a brilliant combination that had her staring in awe at her Mac.

In a small sans seriph font on the flush-left page menu read the word "contact." She stared at it for so long it was as if the pixels became separated, floating like blurry dots that both tantalized and paralyzed. She took a deep breath and clicked on it. Address, various company e-mails, a phone number. E-mail would be too insane. She couldn't send him psychotic volumes and she couldn't simply shoot off a few lines, either. Both would be odd, and she concluded it was not the medium to reconnect through. She thought of Voltaire: "I didn't have time to write you a short letter so I wrote you a long one."

That left the phone. For the first time in her life, Eden was stressing like a normal teen girl, the insecure awkward wreck that she had never been. She had never been one to dial and hang up, yet here she was, almost forty, freaking out, as if the buttons on her phone were electrically charged and would zap her. Her fingertip hovered, then retreated back into a nervous fist, which Eden pumped into the table, nervously. Fuck. What was her problem? Okay, deep breaths. She dialed, her heart pounding with the depression of each key.

"Bennett Associates."

"Hi, yes, hello. Um, may I please have Wes Bennett's office? Please?" IDIOT! She couldn't speak normally to the receptionist! Eden almost hung up.

"Wes Bennett's office."

"Hello, hi. I'm calling for him? Wes Bennett?"

"He's in a meeting with a client right now; may I direct you to his voice mail or take a message for you?"

"Uh, sure . . . ," Eden stammered.

"Which do your prefer?"

"Um, I'll take his voice mail. Please. Thank you so much."

"Sure thing, I'll put you right through."

Eden was about to press the button to hang up when she heard his voice. Grainy yet soft, his familiar tone floated over the receiver. It was real—he was within her reach. When the beep sounded, she almost threw up.

"Wes, hello, hi, sorry, um, this is Eden calling, actually." (Fuck!) "I . . . sorry to call so randomly." (OMGOMGOMG) "I just had bumped into your mom, who is just incredible and we had this really amazing time and she told me all about what you've been up to, and I'm just blown away, really. So anyway, I know you just moved back here, to New York, um" (Idiot! Idiot!), "and

I just wanted to see if maybe you would ever want to, like, maybe get together and catch up for, like, a drink or coffee, or whatever. Dinner?" (Oh no, too forward) "Or whatever you have time for, if you want. If you would like to." (ARGHHHH FUCK!) "Anyway, um, let me know!" She left her number and hung up, shaking.

Great: She was officially a teenager. Was this *Freaky Friday* or something? She felt so ridiculously upside down. She had to call Allison.

"I can't believe you did that. Why didn't you tell me?"

"I don't know. I was stalking his Web site—"

"Send me the link," Allison ordered.

"Okay, sending it now." Eden obeyed.

"Question: What are you trying to get from this?"

"I don't know. Nothing, really. It's just coffee."

"Hey, breaking news: It's never *just coffee*."

"I told Penelope I would reach out to him and catch up. As *friends*."

"Good luck with that. Tell that to Ross and Rachel."

"I sounded like such a loser dorkadelic idiot. I swear I will never hear from him."

"I'm not a betting man, but I'll stake you a massage at Exhale."

"Done."

61

Time may be a great healer, but it's a lousy beautician.

—Anonymous

Chase pondered the globe at his fingertips. *Where to whisk Eden off to for her birthday?* The Ocean Club? Skiing in Aspen perhaps? Or maybe some exotic destination resort, an Aman in the hills of Bali or on the shores of Thailand? What to do. Chase mused at his desk, clicking away on the Internet, from page to page, not wanting to repeat any of the countless destinations he'd traveled to with Liesel. And if he thought being with Eden in her apartment was so magical, he could only imagine what being with her far away would be. He wanted to go somewhere that was fresh to both of them, so they could experience the exotic sights and smells together. Though she had seen the world, Eden mostly traveled to cities where art galleries lined streets rather than scattered isles known for their hotbeds of hedonism.

"Hi, son," Grant said, popping his head in Chase's office doorway. "Can I come in?"

"Sure." Chase quickly clicked away from the pages he was perusing, filled with aqua oceans and palm trees hanging lazily in the sun.

"Got a sec?" he asked, taking a seat.

"Of course," said the dutiful son with a nod. Grant rarely popped in for a chat.

"I'm sorry to interrupt you. I just wanted you to know," Grant said seriously, causing Chase to wonder what was coming next. "I support you. Whatever you want to do with Eden. I don't want you to think about your mother or any of that nonsense. I know you're happy."

Chase smiled in grateful surprise.

"I am, Dad. Really happy."

"I can tell," Grant said, nodding. "Do you think she could be the one?"

"One hundred percent. She's it," Chase said, without even having to consider such a large question. "I love her."

"Then I'm sure I will, too, son."

"That really means a lot to me, thank you," Chase replied, touched by his father's unusual understanding. His father's eyes made him wonder if once he had his own passion he perhaps didn't follow. Maybe Brooke was his Liesel whom he felt compelled to marry? A second later, though, the look in his eye had gone, replaced with a sly smile that was clearly where Pierce and Price got there constant Cheshire Cat grins.

"Chase," Grant said with a twinkle as he reached into his inner coat pocket. "Don't worry about asking your mother for the key to Ruthie's box," he said. "Your grandmother had a feeling that perhaps you might not choose a bride to Brooke's liking and saw to it that I got a second copy."

Grant slid the key across the desk to his son as Chase's eyes widened.

"She had left me an envelope of my own as well," Grant explained as his son reached for the key. "This was in it, along with the instructions to make sure you are free to do as you wish."

Chase exhaled, his love for his late grandmother overwhelming him.

"Thank you," Chase said, standing up.

Grant, as habit had it, stuck out his arm to shake his son's hand.

And Chase, as his new habit since meeting Eden had it, ignored the hand and hugged him instead.

After work, Chase walked to his company travel agency, which catered to posh, upscale clientele, mostly businessmen and heirs, or both.

"Oh, hi, you're new," Chase said to the sweet-faced, cheerful redhead at the reception desk.

"Yes, hello!" she replied warmly. "Kara is on maternity leave so I'm just temping for a few months. How can I help you?"

"Well, I have a mission for you," Chase said with a smile, leaning in conspiratorially. "I need to plan the dream trip."

62

Don't just count your years, make your years count.

—Ernest Meyers

It was pouring freezing rain outside and Time Warner was coming to fix Eden's cable sometime between noon and five and she was chained to her apartment. At least she was imprisoned on a shitty day instead of a gorgeous one. She was happy to shack up and wait, cozy in sweats. When the harsh *brrrring* of the phone punctured the silence of her TV-less home, she lunged across the bed like a wide receiver, grabbing it after one ring. It was Allison.

"Thanks a lot; you sound so not psyched to hear from me," Allison scoffed. "Chopped Liver here."

"No, no, just, he still hasn't called."

"It's been A DAY. God, not all the nuts are in the nuthouse. You're being CRAZY."

"I know. What is my problem?" Eden shook her head, climbing under the covers.

"Everyone has to wait by the phone sometime; it's like a rite of passage. See, most girls pay in their teens and twenties. You're paying now, I guess."

"I guess," Eden lamented. "It's so stupid, anyway. I'm with

Chase. I just wanted to, you know, nip this whole Wes thing in the bud. I'd hate to bump into him or something. I'd rather be two adults and meet up."

"Okay, I'm sure you will," Allison said. "What are you doing today?"

"I'm just hostage to the cable guy. What are you up to?"

"I'm going to pick up Kate and then schlep to the flower market and a few sample sales in the thirties. Sh'I stop by on my way home with some dumplings?"

"Awesome. I'd love it."

Eden hung up the phone. Then looked at it. God, she really was acting like a nervous ninth grader. She detested the aggravating click of call-waiting so had never subscribed; maybe he called while she was on the phone with Allison? She picked up the receiver. Bingo: a studded dial tone. Voice mail.

She punched in her code and heard she had One. New. Message. She hoped it wasn't an automated recording from the Time Warner robot lady. It wasn't: jackpot!

"Hi, Eden, it's Wes. I got your message. It was really nice hearing from you. My mom said she really had a great time catching up with you. I'm finally settling in; I live right on Gramercy Square and would love to meet up for coffee and catch up. That would be great. Maybe tomorrow or the next day? I just went to a very charming bar at the Inn at Irving Place if you'd like to meet up there, or that Seventy-one Irving coffee is really good. Let me know. Bye."

Eden played it once more. Platonic in tone. No nerves, no weirdness, just friendly, happy, chill. Shit. She decided to leave him a message at the end of the day so she could get straight into his voice mail from the company directory. She confirmed tea at the Inn for the next evening at six.

When Allison showed up with takeout, she found Eden hyped up, watching VH1 Classic and cleaning like a madwoman.

"What's with you, Martha Stewart?" she asked as she laid out the low-so soy sauce.

"He called. I'm seeing him tomorrow night. Inn at Irving Place."

"NO WAY! Perfect! That place is so hot."

"It is?" Eden asked. "Is it going to be all these hipsters packed in with their skinny jeans and flats?"

"Noooo, the opposite. It's hot like old school pent-up emotions sexy. Like Daniel Day-Lewis and Michelle Pfeiffer in *Age of Innocence*."

"Why am I so nervous?"

"You're seeing an old flame!"

"I've got to chill out. I told Chase I was seeing a friend tomorrow night. That's all it is. He talked to me like I was a lost cousin or something."

"What do you expect? Did you want him panting through the receiver? Phone sex? It's been two decades, E."

"I know. I just hope I can be normal tomorrow. I feel so off-kilter."

"I'm going to wallop you with an old cliché. Just be yourself."

"Thanks, Whitney Houston."

Eden played The The on her iPod for a pre-drink rev-up, ultimately selecting a little black dress after a movie-style montage of outfit tries that resulted in a Kilimanjaro-sized heap of dresses on her floor. She breathed deeply and walked out down the street for the subway.

When she arrived, she walked up the stairs into the charming Old World hotel, scanning the mahogany lobby and bar room. She picked a small couch in the corner and plopped down, surveying the scene. Allison's description was on the money: The spot did not disappoint. Typical Wes. He knew about a jewel like this while he had been away for ages, and she didn't even know it existed.

"Eden." Wes smiled, approaching her. "Sorry I'm late."

"No, you're not at all." He looked the same. A bit older, but the same. His eyes seemed bluer.

"I'm so glad you're still in glasses," Eden said. "Everyone's succumbing to lasers. I miss specs."

"Gosh, I barely recognize myself without them! If I took them off, my whole head would probably roll onto the floor."

Eden laughed. "Well, I like them."

"It's so nice to see you," he started with a genuine, friendly smile.

"You, too. You look exactly the same. Time is not only your friend but your close buddy, I see," Eden said.

Wes smiled. "Can you believe we are turning forty?"

"It's all I think about," Eden confessed, looking at her lap. "I'm afraid for a single woman it can be a bit of an emotional reckoning." A fleeting guilty thought of Chase crossed her mind.

"No, it can't be for you. You've always had the world on a string," he said matter-of-factly.

"I did, didn't I?" she said, almost zoned out. "Somewhere along the way, I don't quite know when, but . . . the string snapped. The world kind of rolled away from me."

"Are you okay?" he asked genuinely as he picked up on the ever-so-slight signals of sadness behind her beautiful eyes. She appreciated his concern but naturally he felt distant; it had been a long time, and the chasm of their years apart rivaled the San Andreas. He seemed happy, relaxed. She knew he detected her sore muscles, laden with baggage.

"Yeah, sure. I'm fine. I mean, everything's fine. It's just, the past few years have been very tumultuous," Eden said.

"I'm sorry. My mother told me about your breakup, your son moving away."

"It's been hard. But I really knew I had to leave, you know. I'm getting my sea legs back; it's probably good for me." Eden looked at her lap and was dying to change the subject. "So meanwhile you're doing great, congrats on your new firm! How is it coming? I hear you're swamped, which I guess is a good thing?"

"It is a great thing," Wes said humbly. "I can't believe it. I am pinching myself, really. Even though I usually am there until midnight."

"You work till *midnight*?"

"Pretty much every night these days, just until we get all these plans approved. But every project is a passion project now. I'm really immersed in my clients. Actually, I'm working with Max Hadley, our old landlord, remember him?"

"Sure! Max, you used to take him on architecture tours."

"He inherited an old turn-of-the-century building that was used as a storage facility," Wes said, leaning in excitedly. His eyes blazed. "It's just incredible—we discovered these old moldings and seven-wood intarsia inlays; it was amazing."

"Wow, where?" Eden asked.

"Lower East Side, near an old synagogue. The work in this two-block radius is extraordinary. It's like this abandoned pocket of hidden gems. I felt like a dorkier Indiana Jones exploring the space."

Eden laughed. Wes was always self-deprecating, even way back when. But through the lens of his success and still-good looks, he had the aura of a player in Judd Apatow's entourage, gorgeous in a deliciously nerdy way.

"Anyway, so Max hired me to come in as a partner on the project to convert it into really awesome apartments. Some guy on *Top Chef* already signed for one."

"Ooooh, I love that show."

"You do?" Wes sounded surprised. "I've never seen it. I don't really do reality."

"I've only seen a little. But Allison knows who every random contestant on every *Survivor* island or *Bachelor* mansion is."

"How is Allison?" he asked, his face brightening.

"Great!" Eden nodded. "Married, three kids. A five-year-old girl and boy-girl twins who are three."

"Oh, that is so great. I always really liked her. I'm glad you guys are still—"

"Thick as thieves." Eden smiled.

"Yup."

"She always loved you, too. In fact . . . she kind of calmed my nerves about seeing you."

"Nerves? Why?"

"I know, it's silly," she admitted. "It's just been so long . . ."

"I know, so much time has gone by, it's nuts."

"So, Wes, it's so cool what you've accomplished in that time. I mean, could you have ever imagined? Way back then in that little walk-up where you'd play chess with Max, did you ever think that he would come to your own firm twenty years later as a client? You as his designer and partner?"

"Life is weird." Wes smiled, shaking his head. "It's a strange road."

"It sure is," Eden concurred, choking on wistfulness. "I mean . . . look at your parents."

"Yeah, talk about twists and turns. My mom went from single and pregnant to married mother of four. I got a dad overnight. It's so funny, there's so much you can't predict. I never thought I'd live abroad. Then I thought I'd never leave London. I never thought we'd be here talking."

Eden and Wes talked for an hour, about his life in London, his travels to every continent, finding inspiration for his work, and about what he wanted to be doing. He was so much more assured, more open than he used to be. He was still the same humble Wes, but his shyness had been exchanged for a grown-up, down-to-earth humor, dry at times, and lighthearted. He remained un-jaded, somehow youthful, though even at twenty he had always been an old soul, appreciating a lofty archway over a lap dance, coffee over a brewski.

As Wes spoke and asked Eden questions about Cole and the trips she had taken with Otto, his kindness wasn't even remotely laced with nostalgia. He seemed interested to know what she had been up to, but he was emotionally detached. She could tell he was happy to see her, but it felt like reuniting with a much-loved cousin you used to spend every Thanksgiving with, or a close camp friend, an old roommate. He seemed 100 percent content with how his life had turned out. It was strange that Eden, always the dumper, not the dumpee, appeared far more tortured in his presence. Would he still laugh at her goofy dancing? Would he recognize the map of her moles that dotted her back?

Eden was trying to mask any sign of pain or regret. She sat up straight and tried to seem composed, listening to his description of a hotel he renovated in Italy, which she tried to imagine, lake-side and gleaming. After a while, Wes's comfortable, easy vibe made her feel more and more relaxed, so that little by little she started to feel more like her old self again.

"I'm really glad we're here," Eden said. "It's so nice to see you."

"Are you kidding? It's my pleasure. I was so happy when you rang—" He caught himself. "Shit, that was a Brit holdover," he said as he laughed at himself, putting his forehead in his hand. "I hate when expats come home spewing stuff about a *flat to let* or taking the *lift*."

"Don't worry; I know you're so not *that guy*."

"Sometimes you just get so used to something it becomes in-grained." He smiled, then looked at his watch. "Oh shoot, I have to run—"

"Time flies," Eden said, marveling almost ninety minutes had passed. Shit, that sounded so stupid.

"I already took care of the drinks when I arrived so we're all set," he said, standing up.

"Oh, wow, thank you so much—you didn't have to—"

"No, it was really nice to see you," he said sincerely. "I'm so sorry, I just had this plan scheduled beforehand."

"Client dinner?"

"No, a date, actually," he said casually, as if it were a haircut or shoeshine.

Eden felt a zap like a spark on a cold metal banister. "Oh, great—"

"It's a friend of a friend; she just finished architecture school. I haven't met her yet, actually."

"Ah, blind date," she said, forcing a smile. *Just finished school, eh?* By Eden's calculations, that put said date at about twenty-six. Not that she was one to talk, with Chase coming over the following night.

"Yup. Who knows, right?" He shrugged with a grin.

"You never know," Eden said, not wanting to say farewell.

Wes leaned in to give her a warm hug good-bye. "It was great to see you."

"Have fun," she said, almost emotionally electrocuted by his arm around her. "Stay in touch."

Wes flashed her a big, kind smile with a wave and turned to walk away. Eden watched after him as he exited without looking back.

63

Life is a moderately good play with a badly written third act.
—Truman Capote

Eden arrived home to find a shocking delivery. Flowers. Held not by the guy from L'Olivier but by Otto.

"What are you doing here?"

"I fucked up. Royally," he said, walking up to her.

"Otto, what's going on?"

Eden took out her keys and walked upstairs, her ex following her.

"Come back," he pleaded. "Mary is gone. Everyone's gone. I'll change. . . ."

"Please. If a woman got even one tenth of a penny every time a guy said those words, we would be ruling the world right now," she replied coolly.

"Eden, I'm sorry. I screwed up." He walked over to her and looked into her eyes. "Since you cut me out, I can't paint. I did a new series of sketches of some still lifes, and Lyle, who is usually up my butt, said he hated them. He said in this economy they wouldn't sell; people want 'iconic' investments. . . ." He rolled his eyes and mocked his gallerist with melodramatic finger quotes.

"Oh, so you're here because I'm better for business?" Eden laughed. "Otto . . ."

"No. I'm here because I miss you."

"Yeah, more like you miss sold-out shows."

"That's not true. I miss *us*."

"I told you already," Eden said, looking him in the eyes. "It's too late."

"So that's it? Even my apology isn't good enough? That fucking loser boy toy you've been screwing doing it for you, eh?" Just when she was feeling a flicker of guilt, a glimmer of how easy it could be to just go back downtown, back home, back to the father of her child, Otto reminded her exactly why she got the fuck out of there.

"Otto, calm down, please."

"You know what you are? You're a fucking whore. You were always a whore! Look how fast you ditched that poor schlepper you were with when I came along! You got what you wanted with me. Next you're going to bleed this Lydon chump dry?"

His harsh words stung Eden's soul like searing hot needles as she recoiled in horror.

"You were nothing when I found you and plucked you from the shadows of obscurity! You were a little trailer trash slut," he screamed. She jerked back. "I fucking MADE YOU."

Just when she was about to start crying from the verbal stab wounds, Eden took a deep breath. "YOU DIDN'T MAKE ME! And quite frankly, that poor schlepper is more of a man and more of an artist than you could ever be." She started crying not from Otto's harsh words against her but because of the thought of what she had done to Wes. "NOW GET OUT!"

He didn't see it coming . . . neither had she. The two stared at each other, and Otto dropped the bouquet to the floor. He turned around quietly and walked out, slamming the door behind him.

Panting, Eden staggered to the phone to call Allison, who talked her down.

"Good for you!" Allison cheered. "I'm so glad you told him off. Fuck him!"

"I mean, what a fraud he is! He claimed he wanted me back, that he missed us, but I know he doesn't; it's a power thing and he needs me to pose. Then when I say no, he goes from supposedly loving me to calling me a trailer trash whore."

"Fuck him. He's done. Move on."

"I want to. I really do. I'm just so . . . spent. I'm exhausted by life."

"You're just in a rut! You'll get out, Eden."

"You remember when we used to play video games for, like, hours on end at the Gas 'n' Sip?" Eden asked Allison in a dazed voice.

"Sure, I was the Kong goddess," Allison bragged. "I had top scores one through seven at one point."

"Well, you know when Ms. Pacman dies?"

"Yeah, she kind of fades back from most of the pie to just a pie slice and then there's that fizzle squirt sound of doom?"

"Exactly."

"Yeah, so?"

"That is what my heart feels like," Eden said. "When Ms. Pacman bites it."

"Because of Otto?"

"No. Because of Wes."

"You said on my voice mail you had a great time with him."

"I did. Too good a time." Eden crawled under the covers.

"What happened?"

Thinking about him gave Eden goose bumps. "I have this really sinking feeling that I made the wrong choice when I left him. I mean, of course I'm glad because I had Cole. But seeing him tonight just felt like . . . home. I know, it sounds crazy."

"What are you going to do?" Allison asked.

"What can I do? Nothing. He had a date afterward, some chick who just finished school for Christ's sake."

"So there were sparks?"

"No, it was worse than that. I saw him and I was obviously so attracted to him. He's still gorgeous," Eden said. "But it wasn't like I wanted to club him on the head and drag him to a room upstairs and screw him."

"So that's good."

"No, see . . ." Eden shook her head. "What I wanted was to tell him I was madly in love with him."

"Oh, boy," Allison said, sensing disaster. "So what are you going to do about Chase?"

Eden felt guilty about Chase, whom she genuinely cared for, but she had to face reality. "I adore him, I really do. It's just that seeing Wes showed me that I should have that feeling, that uncorked mad kind of love. And even though it's obviously too late to rekindle that with Wes, at least I know that it's out there, that I'm capable of having that kind of affection again."

"Poor Chase," Allison said.

"He has a whole life ahead of him," Eden said. "He will make some woman so happy. He'll have children, he'll have it all. . . ."

"And what about you?" Allison asked.

"Me? Who knows." Eden shrugged. "For the first time in my life, I don't have a clue what I want."

64

No wise man ever wished to be younger.

—Chinese proverb

"Hurry," Chase said eagerly as Eden quietly finished preparing dinner at the stove. "I have two very special things for you. I feel like it's Christmas morning!"

"Hold on, I'm coming," she said, plating the chicken française and haricots verts in mustard dressing. She lay the plates down on the trunk and noticed Chase had opened a bottle of Dom Perignon.

"Wow, that's some nice stuff," she noted.

"I stopped by Sherry-Lehmann on the way home. We have something to celebrate."

"Oh?"

Chase tossed the ticket folio down next to her fork.

"What's this?" Eden asked as Chase beamed, awaiting her reaction.

"It's a voyage. For you and me. How does your birthday in India sound?"

"My birthday?"

"And if you don't want to celebrate that, it'll also be our eight-month anniversary."

Eden was not into milestones. She loved them with Cole; his every birthday was a candle-blowing festival in the studio packed with kids and adults and friends and friends of friends. But as her own fortieth birthday loomed, she really didn't care to mark any occasion, not the holidays—nothing that would officially seal her youth in the past.

But here Chase was, itinerary in hand.

"I spent the past two days at my company's travel agency. We pored over all these brochures and Web sites, and the travel agent said this is the most incredible trip: It starts in Goa in India, a beachfront resort where they filmed that movie *The Beach* or something. It's totally unspoiled and there's an out-of-the-way spa there. We can relax for a few days before touring the country with private guides at Oberoi resorts. We'll be so far away. We can just enjoy each other, away from everything."

"Chase," Eden started carefully.

"Wait. There's something else," Chase said. "I want to tell you something."

"What's that?" she wondered.

"Before we go away together, before we see the whole world that's out there, I want you to remember that this room, this apartment, is the only place I ever need to be."

"I know," Eden said, touching his chin as if he were a beloved nephew rather than her boyfriend. "That's so sweet."

"This is the place where I fell madly in love with you. And while I could do this on a mountaintop or in the clouds with sky-writing or even on our trip, with a thousand orchids . . ."

"Do what?" Eden said, stepping back.

"This."

Chase knelt down before her. Like a little kid with a trick up his custom-tailored sleeve, he reached mischievously into his inside jacket pocket. He pulled out a small red leather box, un-mistakably Cartier. With a huge beaming smile, he handed it to her.

"Oh my God."

"Open it."

Slowly Eden opened the red box, revealing a beautiful square solitaire diamond ring. But before she could even look up into Chase's pleading eyes, one crystal thought appeared in her head, as clear as the flawless D stone that shone before her. A thought that brought her back to Wes. And made her heart shatter the way she had broken his so long ago.

65

One of the many things nobody ever tells you about middle age is that it's such a nice change from being young.

—Dorothy Canfield Fisher

Eden took a deep breath. She had no idea this was coming. She reflected on how this man kneeling before her had given her affection, confidence, and, most of all, strength to put herself back together after Otto. She adored him, yes, but her answer . . . was no. He simply wasn't the right match for her, despite all her affection for him and the great times they'd shared.

Like Robert Smith from The Cure once sang, Chase never set her soul on fire the way that Wes had. Even though she knew Wes was lost to her, along with her youth, seeing him ignited in her a quest for something inside herself, a longing for true love that needed to be fulfilled. She didn't decline Chase because of Wes, but because deep down she knew Chase would never finish her thoughts, read her mind, be in sync with her. Wes had set the bar so high, so long ago, that Eden knew in that moment that no one could ever vault it.

"I can't," she said, wiping the tears gushing down her face.

"You have given me so much, Chase. You went against your family's wishes, the world's expectations, only to give me love and I'm truly so, so grateful. It takes such guts to do that, real courage to be with me when you deserve so much, but I can't give it to you."

"Eden, don't cry," he said, rubbing her back. His reaction was surprisingly calm and sober. It was almost as if he knew she was like a comet or shooting star, brightening his galaxy for only a short while. "I understand."

"You do?" She loved him even more for allowing her to set him free.

"Yes. I just want you to be happy. To have everything you want. Even if it's not me." He smiled.

"Chase, I don't even know what I want. I'm just a confused mess," she said, smiling as she wiped her tears.

"You're a beautiful mess," he said, kissing her forehead. "I must admit, while I kept hoping we would end up together, I saw this coming. I knew you would slip away. Can't blame a guy for trying, though."

His words made her cry even harder, since she saw their demise in the distance as well. Chase hugged her, then looked at her face. Her vulnerability made her even more beautiful.

"I only want your happiness, Eden. I'll never forget you. You made me a new person, a better person, more adventurous—"

"Less anal."

"Less anal, yes," he said with a smile. Chase realized this would be the last time they would be together, and he felt suddenly heavyhearted. Chase knew deep down that they needed to release each other, but he ached for her so much he felt like even his blood hurt. The tides were rising to a boil inside him, his normally fortified levee about to burst.

"I'm going to miss you so much," he said, his voice almost cracking.

"Listen, Chase: I have one final request."

"Anything," he replied sadly, spent but ready to give her the world.

"I want you to take that trip," she insisted. "It's time you break away, too. Go for it. You need more adventure in your life. Dating me has been the craziest thing you've ever done, which is not that exciting."

"Yes, it was," he said soberly.

"I'm serious," Eden said, in an almost maternal tone she would use when instructing Cole. "I want you to go to India, okay? Promise?"

"All right."

"Have some tikka masala for me. Promise?"

"I promise."

The unlikely pair hugged, both on the emotional Jetways of two different but life-changing journeys.

"It's funny, I helped you be young, but you helped me finally grow up," Eden said, leaning in to kiss him on the cheek, holding his two hands in hers. "Thanks to you, I'm now ready to take charge of my future. I now know what I have to do."

66

Few women admit their age. Few men act theirs.

—Anonymous

The next morning before heading to the office, Chase walked forlornly to the travel agency, hoping to get a refund for Eden's part of his exorbitantly priced trip.

"Oh my gosh, what happened?" asked the pretty redhead. "I'm so sorry!"

"Yeah, well, it was great while it lasted but it wasn't meant to be, I'm afraid." He shrugged and sat down in the chair facing the girl. He noticed her shiny red hair flowing past her shoulder and her stylish shift dress. "I'm sorry, but I, uh, I apologize, remind me of your name again?"

"It's Piper," she replied, smiling. "Nice to officially meet you."

"That's a great name," he remarked sadly, remembering Eden loved it.

"Thanks," she said, noticing his downward glance. "Listen, I know this is none of my business, but I'm really glad you're doing this trip, anyway. I've seen so many people who just cancel altogether when there's a breakup. Good for you."

He smiled. "Thanks, Piper."

"You know," she said. "Sometimes it's good to take a chance. You never know what you'll come across, who you'll meet."

"Yeah, I guess," Chase said.

"I had a friend who was all signed up for a bike trip through Italy with her ex-primate and he totally assholed out and dumped her the night before and she went anyway and met her now-husband."

"Really?" Chase brightened. Not that he was on wife-safari or anything, but he felt comforted by Piper's optimism.

"Totally. That's what I'm saying, you just never know! Life's so crazy, you know?"

"I do." Chase nodded. "Thanks so much. I'll let you know how it goes."

"Please do! I really love hearing about people's trips. I'm always bound to the desk here, so I sometimes look at my clients' itineraries and wonder what they're up to that day. It's silly, really. But I just love sending people on these adventures. Hopefully one day I'll get to go on one."

"I'm sure you will." Chase smiled. "Thanks again for dealing with the cancellations for the other ticket. I really appreciate it."

"It's my pleasure. Don't worry. You're going to have a blast."

Chase walked down the hall and pressed the elevator button. He entered the packed car and rode down with the hordes of businessmen and women who were sprinting for their twenty-minute lunch hour to one of the myriad take-out joints in the two-block radius. When the steel doors opened in the grand lobby, bodies flooded in and out of the vast hall, lined with large-scale sculptures. He headed for the middle of five revolving doors, turning and turning, new suits coming in with lunch bags, others headed out. Everyone was running, cycling, buzzing, talking, charging. Chase's metered steps got slower and slower and slower. Until he stopped right in front of the revolving door.

"Hey, buddy, you going or what?" a harried executive asked behind him.

"Oh, yeah, sorry," he replied distractedly. He pushed through the revolving door to the outside and then . . . he revolved back in. He ignored a raised eyebrow of the person waiting for his side of the door and walked back in, through the bustling lobby, to the elevator.

For the second time in his life, Chase was taking a plunge. The first had been standing outside Eden's apartment that cold rainy night, defying his parents and charging to the side of the first woman who had truly changed him. The second was even more bizarre and risky because his bold gesture was based on little but gut instinct, something that Eden had taught him, for the first time in his life, to trust.

He pressed the button to go back to up to Piper's office.

For some reason, while his heart missed and longed for Eden, he had heard her parting words loud and clear. They had helped each other but perhaps were not meant to stay together always. And so, released by her command, his thoughts meandered, or skipped in fact, to the girl whose wide eyes drank in the world only though the golds and cyans of beautifully printed brochures.

Eden had traveled the whole entire world and was weary, wanting a rock, a touchstone to return home to be whole. And conversely, here was Piper, beginning her journey, bursting to get out from behind her desk, away from the fluorescent lights of Midtown to the moonlight in the tropics. But finances and responsibilities had prevented that. Chase thought back to how Piper's quick e-mails were loaded with exclamations ("Chase! Found this new boutique resort that has outdoor sunset massages and LITERALLY ninety-two species of orchids! Who knew?")

He had sworn to Eden he would go on his trip. But did he really want to go all alone? He had his bag packed. The CDL-monogrammed T. Anthony navy suitcase sat by his door.

"Hi," he said, standing in Piper's doorway.

"You're back!" She smiled.

"I know this is going to sound strange. This is really not like me and don't worry, I'm not some deranged lunatic or anything," he stammered.

"Yeah, I'm not worried." Piper winked, looking at his gentlemanly apparel. "You don't seem like the menacing type."

"You planned this whole dream trip and . . . I was wondering if you would want to join me?"

"What do you mean?" she asked, brow raised.

"I mean . . . come with me. I'm serious."

"Like, now?" Piper beamed in shock.

"Like, now."

Chase smiled.

Without a nanosecond's pause, she stood up, picked up a cherry-hued stapler from her desk and followed him out, like Renée Zellweger's character caught in Jerry Maguire's charismatic tractor beam. He looked at her, curious as to why she had chosen that particular office accessory. "I like red things," she said casually. "It's my favorite color."

"Okay, then," said Chase. "We'll be sure to get you something red on our trip."

The two were off and running. His parents would be aghast. Could anything be so insane? To jet off at a moment's notice with a complete stranger?

So there they were: going to her apartment as he waited for her to chuck clothes into a bag, heading to the airport, going through security, having passports stamped together, getting seated side by side. If there is anything that presses the fast-forward button on a relationship, it's travel. Not for a moment was there an awkward pause or a nervous stammer. They didn't kiss until the third day, when Chase marveled at the way Piper seemed to have already been to Indonesia not only through her extensive research but also through her vivid imagination. Her gratified sighs at each marvel they beheld made him beam with pride, and it was refreshing to be with someone who relished every sight, bite, and breeze. They swam under the moon, they hiked under the sun, they danced by torchlight and kissed as the Balinese waves lapped their toes. In that moment, with Piper in his arms, their four feet wet with faraway waters, Chase smiled to himself: Eden would have been proud of him.

67

A truly great book should be read in youth, again in maturity and once more in old age, as a fine building should be seen by morning light, at noon and by moonlight.

—Robertson Davies

O n the night Chase was boarding the plane with Piper, Eden was home alone. She sipped a glass of wine as she looked out her window at the wet streets. She hoped Chase's flight wouldn't be forever delayed. She meandered to her computer, where she clicked on Wes's Web site, looking at the various buildings he had designed and restored. Should she call him again? E-mail? She was so confused. She got in bed and watched TV until before she knew it, she had dozed off in front of some gossip show—or as they called it—"entertainment news."

She was startled awake by one of those ominously loud commercials. She got her bearings as she saw it was eight o'clock. Shit, now what? She flopped back down in bed and thought she would choke on self-pity. But then she stopped. How could she dole out advice to Chase and not practice what she preached? She could never be at peace with moving forward in her life until she fought for what she really wanted. Who she really wanted. She threw on jeans and a black blouse with a bow, wrapped a scarf around her, and put on a gray coat and headed out. She walked all the way to Wes's Park Avenue South office building and buzzed from the lobby.

"A Miss Eden Clyde is here," security told reception. "Okay, he says go up."

Eden rode up in the elevator, shaking. Holy shit. No going back now.

Wes stood in his glass entrance doorway.

Mother Love Bone played in the background as young people carrying rolled-up blueprints walked around in jeans.

Shit. She knew he worked late but she didn't realize he had a whole crew of people there.

"Eden, hi—"

"Okay, I'm sorry to just show up here. You must think I'm a stalker, a total crazy person," Eden gushed. She took a deep breath and looked at his face, which remained largely unchanged, still the same gorgeous blue eyes, a more weathered but much sexier countenance. *Breathe*, she told herself.

"No, don't be silly, come in. I'm just wrapping up a meeting with—"

"Oh my God, you're with a client? I'm so sorry." Her face burned with embarrassment. "I'll go. I'll call you another time."

"Don't worry, it's actually with Max. He'd love to have you join us; come on in."

She followed him nervously across the spacious reception area to an all-glass conference room where Max sat. His fingers ran over the scale model of the buildings as Eden and Wes walked in.

"Max, Eden is here," Wes explained.

"Max, I'm so sorry to barge in. I just . . . I was nearby, and, um—"

"Eden, sweetheart, so lovely to hear that voice," he said as he held out his hand, which she took, sitting next to him.

"It's really good to see you," Eden said, wanting to cry. She looked back at Wes, who was clearly surprised by her sudden arrival.

A rising tide of emotion welled within her chest. She looked at both men, two of the most genuine people she had ever met. And in that moment, she felt safe.

"I . . . ," Eden started but couldn't speak.

"Eden, are you okay?" Wes asked, sitting down next to her.

"I lied," she confessed, looking up at Wes. Her eyes were glassy with the thick veil of tears on deck. "I wasn't nearby. Not at all."

She blinked and all the levees of her eyes cracked. Then broke open.

"Wes, I am here because, oh God, I am so, so *sorry*. Ugh, that word is so weary with overuse, so weak. Okay, I am not sorry: I am gutted. I am sorrier than I have been about anything else in my entire life," Eden spewed. "You must think that I am raging nuts to show up here, but just because I haven't seen you in forever doesn't mean that I ever stopped thinking about you or caring or lately, since our coffee, even obsessing! Okay, that sounded scary. I swear I'm not Glenn Close and I swear I won't boil rabbits on your stovetop, but after I bumped into your mom and then saw you, I thought so much about how your mom fought for your dad and I was haunted by your mother's boldness, her choice to go for what she wanted and I had to come here to tell you something," she said.

"Okay," Wes answered softly. He faced her, arms crossed. Eden noticed that his rich brown hair was flecked with gray.

"You know the guy I mentioned I had been seeing. Chase?"

"Yes," Wes answered.

"After I saw you, I started thinking about you, about us. Nonstop. And soon afterward, Chase proposed. He gave me a red Cartier box. And do you know what popped into my head?"

"What?" asked Wes.

"I thought . . . *I wish it were a box of raisins.*"

She burst into tears and knew she seemed utterly nutso. She knew he wouldn't actually dial the police and have her whisked away in a straitjacket, but she was worried he definitely thought she was mildly insane.

Trying to digest this shocking soliloquy, Wes simply sat there, silent.

Eden was mortified. "I'm sorry, I shouldn't have come. I'm so embarrassed. I'm so sorry to have interrupted." She turned and ran out.

"Eden, wait!" Wes called after her, but she was on her way to the door.

Wes turned to Max.

"Come here," Max said to him. "I have to tell you something."

Outside, Eden was furiously pushing the down button for the elevator, which could not come fast enough. Maybe the cable would snap and she'd be out of her misery. Eden, in total meltdown mode, burst into convulsive tears. Chase had helped her crack her hardened veneer. He had cracked the dam, but seeing Wes was the battering ram that unleashed a flood of tears. She had her chance and she threw it all away for nonsense, for fame, for security. And now she looked like a total fool. *Where the fuck was the fucking elevator?*

Wes came through the double doors and walked up to her, and took her hand. "Come with me," he instructed.

Sobbing, she followed him back inside, turning to the left as opposed to the conference room. She followed him down a long hallway, feeling like her life was slipping away, swirling out of control.

"Please don't think I'm some psycho stalker." She wept. "I'm so mortified."

Wes led her into a huge, sleek office with views of the city and a book-covered desk. He closed the door behind them.

"Turn around," he instructed.

Eden spun around in her thick, all-enveloping fog. Hanging on the wall was *Beside Eden,* Otto Clyde's last masterpiece, which had sold even before the gallery doors opened. Eden's jaw dropped. She turned to look at Wes.

"*You* own this painting?" she said in shock. "I thought it was some fancy Midtown lawyer that bought it!"

"It was," he said with a sly smile. "My lawyer."

"Oh my God," she marveled. "I can't believe it." She stared at the image of herself in repose, her languid eyes seducing the viewer. "Wes, I'm so sorry."

"Eden, don't be *sorry*. Don't worry about the past. We were young. I'm totally content. I have a thriving business—"

"It's not just that I'm sorry," she interrupted. "It's that I *love* you. After I saw you I knew it for sure. I love you, Wes. And now I know I never stopped."

Wes walked closer to her and moved the hair from her face.

"Do you know what Max just said to me?" Wes asked, grabbing Eden a tissue from his desk and handing it to her.

"No, what?" she asked, wiping her eyes.

"He said, 'Son, I may be blind but I can see well enough that you two are the loves of each other's lives'."

Eden looked at him and threw herself into his arms, crying into his warm soft sweater.

"I know that you are for me," she said. "When your mom told me you never married, I practically choked on my relief."

"It's hard to get married," Wes said, looking at her, "when deep down you know you'll always love someone else."

He kissed her and she felt the charcoal clouds that had shadowed her for years suddenly open up. They kissed like twenty-year-olds on the street, as though no time had gone by. But they also kissed like tons of time had gone by, time that made this moment all the more like a fireworks finale, blazing, deafening, bright and bold. She put her hands up the back of his sweater, and he held her neck and shoulder.

"Can you believe this?" she asked him. "From twenty—"

"To double that," he said.

"Actually," she said, eyebrow raised. "I'm thirty-nine for seventy-two more hours."

"That's right," he said, recalling the date. "Any plans?"

"I was hoping to have a party," she said, looking around the charming office.

"Oh yeah?"

"Yes. A very, very small party, with a very exclusive roster of invitees. There's exactly one person on it, in fact."

Wes smiled. "Do I make the list?" he said, stepping toward her and taking her hand.

"You are the list."

The pair stood staring at each other for a moment. Eden was so overwhelmed by emotion that she could barely move, but she summoned everything she had just to lean into Wes. They hugged, and they fit right back together like an ancient, long-buried lock and key. They clicked. It was in that warm melding of her cheek on his chest that she suddenly knew the feeling people always talk about: coming home.

"I thought you never cry," he remembered, wiping her tears and kissing her forehead.

"I've been crying a lot lately. I think these last few years I made up for all the time I never did," she said. "I think that finally in my ripe old age, I am free to weep," she sniffed. "Being a hag is quite liberating actually."

"You're not a hag. You know, you're more gorgeous now than at twenty."

"Okay, Pinocchio," she said, giggling through her tears.

"I'm not lying. Experience is sexy."

"Well, then I guess at eighty, I'll be smoldering."

"You will be," he said with a smile.

"Will you really spend my birthday with me?"

"Of course," he said, putting his arm around her and squeezing her. "What are you going to wish for?"

"I can't tell you that!" she teased, her tearstained face coyly smiling.

"Okay, don't." He smiled, touching her neck as he studied her face. Her laugh lines by her eyes were defined, her cheeks a bit hollowed, but Wes believed she was even more beautiful than ever. The years had given her character. Her soul was richer, her heart bigger. She was a better, more centered person for their time apart. Perhaps his mother had suspected this day would come, but as for Wes, he had no idea. Their instantly uncorked affection and honesty transcended his wildest hope.

"All right, I'll tell you my wish," Eden said, putting her arms around his waist and looking through his little gold glasses into his eyes. "My wish, for my fortieth birthday, is that I am, somehow, after all that has happened, after all I did to fuck everything up," she continued, glassy-eyed, "that I am lucky enough to be with you. That I can earn back a place in your life."

"You never lost it," he said, kissing her.

"Really?" she asked.

"Really."

"I hope so. That was my wish. Oh, and also that I can spend my eightieth birthday with you as well."

"Maple," he laughed, kissing her. "It's a date."

Epilogue

Grow old along with me!
The best is yet to be, the last of life, for which the first was
made.

—Robert Browning

VOWS

Eden Clyde and
Wes Hutcheson Bennett

Eden Clyde, best known as the muse to world-renowned artist Otto Clyde, wed award-winning architect Wes Hutcheson Bennett last Saturday evening. The bride and groom dated and lived together for one year, two decades ago, and reunited after the bride's relationship with the artist ended. "I was devoted to someone older, then I met a wonderful person who was much younger," she said, touching on her much-written-about relationship with DuPree family scion Chase Lydon. "And then I returned to my first love, someone my exact same age," she said and smiled. The groom, 40, was conceived at Woodstock, "the ultimate love child," his beaming wife, Eden, also 40, explained, replicating history as she

---

stood aglow, and six months pregnant, at the cherry-blossom-covered altar. It is the first marriage for both. They recited their vows at the Bowery Hotel ballroom, which now stands at the site of an old diner where the pair first met. "I always knew they were meant to be together," the bride's best friend, Allison Rubens, said. "It's like this fairy tale that someone read only halfway through, and then picked up again years later." Mrs. Bennett's son with Mr. Clyde, Cole, concurred. "I've never seen my mom so incredibly happy," he said, beaming. Mr. Bennett's profession in architectural restoration is all about rebuilding, and the parallel to their relationship is not lost on the couple. "He takes something old and beautiful and breathes new life into it," his wife said, looking at her husband. "And now, we had our own renovation. Our history remains, but we're stronger and better than before."

Artists, actors, friends, and family gathered to toast the couple, whose ringed fingers and first marital kiss were twenty years in the making. "I have no regrets about the lost time," Wes said, his arm around his new wife's shoulder. "Whatever she needed to do to get back to me, to get us here tonight"—he paused to kiss her hand—"it was worth it."

Acknowledgments

This is my first book where I have *zero* in common with the protagonist: a stunning model from the tumbleweed sticks (her) versus an ordinary-looking city rat (*moi*). Not to be cheese, but this "journey" would not have been possible without editrix extraordinaire Erika Imranyi and my agent, Jennifer Joel. Thank you both for your notes and guidance throughout. Ditto to Dr. Lisa Turvey, devoted pal slash longtime first reader: Your help is essential to this process, and I'm truly grateful for your time, especially when you were knocked up and probably fighting zzz's.

I also wanted to thank the *Ex-Mrs. Hedgefund* cheerleading squad of amazing supporters. Your emotional pom-poms meant the world to me: Jeannie Stern, Vanessa Eastman, Dana and Michael Jones, Trip Cullman, Dan Allen, Laura Tanny, Lauren Duff, Tara Lipton, Alexis Mintz, the Heinzes, the Bevilacquas, Jenn Linardos, Nikki Castle, Lynn Biase, Lisa Fallon, Michael Kovner and Jean Doyen de Montaillou, Carrie Karasyov, Julia Van Nice, Kelley Ford Owen, Robyn Brown, Jacky Davy Blake, Vern Lochan, the amaaaazing Beth Klein (who planned a party mid–stork flight), Fréderic Fékkai, Tory Burch, Nanette Lepore, Mark Badgley, and James Mishka. And of course: the fabulous Amanda Walker, and finally, Carol Bell and Barbara Martin, who actually make touring fun.

To LC and the nuggets, you make my return so happy every time. Love you so.

And

To Mom, Dad, and Will: you made the heinous zitty teen years actually fun and formative versus awky and miserable! I'm so glad you cultivated in me the realization early on that the real Beautiful People are the ones who make each other laugh.

Also Available from Jill Kargman

The Ex-
Mrs. Hedgefund

Divorce may be pricey, but second chances are free...

a novel

JILL KARGMAN

Author of *Arm Candy*

978-0-452-29594-0

Plume
A member of Penguin Group (USA)
www.penguin.com